ONE LIFE TO LOSE

QUEERS OF LA VISTA

KRIS RIPPER

RIPTIDE
PUBLISHING

Ripper

Riptide Publishing
PO Box 1537
Burnsville, NC 28714
www.riptidepublishing.com

One Life to Lose
Copyright © 2016 by Kris Ripper

Cover art: L.C. Chase, lcchase.com/design.htm
Editor: May Peterson
Layout: L.C. Chase, lcchase.com/design.htm

ISBN: 978-1-62649-440-4

First edition
December, 2016

Also available in ebook:
ISBN: 978-1-62649-439-8

ONE LIFE TO LOSE

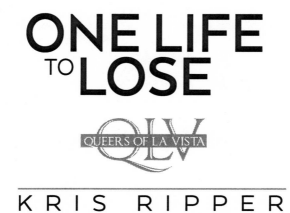

QUEERS OF LA VISTA

KRIS RIPPER

RIPTIDE
PUBLISHING

For all the Cameron Rheingolds. Love will find you.
Be brave.

TABLE OF
CONTENTS

CHAPTER 1

Three minutes until go time.

I relaxed the death grip I had on my index cards and took another look at the computer screen currently showing four of the theater's security cameras. The lobby was almost cleared out and the theater was almost full. I felt dizzy.

I don't experience anxiety as a jumpy heartbeat or damp palms. When I am most nervous, the color leeches out of the world, leaving me walking through a grainy black-and-white film. As a coping mechanism, it works well; I'm comfortable in that state, navigating the gray areas, finding a home between shadows and light.

One final breath. I double-checked that the booth was locked, accepted nods of support from my ticket taker and concessions staff, and made my way to the stage.

My earliest memory is standing on the stage between my parents on the night we opened the expanded concessions store, serving sandwiches and soups. I was four years old, holding my father's hand, staring out at all the people. All I really remember is how high the stage felt and how loud the people were, but they told me later that I smiled and waved at the crowd. I can never be certain if my parents misremembered (projecting their general love of chaos on their young son), or if there was a time when my world did not drop into grayscale at the first moment of overwhelm.

I knew *An Affair to Remember* backward and forward. It was the obvious choice to start the Cary Grant Film Festival. I probably knew my speech even without the index cards. And it was short, so there shouldn't have been a problem.

Then I tripped.

I tripped walking from the stairs to the microphone. Four steps. I'd carefully put the podium off to the side where I wouldn't have to move it and it wouldn't be in the way. Four steps from the point where I reached the stage to the point where I turned toward the crowd.

On the second step I tripped and my index cards flew everywhere.

People gasped, giggled, made other sounds of commiseration and nerves and gentle mockery, a distant, muted soundtrack to the white noise buzz of my brain registering that even if I could pick up all the index cards, I hadn't numbered them.

It would be impossible to piece my speech back together.

I closed my eyes for a split second, wishing my dad were there to hold my hand. He'd squeeze it and say, *What would Cary do, Cameron?*

Cary would get off his knees and pick up the microphone. So I did.

A great many people. The first night of the film series hadn't sold out, but it had come closer than any event I'd done in years. I tried to blur my vision so I wouldn't recognize anyone.

"Hello. I seem to have had . . . technical difficulties with my teleprompter."

Laughter. No one turns to Cam Rheingold when they need a joke, but I can do dry. At least a little.

"Welcome to the Cary Grant Film Festival. Each Saturday from now until mid-December we'll show a film starring Cary Grant." A few claps. I smiled, carefully not-looking at any of the faces. "Mr. Grant has been my absolute favorite actor since I was a child, and I'm so pleased to present to you Leo McCarey's *An Affair to Remember* for our first film in the series."

I'd had a whole mini lecture planned—about how the film was a remake of McCarey's earlier *Love Affair*, and how most people agreed the latter was the better movie—but if I launched into it without my notes, I'd fumble. The sequence would be wrong, and I might potentially misstate my facts. I couldn't take the risk.

"This is widely considered one of the greatest love stories of all time," I said instead. "A story about how terrible timing is sometimes perfect timing, about the radical notion that two wealthy individuals might love one another so much they'd decide to work for a living, and of course, about the power and intensity and endurance of romantic love."

More clapping this time. Perfect.

"Please enjoy *An Affair to Remember*. And do join me in the lobby after for refreshments. If I don't see you then, I hope to see you next week, when we'll be watching *North by Northwest*." I bowed to the lights, caught a disturbingly distinct view of eyes and smiles and hairstyles, and quickly walked down the steps and out the long hallway to the doors while the intro started to play.

I pressed myself against the wall in the dark until the credits had finished and the picture really began. Then I escaped to my booth and watched it on the monitor instead of the big screen.

I'd promised myself I wouldn't hide, but I had failed to factor in dropping my index cards. I needed the security of the booth, at least until the next particularly gruesome act of this event would begin.

Refreshments. Small talk. Perhaps I could redirect every conversation back to Mr. Grant. I'd certainly try.

I didn't know why I'd noticed them. I hadn't right away; they intruded into my awareness gradually, like a sound in the distance that you only realized you'd been listening to all along. Their voices mingled with the familiar voices of people I knew—Zane Jaffe, who had recently shaved half her head, leaving only the half that was purple. Anderson Philpott, with whom I sometimes discussed books at Club Fred's. Obie Magoveny, who'd made the necktie I was wearing that night: a classy, subtle reel of film print. Countless voices I recognized, and others I did not.

First I saw them from the back, then their profiles as they stood beside each other, occasionally inclining their heads or brushing hands.

My system was on overdrive, and despite the grayscale, certain things were in sharp focus. Alisha's laughter at something Ed said, followed by the laughter of the two young men standing with them. Ed caught my eye and smiled, gesturing me over.

It was simple to excuse myself, to approach, to ready my nerves for yet another handshake, another greeting.

"Cam, you've met Josh and Keith, right? They run QYP down in the Harbor District."

I shook Josh's hand while parsing *QYP*. "Is that the drop-in center?"

"So you've heard of us." He smiled. Handsome, African American, with a certain twinkle in his eye that I, veteran of so many old movies, immediately found attractive. Not that I betrayed my reaction. I was used to seeing that kind of charm transmitted via a screen at a safe distance away. It didn't occur to me to respond to it.

"I think I must have read an article in the paper." I raised an eyebrow at Ed, who laughed.

"Guilty. I wrote two, actually, though the second one was online only."

I reached for the other man's hand. He looked far younger up close than he'd appeared from across the lobby. "I regret missing your open house. Sounds like it was interesting."

"You missed Josh giving a depressing speech and correcting an audience member about misquoting Gandhi." Hard to gauge his age. Blond, blue-eyed young men had a certain quality about them sometimes that made them seem frozen in time. They were often the same men who one day woke up having aged twenty years overnight.

In my line of work, you see people intermittently over a long period of time. You notice things like that.

"I can't judge. I just had to remind a woman nearly three times my age that it was Gregory Peck in *Roman Holiday,* not Cary Grant. Very awkward."

Josh waved a hand in my direction, as if I'd proved some kind of point. "What's the alternative, really? Let people wander around misquoting Gandhi and skewering film history?"

"It was a great speech, anyway," Alisha said. "Ed's still mad he didn't record it."

"I don't know what the hell I was thinking."

"One of the kids took video," Josh said. "Search YouTube."

"You're on YouTube?" I was utterly fascinated by YouTube. I'd been raised to believe that narrative belonged to experts, and I was entranced by the idea that people simply took it for themselves, molding their own stories however they wished.

"Only by accident." Keith grinned at Josh, and their shared expression might as well have been a gesture for as tangible as it felt to me. It was only a smile between two men, but it seemed to me that they held hands in that smile, perhaps even kissed.

I shook my head, trying to clear it of unwelcome images.

"How're you holding up?" Ed asked. "Is it as bad as you feared?"

"I started the night off by tripping over my feet and losing all my index cards. It's improved since then."

Keith cleared his throat, flushing pink, and reached into his little shoulder bag. "I, um, picked them up. At least, I think I got them all." He produced my stack of cards and handed them over, but it took half a beat of silence for me to realize I actually had to stretch my arm out to take them.

I was so captivated by the color in his cheeks. Sometimes people as pale as Keith blushed blotchy, but he glowed, rosy and sweet.

"Thank you." I didn't mean to brush against his fingers, but it happened anyway. "I think I was attempting to forget that part of the show."

"You did all right without them."

"I hope so. I had all these notes about the film . . ." Now was not the time.

"Can I ask you—what was your favorite part?"

"My favorite part," I repeated.

Alisha clapped. "Oh, good question."

"I mean, if you don't mind my asking," Keith murmured.

"Oh no. Not at all. Hm." I should have said something obvious, but for whatever reason, perhaps because I could see how blue his eyes were, I told him the truth. "Ah, it's a two-part answer. The first is the scene when Nickie goes to visit his grandmother and looks around her empty villa. I like that they allow all that space for his grief, for his pain."

"He touches her chair," Josh said. "I cried."

This time Keith reached out and physically took his hand.

"I hold out for my second favorite moment, which is when he hands over the stole to Terry and she knows that his grandmother is dead, without anyone using words or euphemisms, without any explanation. She just gets this . . . look on her face, this understanding." I swallowed, trying to cover the intensity of my feelings. "That's when I cry. Because she grieves, too."

Alisha hugged me, hard, and her hugs were comforting, even though I didn't find hugging comfortable. We must have spoken more, but I was distracted, thinking about grief and loss and the empty spaces left by people I'd loved.

I was hailed by a very old friend, and in the spirit of escape I made more excuses and went to say hello. The first words out of Hugh's mouth were, "Your parents would be so proud of you, Cameron," and I had to bite my tongue to keep the threads of my composure from unraveling.

The beautiful thing about having an old friend around in a moment like this was in the way he changed the subject to the film series, asking me when *Penny Serenade* would play, and promising to return for it.

Of course, the liability inherent in the presence of someone who remembered one as a fumbling, slightly besotted adolescent, is that when Hugh took my hand to say good night, I blushed.

"You should be very satisfied with tonight." His eyes, amused behind his glasses, glinted. "You might even consider being outright pleased."

"Next week is when we'll know if it worked. And the week after."

He gestured to the room, full of happy movie-goers and laughter. "It worked, Cameron. I'll see you soon."

"Good night."

I really had no idea how I made it through the rest of the evening. The reception in the lobby lasted only an hour and a half, and that was including the staff's quick efforts at throwing everything away after, but it seemed like an epoch, or perhaps like the spinning of the earth; I could tell myself time passed, but my experience of it did not reflect that reality.

When I finally locked the theater and walked up the steps to my apartment in the building next door, I felt exhausted and somehow violated. Not in a cheap way. Not in a way that trespassed on other uses of the word. But I'd taken a movie I felt intimately connected to, engaged with, and opened it up to La Vista, inviting everyone inside. It might have been a slip in judgment, to begin with a film I loved as much as I loved *An Affair to Remember*. Next week would be *North by Northwest*, a film about which it was possible to have a sense of humor, though my favorite anecdote about the movie was that Eva Marie Saint had to re-dub a line to avoid mentioning "making" love, which wasn't a story I planned to share with a crowd largely made up of people my late grandparents' age.

I didn't turn on the lights in my apartment. I toed off my shoes and walked in darkness. First to the bathroom to shower, lighting only a candle. Then to the bedroom. I didn't have the energy to deal with shapes and colors, and my anxiety-infused silvers and grays had worn off, leaving me with oversaturated hues and too much definition.

Far easier to feel my way by touch and familiarity, to slide into my sheets, to trust myself to textiles and the peaceful traffic on Mooney, which never truly went quiet.

Into my pleasant darkness, their faces intruded, their eyes. Josh's brown and twinkling. Keith's blue and seeking. Why did I project so much on two men I hardly knew? I shouldn't. I knew that. But I couldn't seem to help myself.

I hoped they'd come back next week. If only so I could see them more clearly and reassure myself that any pull I'd felt toward them was entirely misguided.

A week. I had another week in which no one would expect me to leave the safety of my ticket booth. I inhaled and called upon the vague sense of God that thirteen years of Catholic school had not quite burned out of me. *Thank you. I'll try to need you a little less next week, but no promises.*

God, if such a being existed, seemed inclined to treat my gratitude with calm benevolence. I'd long ago realized that my internal God was probably just a wish for the man I longed to be, who greeted the present moment with wonder and acceptance. Maybe I would someday learn how to do that. Until then I allowed myself the comfort of my prayers, infused my dark bedroom with as much peace as I could manage, and fell asleep.

CHAPTER 2

I went to Club Fred's at least once a week. The tradition—custom? habit?—stemmed from my parents, who used to mandate I go out for two hours each week to somewhere other people would be.

I'd argued that high school was enough mandated social interaction, but they'd told me that I didn't have to interact, I just had to *be*, which was an opportunity not really allowed at St. Patrick's. Certainly not being me, in any case.

By the time they died when I was twenty-four, I didn't mind going out once a week. And I'd never have gone to Club Fred's for any other reason. I occasionally met men there, but I actually preferred the understandable communications ascent of internet dating to the murky in-person variety. Emailing, phone calls, the awkward coffee date. It took me some time to work out how to present myself as a man interested in dating before hooking up, but now that I was comfortable asserting myself, I'd had a few decent (if brief) relationships resulting from my online forays.

Club Fred's was about something else. Sometimes I talked to people, but most of the time I sat at the bar and read whatever book I currently favored on my Kindle app. I ordered exactly one drink, a Scotch on the rocks, and sometimes I barely spoke to anyone. Because social interaction wasn't mandatory.

Except, on the Friday after my first somewhat disastrous attempt to introduce *An Affair to Remember*, I happened to hear a familiar laugh as I let *Rebecca* wash over me. Something about du Maurier got to me so deeply that I couldn't even say I loved her books. From the minute I opened them until I put them down, I felt a slightly painful tightness in my chest, no matter how many times I'd read them before, and it was so . . . present. So real. I hardly had to pay any attention to *Rebecca*, I'd read it so many times; my eyes scanned the pages and the book played out in my mind as if it were a film. (*Not* the adaptations, which might be all right, but were nothing compared to how viscerally I became immersed in the book.)

There I sat, nursing my single drink, lost in Manderley, when I heard Josh's laughter somewhere nearby.

There was something magnetic about each of them, or maybe it was about both of them together. I heard his laugh and immediately searched for him in the crowd, finding Keith's fair hair first.

They touched each other so much. Not in such a way that it seemed to be an advertisement, a flashing neon sign of righteous couple-hood. The way the two of them touched wasn't merely subtle, it was practically invisible. Josh might drag his knuckles across Keith's jeans, at the side where his hand happened to hit, almost a subconscious *I'm here*. Keith might sit in a certain way so that their arms met for a second, a split second, probably so quick and gone that no one who wasn't watching specifically for it would notice.

I watched. I'd watched in the lobby, but at Club Fred's I watched with intention, to prove or disprove my theory about how frequently they touched. I tried not to be creepy about it—I hardly knew them, and they were clearly younger than I was, and clearly devoted to one another—but I wanted to understand how it worked, that kind of togetherness. I'd had the odd boyfriend here or there, but I'd never made it to moving-in status. I'd hardly made it past spend-the-night status, and that had been . . . rare.

And distantly past. My mind could not make it back to the new Mrs. de Winter, as alluring as she was in her determinedly unalluring way. I could, of course, go home. I'd left the theater in the care of my loyal staff, who didn't expect me back in tonight. I enjoyed being alone in my apartment, listening to traffic, reading or browsing my usual online haunts for new films to lease. Not *new* in the sense of *recent*, of course. *New* in the sense of *I haven't shown them before*.

But I didn't want to go home. Josh laughed again, and I turned on my stool to see them more clearly than I could with a glance.

Laughing with Obie and Emerson, whom I at least knew. I could approach, say hello.

But why? Social interaction wasn't mandatory, after all. And I'd already talked to Tom the bartender for a few minutes.

Still, I *did* want to say hello. I couldn't figure out the reason I felt drawn to them, or what it meant, but I could now sense their presence in the room and I didn't want to let go of that awareness.

What would Cary do?

Find an angle, of course. The way he did everything. I wasn't Cary Grant, though; I was odd, slightly awkward Cameron Rheingold, who read at the bar and counted nontheater social interactions per week in single digits.

Of course, the entire point of the film series was for me to start reaching out more, cultivating the theater as the kind of community hub it had been when my parents ran it. That this wasn't the theater seemed beside the point.

Social skills were social skills, and I could practice them wherever I liked.

I stood up, embracing the way my brain visually dimmed the rest of Club Fred's until I could focus on the small group of men standing at a high table. I would say hello. If it was intolerably awkward, I'd then say good-bye. Having a reputation for being a little strange meant there wasn't that far to fall in other people's opinions, so I made my way over and braced myself for eye contact.

Keith saw me first. Keith, whose blue eyes had penetrated my protective grayscale. He smiled. That was it, nothing overwhelming. He smiled in greeting, or in welcome, and I smiled back without thinking.

"Cameron, hey," Obie said. "You've met the QYP guys, right?"

"I have."

Josh grinned, his all-out tooth-baring grin, and slightly inclined his head toward Keith's. "Babe, we're 'the QYP guys.' How cool is that?"

"It's cool. Hi, Cameron. Nice to see you again."

I shook hands all around and stood beside Obie's entertainingly prickly boyfriend, Emerson. Where you would look at Josh and Keith and see an unassailable air of projected togetherness, you'd look at Obie and Emerson and wonder how two such different people even managed to have a conversation, let alone a relationship.

It was always so fascinating to study people. Obie and Emerson gave me a lot to watch.

"Did you see I wore the tie on Saturday?" I asked Obie. He was one of the people I hadn't managed to say hello to for longer than a moment after *An Affair to Remember*.

"Of course I did! You looked great. Are you excited about this week's movie?"

"You can't go wrong with *North by Northwest*," Josh said. "We're looking forward to it."

"It doesn't matter how many times you've seen the crop duster scene," Keith added. "You always think that this time he might, you know, not get out of that field."

I blinked, a little impressed they knew the upcoming film. "Yes. I planned the film series hoping to seduce people with a few pictures they already know they like in the beginning."

"And lock them in," Obie agreed. "Sounds good." He poked Emerson. "Shouldn't we be seduced by Cam's film festival?"

"We're watching James on Saturday." Emerson didn't exactly look heartbroken. I enjoyed the idea that he'd prefer the company of an infant to being out in public. Having never been around children, I couldn't say if I'd make the same choice, but maybe I would.

Of course, the movie theater didn't feel like "public" to *me*. It was more like a large extension of my living room. Especially when I was showing Cary Grant.

"Will you tell me more about QYP?" I asked a few minutes later, after Obie and Emerson excused themselves to the dance floor. I'd hesitated—the role of third wheel is often more acutely tricky than that of fifth wheel—but neither Keith nor Josh seemed inclined to be irritated by my presence.

"Fair warning," Josh said. "If you open that door, we might not be able to control ourselves."

That strange bubbling sensation in my chest, which usually only arrived when I was flirting—or considering it—made no sense in the current context of Josh's smile. He and I could not be flirting. And why did the bubbling intensify when Keith laughed?

"So true. Josh's mom said we're like people with a new baby except we have fewer pictures."

"But not none." Josh pulled out his phone and paged through before holding it out to me.

I obliged him by taking it. "That's . . . a very nice kitchen."

"It's the kitchen at the center. We cook there as much as possible, since it's way better than ours."

"Oh." I looked more closely. The long peninsula seemed like the perfect place to sit. I wondered if the rest of the room held up to the kitchen's large scale. "I think someone said you're down in the Harbor District?"

"At the edge of it, yeah, in one of the warehouses down there. You should really come by, Cameron."

Keith nodded. "We're open noon to nine, though we're hoping to expand those hours at some point."

"And get staff coverage."

They smiled wryly at each other.

"Is it just the two of you at the moment?"

"Mostly." Josh shifted his beer on the table, marring the damp ring it had made. "We have some volunteers, but we're just not established yet. And we definitely aren't in a position to hire anyone, which is what we'll need to do eventually, as my chief financial officer keeps telling me."

Keith elbowed Josh. "Don't call me that unless you're paying me like a CFO."

"Partner, partner. My significantly more financially astute partner."

"It's not financial, anyway. But I know that you and I together can't work twelve-hour days six days a week without burning out."

"Do you actually take a day off?" I knew that routine. I'd done it after my parents died, running myself into the ground.

"Well, we don't open to the public on Sundays," Josh said. "I go to church. Keith goes to the center and does paperwork."

Keith shot him a look. "Paperwork can be sacred. It's a ritual, anyway. What about you, Cameron? Do you take days off from the theater?"

Both of them had said my name, and I liked the sound of it in their voices.

"I do." I fought, with every fiber of my being, the flush that wanted to steal over my skin. So ridiculous. They were simply kind, and attentive, and absolutely not interested in me, no matter what my unusually overheated body seemed to think. "We've had the same Thursday, Friday, Saturday, Sunday crew for years, so I can work shifts on those days without worrying about opening or closing, filling in where I'm needed."

"So which day do you actually take off?" Keith had dimples— not wildly flashing dimples, just two little points that showed up with each smile and promptly disappeared again.

I needed to stop thinking about his dimples.

"Oh, whenever we have coverage. We changed over to the digital projector about five years ago, which makes it somewhat easier to staff."

"Because newer equipment means less training?" Josh asked.

"I served as projectionist a lot before, since I'd grown up doing it and knew how to fix things if they stalled out in the middle of a picture. Or if the projector decided not to run. But the digital system is much less fussy, so we have a lot more folks who can run it." Their eyes didn't appear to be glazing over—yet—but I was still relieved when people suddenly crowded our table, eager to say hello.

Zane, Jaq, Jaq's girlfriend Hannah. People I knew. Jaq and Zane were bickering as usual, and I scooted closer to Josh so they could all squeeze around the table.

"I'm just saying it's too big a risk," Jaq argued. "Philpott! Anderson Philpott, get your skinny ass over here!"

We made room for one more, and I smiled apologetically at Josh as I accidentally brushed against him.

"Hon, you can't save people," Hannah said. "Even canceling the Halloween event won't save people."

Zane, from Keith's other side, leaned toward us. "Jaq's on kind of a rampage, don't mind her."

"I'm not on a rampage, damn it. Philpott, back me up— Don't you think the only thing that makes sense is to cancel the next Club Fred's theme night, you know, since people keep getting murdered at them?"

"Technically they're murdered after them." Philpott nodded around at all of us, standing a little apart from our table. "And I assume unless Fredi closed the bar completely, the killer could still recruit a victim here."

"Then why doesn't she close the bar?"

"Oh my god," Zane said. "We had this fight last time."

"And someone fucking *died.*"

Hannah put a hand on Jaq's arm. "Breathe, Jaq."

"I'd close the bar if I owned it," Josh said. "But I don't think it would have any effect on what's going on here. They, whoever they are, would still find someone to target, don't you think?"

"So why would you close the bar?" Philpott asked, raising his eyebrows.

Zane added, "Close it for good, or just for that night?"

"Just for that night, since it's already been promoted, though I guess I'd hate for Fredi to lose business on a Friday night. And I'd do it for my own peace of mind." Josh gestured to the bar. "After Tom getting arrested, and information coming out that the victims were all here the night they died, Fredi looks older."

Jaq nodded. "Like presidents at the end of their term, not the beginning. She looks grayer. Than she used to."

"No doubt it's taking a toll, but I'm not sure how even closing for the night would impact anything." Philpott shrugged. "A serial killer doesn't stop killing because their favorite hunting ground shuts down for a night. They simply hunt on a different night, or in a different place."

"Plus," Keith said, "someone needs to mention acceptance of risk. We're sitting here now knowing that someone's out there thinking about the next person they want to hurt." He made a space-limited gesture at the table. "We've all knowingly accepted the risk, haven't we?"

"Risk aware and consenting," Philpott agreed. "I'm with Keith on this one. I think the only thing we can do is be vigilant and watch out for each other, and hopefully defeat this guy that way. It seems clear that people willingly accompany the killer at least part of the way, so the best thing is to work it from that angle."

Jaq shook her head incredulously. "Are all of you nuts? If there's a direct connection between theme nights and people dying, how can you sit here and say we keep having theme nights? I just— What else can we fucking do?"

I thought about something Ed had said to me the last time we talked about it. "But if they keep killing on theme nights, that might actually help catch the person. There are only so many people who come here, and most of them use credit cards." Ed had told Fredi and Tom to pay attention to anyone using cash, though they said enough people did so they couldn't remember them all. I decided not to share that with the group. Jaq might scream.

"That's grim," Josh murmured. Philpott nodded and seemed on the verge of speaking, then didn't.

Jaq's fingers drummed on the table. "So we're bait. That's the silver lining?"

"Well, *we* aren't bait," Hannah said. "You're not going anywhere with anyone who isn't me."

"You know what I mean."

We all knew what she meant. And for a moment we all looked around, thinking about that.

Josh shifted, slightly, not in a way that anyone would notice unless they were physically standing against him. I glanced down in time to watch him skim his fingers over Keith's. "And on that note, we're dancing. Anyone else?"

"You betcha." Hannah finished off her wine. "C'mon, sugar."

Jaq might have stayed longer, but Hannah tugged her, and she went. Josh and Keith waved good-bye, and I waved back.

"I'm dancing too," Zane said. She eyed me, then Philpott. "Let me guess: that's a no from both of you."

"I don't dance." He grinned.

She rolled her eyes. "Cameron? Keep a girl company?"

"I'm about to head home." Which was true. I mentally reminded my parents that they hadn't mandated dancing, either. I'd been on the dance floor at Club Fred's a few times, with various dates, but not generally if I could help it.

"I'll have to dance alone, I guess! Bye, boys!" With a flip of her purple hair over the shaved part of her head, she was off.

"Are you really leaving?" Philpott asked. He wasn't quite smirking. "Or can I ask you about your film festival?"

"Ask away."

"Tell me you're showing *Notorious.*"

"That's how we're closing out the series. You like Hitchcock?"

"I do like Hitchcock, but *Notorious* is my favorite Cary Grant. I think because his role could have been played by any leading man–type actor, but he brings it more depth than it had at the textual level."

"I completely agree. You could plug in any man and Ingrid Bergman would still have sailed through the story. But the way he plays passionate and snubbed and aloof all at once is perfect."

"I've never seen it on the big screen, so I can't wait." He drained his beer. "See you around, Cameron."

"You too."

He turned away and a young man I didn't recognize sidled up to him. Both of them smiled, familiarly. I'd never seen Philpott with anyone, though I'd always assumed he was gay, or bi, or queer in that way people are now when they don't define themselves. I sometimes wish I'd been slightly less certain so early on, that I'd embraced a wider idea of who I could be.

But perhaps I would have always ended up the way I ended up.

I walked out of Club Fred's and shivered in the chill, though not exclusively because of it. Five people had died. I knew this only because I paid a very small amount of attention. You didn't have to be that up on current events to know the basic facts, which were that on five separate occasions, over the last eight months, Club Fred's held theme nights that ended in deaths.

Five people. I hadn't known any of them, really, but I'd bought a young man a drink on his birthday only to discover weeks later that he'd been killed that night. I couldn't grieve him; I hadn't known him. But I stood on the sidewalk, flipping my collar up against the wind, and thought about that night, and that boy, who'd left by this exact door in the company of someone who had betrayed his trust so fundamentally that he had not survived it.

I went home, turning my mind to Saturday. *North by Northwest* would be fun, and this time I would not drop my index cards.

CHAPTER 3

The second week of the film series went well. No index cards were dropped. I told the story of the journalist who'd originated the idea of the fake agent pursued across the country, and how he'd made ten thousand dollars when Hitchcock bought the story from him. I also encouraged the audience—again, filling most seats in the theater—to keep their eyes open for Hitch's possible second appearance in the film. (The first was during the opening credits, when Hitch missed his bus.)

I settled in to socializing in the lobby after, without the world being quite as gray and black as it had been the previous week, which meant I was a little more raw, a little less protected by my pleasant celluloid shield.

Less prepared for Keith to touch my arm, casually, as I stood in front of an old *White Christmas* poster I superstitiously never took down. The two of them had approached, slowly, but I'd seen them coming. Still, the touch was a brief jolt to my system. I couldn't feel his fingers through my suit coat, but for some reason I tried to, as if all I needed to do was make a wish and then I'd feel the phantom warmth of his hand.

"I loved the movie," he said. "Not as much as *An Affair to Remember,* but more than *Rear Window.*"

I managed to smile. "Are you a Jimmy Stewart fan?"

"I am, a little."

"He means a lot," Josh added.

"Then I'm sure I'll see you for *The Philadelphia Story.*"

Both of them smiled, satisfaction in stereo.

"You'll see us for all the movies, Cameron," Keith said. "But will you come down to QYP this week? We'd love to show you around."

"Of course." I forced myself to pause for a moment, to still all the twitching thought-stubs in my head (calculating how much longer people would linger, and if we'd run out of snacks, and if I should have petitioned for a temporary liquor license after all, since the array of juices looked so silly on their table). "Yes. I'd really like that."

Keith's eyes were still so blue. A dark and forgiving blue, with flecks of sky and sea.

"When will you be off? Or is that something you can predict at all?"

I had no idea. "Mondays are generally safe. Monday late morning?"

"Great." He patted my arm once. "See you then."

Josh grinned. "Looking forward to it. Good night."

I said good night, and maybe I was searching for meaning in ridiculous things, or maybe there was some magic to the two of them, but opening the door seemed to pierce the surface tension of the room and soon everyone was saying good night and following Josh and Keith out into the cold.

A coincidence, or just that kind of timing. No magic to it at all. But I found myself associating them with the peace of an empty lobby, smiling to myself about visiting their center.

Merely the anticipation of going somewhere new, pursuing more conversations with new friends. Or so I told myself, sternly, with no room for anything else. Even as I pictured Keith's eyes and recalled an echo of Josh's laugh.

It began raining late Sunday night and continued through Monday. I pulled the Volvo to the curb in front of the last warehouse on the row, which had a rainbow-painted sign out front, dripping bits of color onto the sidewalk.

Queer Youth Project - Change the world.

Simple sentiment. Hard to argue with. Too bad about the sign, though. They'd certainly need to invest in one that resisted weather fluctuations.

I got out of my car and straightened my clothes as I walked, wishing I'd worn my longer topcoat. No awnings on this side of the Harbor District, no cover of any kind as I approached the large, horizontally sliding door—suitable for deliveries—which was open three feet wide.

The first thing I saw, before I was even inside, were the colors. More colors. Bright colors, but not garish, not offensive to the eye: blues, purples, and greens, in blocks two-thirds of the way up the high walls. From there to the ceiling they were a warmish gray tone. I slid in through the opening and stood there looking around, appreciating the scale of the place, and the clever way it had been arranged to maximize and contain specific areas. On the far side were little conversational nooks, groupings of chairs and couches, all serviceable, none seeming altogether luxurious or comfortable. A few long tables with folding chairs along the outside wall, and another area beside it with two round tables. Places to work, or perhaps study.

Josh sat at one of the round tables alongside a young man in a coat far too big for him. I couldn't tell if he'd seen me, but he was clearly busy, so I side stepped to get out of the breezy doorway and continued a visual tour.

The kitchen dominated the left side of the room, large and open, and the peninsula I'd seen on Josh's picture had stools, as was only sensible.

Beyond the kitchen, along the back wall, were a couple of thrift-store bookshelves, mostly empty, and a handful of brightly colored beanbag chairs. And a doorway, in which Keith suddenly appeared.

He smiled and waved, but didn't speak until he'd crossed the wide expanse of the room. "Hey, I'm so glad you could come out in the rain."

"I haven't melted. Yet."

"Were you worried that you'd turned into the Wicked Witch? Here, can I get you anything? We have a pot of coffee made relatively recently, and vast stores of hot chocolate and dehydrated hot cider."

I followed him into the kitchen, where he poked around in cabinets until he found what he was looking for.

"Sorry, we keep shifting things around. Here." He handed me a mug and gestured to the little basket with supplies, and the coffeepot.

"Thanks. It's incredibly cold out there today. I thought the rain might warm things up, but this is clearly a cold front." I tapped the pound bag of coffee. "Sobrantes? Your coffee budget must be high."

He grinned. "We make one pot of Sobrantes a day, which is what we'd make in the apartment if we didn't come straight here in the mornings. What you're drinking is actually generic grocery-store brand with a tiny bit of cinnamon at the bottom of the carafe to liven it up a little. But see if it doesn't taste better when you're looking at a bag of Moon Bay Blend."

I appreciated the notion and sipped my coffee, thinking about Los Sobrantes, the best roaster in La Vista. "I think you're right. It certainly doesn't taste cheap."

"See? Now let me show you around a little."

We turned to leave the kitchen when the sound of a chair scraping across the ground made both of us pause.

The young man at the table had stood up fast and was staring down at Josh, body rigid with anger.

"Hey," Josh said sharply. He, too, pushed back from the table. But he didn't stand. He stared up at the boy until the boy's shoulders hunched, and he sank back into his seat.

"I hate it when this happens," Keith murmured. "Intellectually I understand that they do this father-child dynamic in a way that works for both of them, but I find the fighting hard to take." He glanced at me. "That's Merin, our second-in-command. I'll introduce you when they're done with their current showdown."

"Of course." I turned, allowing him the opportunity to turn as well, so he wasn't looking at the round table. "How did all this get started? I'm dying of curiosity."

"It was all Josh's idea. Though he'd say none of it would have happened without me."

They'd met in college. I was surprised to discover that Keith was still in college, his final year before graduating with a BA in business administration. But even as surprised as I was, I could also see his youth in his cheeks, in his hands, constantly gesturing.

"You work around your class schedule?" I asked.

"Most of my professors have been great about it. I mean, I'm applying a lot of what my classmates have only ever read about, so a few of them will let me skip classes and turn in extra work, or attend classes and curtail some of the assignments for other things. I'm actually working with one of my professors right now on our bookkeeping as an independent study project, which is kind of amazing. I should be paying her, but she said she's so delighted to have something real to think about, she should be paying me." He shook his head. "Sorry, you were asking about how we got started. It was Josh's crazy, amazing idea, but he pretty much introduced himself to me one minute, and the next minute told me that we were about to start a business together and was I prepared to be the brains of the outfit? I told him he better not be implying I wasn't beautiful." A smile tugged at the corners of his lips, and I watched, waiting that half beat until it won, fully taking over. "He's so charming. It's obnoxious."

I made my voice dry. "I can see that."

"Oh god, stop." Now he blushed, and it was a lovely thing, watching Keith blush. I could appreciate the aesthetics without being personally invested. Who wouldn't appreciate Keith standing before them in a blue plaid button-down, gripping his coffee and trying to hide his smile?

"How long ago was that? It seems like QYP happened incredibly fast."

"Ha. Not from our perspective. We met three years ago. It took a year and a half to put together the full business plan and really work it all out, though we've had people interested in investing almost from the start. Josh likes to say rich white people can't resist throwing money at him."

I considered his ... obnoxious charm, and agreed. "I'm completely impressed so far. What's the vision for it?"

"We want to save the kids. All of them, but especially the queer kids." His eyes flicked to the round table again. "Hopefully at some point we'll have a good network of shelters, at least for the kids who are over eighteen. But the younger kids are a problem. Foster care isn't a good solution, but everything else is illegal. Sorry. I'm mumbling to myself. We can't anticipate all the needs our community will have, but even just getting started, we have a few people coming in to use the lockers, and more than a few requests for computer use, though we don't have a good system for that yet."

"And are people coming by?"

"Yeah, I know you can't tell by today, but the rain's killer. We get a good little group after the high school lets out, and throughout the day we have a little bit of traffic around meal times. It's getting to be an issue with ages. We don't demand ID, but we're an under-twenty-five organization, for the safety of the younger kids. Food draws in everyone." He gestured to the high windows, where rain kept pelting. "When it was sunny, we brought the food outside. That way we could offer it to whoever stopped by without compromising on our demographics. Harder now."

"And presumably there's higher demand for a place to get off the street."

He held up his hand, seesawing it back and forth. "When we're established, that might be the case. At the moment we don't have too many people lingering. People who live on the streets often have their haunts and their usual places to go in bad weather. We haven't made it into anyone's regular rotation yet, and to be honest, that's not our goal. We exist to catch a certain group of kids *before* they start living on the street." Another glance over. I followed his gaze.

Josh was sitting closer, talking to the young man at the table, leaning in. Not too close, but before there had been an invisible barrier between them, and now there was none, only space. I could see how much the boy wanted Josh's help, and how resistant he was to accepting it, mirrored on the other side by how much Josh was holding back because this wasn't the type of young man you could hug to make everything better.

"I don't know," Keith murmured. "What do you do with a kid whose home life consists of putting their head down and hoping to scrape by safely until they turn eighteen? And then what do you do? Hand them off to a shelter? They'd make Merin go to a women's shelter and—there's no way."

I studied them again, but Merin still read like an angry young man to me. "He'd pick the streets?"

Keith touched my arm, as he had the other night. "We don't use gendered pronouns. But yes. *He* would choose the street over a women's shelter, and even if we could somehow find a men's shelter, I'm not at all sure that would be safe. The world is not set up for trans youth, Cameron."

"I'm sorry." It was the only thing I could think of to say, no matter how absurd.

"Let's make lunch. Do you mind working? Sorry, that's terrible, isn't it? Inviting you down here and putting you to work."

"I don't mind in the least. I don't need to be back at the theater until four, so by all means, put me to work. What are we making?"

"Sandwiches. Peanut butter and jelly, and tuna. Nothing fancy."

I took off my jacket and draped it over a stool, then rolled up my cuffs. "How can I help?"

Keith blushed, again, and lowered his head. "I hope you don't take this the wrong way, but I really like how you wear clothes. Um. God, that's embarrassing. Anyway."

Take it the wrong way? I had no idea how to take it. I had no idea what to say.

He cleared his throat. "Sorry. Um. Here, start on peanut butter. Let's make a loaf of each type. The food's mostly donated, and we bring the uneaten prepared food back up to the soup kitchen on Third and Water Street."

I nodded, still trying to find my tongue. And trying not to look over at my fellow sandwich maker, blush lightly staining his cheeks.

I did not meet Merin that day. When they were done with their conversation, Merin slipped out the door with a vague backward wave I assumed was intended for Keith.

Josh stood up, slowly, as if he ached, and made his way to the kitchen. A few people had stopped by for sandwiches, but we still had plenty left. He grabbed a tuna and jumped up to sit on the counter.

"Sorry about not saying hello earlier," he said to me.

"Not at all. I completely understand."

"That makes one of us. I don't completely understand anything right now." He looked at Keith. "How do you feel about becoming a foster parent?"

Keith winced. "Did you finally figure out what's going on?"

"No. But it's clear Merin's only telling us a fraction of what's actually happening, and I don't like any of it. Neither does Jaq. She called again this morning to make sure we had eyes on Merin, since the little punk skipped school. Sorry, Cameron. I don't mean to leave you out or discuss totally private things in front of you."

"It's really not a problem. Would you like me to step away for a moment?"

"No, no. Stay. How do you like the center?"

"It's incredible. I am . . . impressed and amazed."

Josh's grin was infectious. "Good. Glad to hear it. We do seek to amaze. We're really happy you found time to hang out."

"Absolutely." I didn't have a follow-up, and he was chewing. The moment of silence wasn't awkward, exactly, but I felt awkward suddenly, standing there in what felt like their kitchen. "What's this about?" I asked, tapping a piece of paper taped to a cabinet.

"National Coming Out Day is tomorrow, so we'd hoped to barbecue outside," Keith said. "But the rain's not supposed to break until late, unfortunately."

Josh shrugged. "My dad will barbecue in the rain. It's just a matter of how much of that food we'll end up donating to the soup kitchen."

"True. If you're interested in dinner tomorrow, you should come down again, Cameron."

"I'm on from noon until closing, actually," I said with some regret. I wouldn't mind another excuse to sit and talk to them. Then again, maybe I could do one better. "National Coming Out Day," I mused. "I think perhaps the Rhein will be donating all proceeds tomorrow to a promising organization helping queer youth."

Both of them blinked at me.

It was last-minute, but I could make it work. "Would you send me an email with your logo? I need to print a couple of signs. Next year we'll work it out a few weeks in advance, but there's still a little bit of time to get the word out."

"Are you serious?" Josh set the last of his sandwich down. "Cameron, are you serious right now?"

"Of course I'm serious. Why not? We've done things like this in the past." And while technically I should wait until I did the books at the end of the month before cutting a check, I knew I wouldn't. I'd estimate. The exact amount mattered less than getting them the money quickly; it couldn't possibly be cheap to have installed the huge kitchen and furnished everything.

Keith bit his lip. "I don't even know what to say. Thanks so much. That means—that means a lot to us."

"Well, don't get too excited. Tuesdays are not huge days at the theater. But between Ed, Alisha, and me, we should be able to round up a couple extra moviegoers. It might be worth dropping a flyer at Club Fred's as well."

"Right, the logo. Give me your email address. And phone number." Keith programmed both into his phone. "Cameron, thank you so much."

"Really, it will only be a few hundred dollars. It's absolutely not that big a deal."

But there was no convincing them. They seemed unreasonably grateful and I finally distracted them by asking if they had a computer in the building we could quickly work up a flyer on so I could stop by the copy store and drop some off before heading back to the theater.

Keith, it turned out, was something of a whiz. In no time he had the Rhein's logo, QYP's logo, and a pleasing invitation to see any film at the theater on Tuesday, October eleventh, and all proceeds would be donated to the Queer Youth Project. He also insisted on printing ten of them, in color, to save me the trip to the copy store.

Both of them shook my hand as I headed out, though I had the distinct impression they wanted to hug me instead.

I would have accepted the hugs.

CHAPTER

I f I'd been able to plan the movie we were showing Tuesday, I would
have picked a film with some relevance. Perhaps coming-of-age, or a
story about redemption.

What we were actually showing: *The Big Lebowski*. You might be
able to make the argument that *The Big Lebowski* was about *something*
(though I wouldn't), but it was certainly not a film I associated with
bringing hope to anyone who wasn't incredibly stoned at the time.

On a normal night we'd still have made a little money. It
was considered a cult classic by a lot of people with disposable
income, and we did well on films like that.

On National Coming Out Day, momentum gathered, slowly,
and by that evening we were having a very good day. More surprising
than a sudden wave of Coen brothers fans was the fact that so many
of them seemed pleased to hear about QYP.

I'd set up little folded cardboard signs along the outside shelf of
the ticket booth, along with posting a few more flyers in the window
so that people waiting in line could read them. I expected it to end
there, but every third person or so wanted to ask questions about the
center, and even more miraculously, very few people seemed impatient
with the explanations.

As a general rule I like to process the line quickly and get
everyone into the theater, where they can pick up their food. We
serve salads and sandwiches and a few basic hot foods, like nachos
and hot dogs and soup. Because it takes a little while longer than the
popcorn and candy (which has its own line), I don't want to hold up
the ticket sales. And I have no reason to; unlike both of my parents,
I do not treat the booth like an ongoing social hour.

Yet on that Tuesday I enjoyed talking about QYP and the plans Josh and Keith had for it. Once or twice I mentioned that I would have liked such a place when I was younger, and I got a few knowing nods.

The 7 p.m. show attracted some familiar faces. It took me about five minutes to realize the group buying could have all been at home at Club Fred's, which was right around the time I noticed Ed and Alisha approaching the window.

"I didn't realize you were coming tonight."

"We weren't, until Tom told us about the fundraiser."

It was a fundraiser, I supposed. I hadn't thought of it like that. "Happy National Coming Out Day." I passed them their tickets.

Alisha pushed a little cellophane-wrapped pile of cookies through the small gap in the window. "You too. I made more, but these were the, um, edible ones."

Ed smirked; she hit him; he claimed he hadn't said anything. I thanked her and waved them along.

More people showed up for the ten o'clock show, as if Fredi had handed out five-dollar bills and bussed them across town. This time the explanations were greeted with less politeness and far more enthusiasm.

"What a great idea. I can't believe I hadn't heard of them," a gorgeous, statuesque woman I vaguely knew from roller derby posters said, handing me a twenty. "Can I give this to you to give to them?"

I started to explain how donations worked, when I saw someone wave from farther back in the line.

Josh. Grinning.

"But," I continued, "you can feel free to trust it to Josh and Keith for safe keeping. They're right—there."

She giggled, taking her ticket and rejoining the line alongside them, seeming somewhat delighted to have the opportunity to meet the men behind QYP. What had Obie called them? *The QYP guys.* Yes.

I could hardly control the pull of a smile when they made it to the window. "Two?"

"Four, actually. My folks wanted to come, but this is too late. And Keith told them they'd hate the movie."

"They would!"

I took their money—and Josh's parents' money—and passed four tickets back. "But with the cut I have to take, it would have made more sense to just give you a donation."

"Nah. They're supporting the theater and the center at the same time. Thanks, Cameron."

"Of course."

They moved out of the way, and I wrapped up sales for the night, vaguely planning what I'd do to keep myself busy until the movie let out. If I wanted to really stay busy, I could send most of the staff home. More to do, good for payroll. I wasn't tired, after all.

And I wanted to see them. Even if only for a moment. I had a small, unobtrusive crush on Josh and Keith. Harmless. The kind of crush you got on people who embodied qualities you admired. They were both so focused, so driven, so hardworking. It wasn't sexual, I told myself, as I puttered in the booth. It was . . . intellectual. An intellectual crush.

A tap on my door. I looked up—the booth, of course, was nearly all window, with no place to hide—surprised to see them standing there. The jolt of heat I felt at the sight of them somewhat betrayed that my crush wasn't *entirely* intellectual.

I fumbled the doorknob. "Are you— The movie already began—"
It was exactly thirteen minutes in, my monitor informed me.

"We aren't really here for the movie," Josh said.

Recognition dawned. "Oh, I'm so sorry, I won't have a check for you until—"

"We aren't here for a check, either." This grin was crooked, lifting higher on the left side. Josh had a strong jaw, which made his mischievous, playful smile even more attractive. "Thank you so much for doing this, Cameron. We appreciate it."

"You two are doing all the hard work." I stepped out of the booth, which seemed less awkward than staying inside it and speaking to them through the doorway. "It's only a small thing, and next time I'll get publicity out well in advance, but I think it went well for a spontaneous attempt. How was your barbecue?"

Keith shrugged. "We managed to give away most of the food, and make some good connections. Not entirely with our target groups, but then again, not necessarily outside them, either. We can't always know who we're talking to."

"And what they're getting out of engaging with QYP," Josh added. "I can see that."

We stood there, not quite awkwardly. A pause that would, should it become a silence, be awkward, but wasn't quite yet.

"I can get you a check later in the week," I said. "If that's all right."

Josh cleared his throat and glanced at Keith before looking back at me. "We'd like to take you to dinner. Whenever is convenient for you, though it will have to be around this time of day, after we close."

"Oh, you don't have to. I figured I'd just drop the check by the center." I'd counted on using it as an excuse to visit again.

"Or on Sunday," he continued, ignoring my equivocation. "If ten is too late. But we'd . . . really like to take you to dinner, Cameron."

Keith shifted, not quite nudging him. "Unless you aren't interested."

Interested? I swallowed, resisting the gentle pressure at the edges of my vision to extract all color. No. I didn't want to lose their eyes. Especially not right now, when both of them seemed slightly nervous. As if they were asking me out on a date, not a thank-you dinner.

"Oh, no, ten is—ten is fine." I pictured the schedule. "I really only have Thursday this week, but next week I'll be free Monday through Wednesday."

"Monday would be great," Keith said. A tentative smile in my direction. "It's a date, then. Do you want to meet up at the Grill?"

The San Marcos Grill was a seafood restaurant perched at the edge of the Harbor District, overlooking the bay. It had been renovated about five years before, earning a title as the fanciest restaurant in La Vista. Top of the list for romantic dinners.

I swallowed so loudly that even over the ambient sounds of the theater around us, they must have heard it. "I— That would be— Of course, that sounds fine. At ten?"

"Let's plan on ten, but I'll confirm it once I make the reservation."

Reservation. I'd gone on exactly three dates requiring reservations, and two were in high school, with young women I'd playfully courted. Young women who'd known that it was all in fun.

Surely this must be as well. My pounding heart—indicating excitement more than anxiety—notwithstanding.

"Thank you." My voice sounded bizarrely formal to my ears. "I look forward to it. But you're missing the movie."

Josh laughed. "Keith *hates* this movie. With a passion."

"Because it's ridiculous and I don't care about any of the characters. I understand watching it the first time, but how can so many people continue to enjoy it? The crime plot is a joke. And the rest of it is absurd."

Josh allowed his knuckles to brush across Keith's. I shouldn't watch such things when we were this close together.

"I think it's cute how much you hate *The Big Lebowski*."

Keith shot an unimpressed glare at him. "Glad I could entertain you. Anyway, Cameron, thanks again. And we'll see you on Saturday for *His Girl Friday*."

"And Monday for dinner."

Their habit of finishing one another's sentences and adding thoughts on the end should have been annoying, except that somehow they did it without seeming codependent. Each of them embellished on the other's ideas without highlighting any previous gaps or flaws, additions without any notion of absence being compensated for.

Or maybe I was inclined to find it charming because they charmed me.

"I look forward to Saturday," I said, still too stiffly.

"So do we. Bye, Cameron." Both of them smiled and backed toward the door.

I waved, uncertainly. I disliked feeling so off-footed around them, but on the other hand there was something refreshing about it, something surprising. I spoke to people all day long and rarely felt that stirring of newness that theoretically accompanied such frequent interactions with strangers. When I wanted to be intrigued, or challenged, I turned to films, books, art, poetry. Those were the spaces in my life that made me consider new angles, or inspired me to form new thoughts.

I felt a nagging sort of hunger to spend more time with Keith and Josh, and despite how little I cared to admit it, part of me wished that this playful date was something else.

Far more in need of a distraction than I had been before, I offered early offs to the two teenagers who were running concessions, and they eagerly accepted.

Good. Closing concessions entirely on my own would give me something to focus on so I would think less about Monday and the date that wasn't.

CHAPTER 5

T ext messaging was a medium I hadn't had much cause to explore. Ed liked to text me, generally if he had a question I could answer, or if he wanted to stop by and was making sure I'd be around. I'd had a boyfriend, early in the texting age, who'd loved it, though I'd found the practice tedious. That was before touch screens or QWERTY keyboards.

Still, it wasn't something I did daily. Or initiated.

At nine thirty Friday night my phone made its odd little sound to indicate a message had arrived. Since it was rare, the sound startled me, registering below the consistent tide of ticket-purchasers requesting tickets and myself citing prices. (The magic of the five-dollar ticket is in its simplicity: my cash customers never needed me to do the math.)

When I had a spare moment, I woke my phone from its usually peaceful slumber.

Unknown number: *Reservation set for 10:30 Monday. Still okay?*

As I stared at it, a second message came through.

Unknown number: *This is Keith. Is that obvious?*

Unknown number: *I probably should have led with that.*

Unknown number: *Do you text? I guess I'll call if I don't hear from you.*

Right, yes, I should reply. I hit Reply and stared for a long moment at the fresh message.

Cameron: *I text. And yes, that works perfectly.*

There. Very straightforward. The message ding went off again as I was saving his phone number in my contacts.

Keith: *Cool.*

Keith: *We're at Club Fred's. Josh is locked in a weird debate about gun control with a straight couple. (?)*

Keith: *I shouldn't say that. One or both of them might be queer and just dating straight.*

Keith: *Or trans.*

Keith: *I might be prejudiced against straight people.*

Keith: *Not prejudiced. But it's weird to see them in "our" space, if that makes sense.*

Keith: *Oh my god, are you staring at your phone totally horrified right now? Sorry, I'll shut up.*

Cameron: *Not at all. Your fingers are much faster than mine.*

Well. That sounded dirty, when I read it aloud in my head.

Keith: *:-) I text kind of a lot.*

Keith: *Sometimes I text Josh from the office at the center. When he's like thirty feet away.*

Keith: *Just for fun.*

I wanted to say something else, to keep the conversation going, but I couldn't think of anything, and my grasp of emojis didn't leave me confident enough to use one.

Keith: *What are you doing right now?*

Keith: *That wasn't a come-on. Even though it sort of sounded like it was.*

Keith: *Or maybe it didn't and I made it weird.*

Cameron: *Not at all. I just wrapped up sales for the final show of the night. Now I'll go clean the arcade and help out with concessions.*

Keith: *When I was a kid I wanted to work at the Rhein. I thought it'd be fun to see movies all the time. I didn't think that much about the actual work that went into it. ;-)*

Cameron: *It's not hard. Sometimes I miss the days when I was more of an employee and less of an owner.*

Of course, had I been an employee, I likely wouldn't have been able to justify sitting in the booth texting.

Keith: *Was it hard to take over? Or did you feel like you'd kind of been groomed all your life to do it?*

I pondered that one, tapping the desk. It wasn't nearly that simple, that dialectical, but texting did not seem like a format conducive to conversational nuance.

Cameron: *Both. I'd certainly been groomed. But the circumstances were sudden, and unexpected.*

Keith: *I'm sorry, I shouldn't have asked. I didn't completely think it out before hitting Send.*

Cameron: *No need to apologize.*

After a moment, and because that felt incomplete, I tried again.

Cameron: *I feel fortunate to have had two incredible, happy, beautiful parents for twenty-four years. I miss them, of course, but I count myself blessed to have known them in the first place.*

All true. No need to mention that sometimes I still cried, bitterly, because they'd been taken from me before I was ready.

Keith: *Stop making me teary at Club Fred's.*

Keith: *I really like you.*

Keith: *That's the beer talking.*

Keith: *No, it's not.*

Keith: *Josh is mocking me so hard right now.*

I reread the messages, not sure what to make of them.

Cameron: *Did he win the gun-control argument?*

Keith: *No, but he did solve the mystery of the straight people at CF's.*

Keith: *Bachelor party for a gay friend.*

Keith: *Whew. Not that straight people aren't allowed, or anything. Just that they were . . . so straight. He looked nervous, and she gawked around at everyone like she was hoping a couple of guys would drop their pants and start humping right there in front of her.*

Keith: *That's . . . really not charitable.*

Keith: *It's the beer talking.*

Keith: *Josh says it really isn't. Stop reading over my shoulder!*

Keith: *I mean, I have straight friends who come in here and have a really good time and don't act like they're at a zoo, interacting with wild beasts.*

Keith: *Now he says actually that's a good description.*

I could practically hear their banter, practically see Josh's teasing smirk, and Keith's answering blush.

Cameron: *Sounds like you're having a good night.*

Keith: *Fridays are good. One more day of work, capped off with the film series tomorrow night, and a day off on Sunday.*

And Monday. Our dinner. Date. Thank-you date? Whatever it was sent my pulse a notch quicker.

Cameron: *I look forward to His Girl Friday. I can't do italics?*

Keith: *:-P No italics. But I knew you meant them.*

Keith: *I haven't seen it. Josh said I'll love it, though.*

Cameron: *I read once that the script was 180 pages long, which meant they shot roughly one page for every thirty seconds of the film. I can't even imagine how much they had to memorize to pull that off.*

Keith: *How long are normal scripts?*

Cameron: *Right around a hundred pages.*

Keith: *Wow. So like . . . eighty extra pages of talking?*

Cameron: *Talking very quickly, and talking over one another. It will make more sense to you once you watch it.*

Keith: *I'm excited.*

It seemed like our conversation had reached a natural conclusion. When he didn't text again, I finished closing down the booth, then went on with the rest of my evening. Texting wasn't so bad, providing I was interested enough in the other person to overcome the inconvenience of the medium. I was actually happy he'd initiated it. He might again, and I wouldn't dread it, because it had been fun.

The movie let out, I locked up, and went next door and upstairs to the blissful quiet of my apartment.

The light on my phone was flashing. I'd received messages without hearing the sound.

Keith: *Fun talking to you, Cameron. You're a good text buddy.*

Keith: *Josh is mocking me again, but text buddies are totally a thing.*

Keith: *Not everyone is a good text buddy.*

Keith: *Are you going on the Ghost Tour? We go every year.*

Keith: *Oh my god, you're probably super busy and I'm like spamming your phone.*

Keith: *I'll shut up now, future you, who'll get all these messages at once and worry that you've opened a can of crazy and I can't be contained!*

There was a pause in the messages long enough for my phone to have registered a time stamp that was about twenty minutes later.

Keith: *It really wasn't the beer talking. Anyway. I'll see you tomorrow.*

I stood in my little kitchen, staring down at my phone, wondering how to respond. Or if I should respond. He'd sent the last message at 11:23 p.m. and it was now 12:14. Was that too long? I didn't want to wake him, if he was sleeping.

Or Josh.

I shut down my brain before it could conjure an image: a long shot of a bedroom, slightly out of focus, and two young men intertwined beneath the blankets.

Cameron: *I haven't been on the Ghost Tour in a few years. I look forward to seeing you guys tomorrow. Good night.*

Did people say "good night" in text messages? I had no idea. But I'd already sent it.

As I was climbing into bed, my phone dinged again.

Keith: *You should come with us. Good night. :-)*

Go with them on the Ghost Tour? Now I imagined the three of us, huddled in coats, with our little glow sticks clutched in our hands, walking through the cemetery behind a tour guide who told us scary stories. Ed had been a tour guide for years. I'd have to ask him if he was doing it again.

My brain was becoming insufferable. I ordered it to cease and desist all fantasies in this vein immediately. Then I made my internal voice British and repeated myself. Something about American cultural immersion made British accents so much more authoritative than other accents.

His Girl Friday would be fun without too much pressure. And I lived for the moment Cary Grant dropped his birth name into one of his monologues. No reason to be anxious whatsoever.

CHAPTER  6

W eek three of the film festival passed without incident. I advised the audience to listen for mention of "Archie Leach," and heard a few delighted laughs when it happened. I shook hands, made more small talk, and met Josh's parents, who'd come to the movie with Josh and Keith.

"I played basketball with your dad years ago," Mr. Walker said to me, shaking my hand overlong.

"Did you? Are you in *that* picture?"

He laughed. "I'm the short black kid trying to see over everyone's shoulders."

"Hold up," Josh said. "Cam, your dad's in *that* picture? The one where they're all in their tux jackets and no pants?"

I registered his use of the shorter form of my name and my breath seized for a moment. I recovered, but not before Mr. Walker answered for me.

"Paulie Rheingold is the joker on the end. About five seconds after that picture was taken, he tossed Anthony McDonnell to the ground and jumped on him."

"Somehow he never told me that part," I said, surprised and delighted by this moment of unknown history.

"He was quite the clown." Mrs. Walker nudged her husband. "And so attractive."

"No argument. Paulie was a good guy. Your mom, too. Really good to meet you, Cameron."

"It's good to meet both of you."

Mrs. Walker kissed my cheek. "*His Girl Friday* is a great one. I'm sorry we missed *An Affair to Remember*."

"I show it every now and then. I'll let you know next time."

She smiled warmly. "You do that. I wish we'd thought to bring you some food, though. The boys say you work long hours."

The boys. I darted a glance to them. "Oh, I'm all right."

"I'm sure you could use some ribs."

I was about to defer, when Josh said, "We'll bring him something next week, Mom. Is that all right, Cam? Keith and I will bring something along that we can reheat after the movie."

"That's my boy." She kissed his cheek, then Keith's. "Good boys."

Mr. Walker also kissed Josh's cheek, and gave Keith a hug. "Be safe out there."

"We will."

I turned back to "the boys." "You really don't have to bring me food. You're already buying me dinner."

"We don't mind," Keith said. "See you Monday." Again, the near-hug, transformed into a handshake.

"Good night." Josh also shook my hand, smirking a little.

It was early yet. I had to entertain for a bit before I could finally close, which at least distracted me from thinking about Josh's smirk.

Monday night came far too fast, and took forever to arrive. Our date-not-date had consumed proportions of my mental energy that made no sense in the context of a thank-you dinner, but I'd enjoyed imagining it on some level I couldn't fully parse.

What would we talk about? I tried to rehearse, but I had no idea how the dinner would go. I could picture them sitting, and if I concentrated, I could hear their separate cadences, the rhythms of how each of them spoke. I knew I'd heard Keith laugh, but I couldn't remember it the way I could Josh's laugh, low and warm and engaging, as if his laughter reached out to include everyone in range of it.

Keith texted once, in the afternoon, to make sure we were still on. I said we were.

And that's when time sped up.

Before I noticed, I was turning over the ticket booth to my closing crew and going upstairs. I went for a waistcoat embroidered in varying shades of dark gray, which looked almost black until you saw it up close and realized the dimension was down to threads arranged perfectly to offset each other.

Someday I would learn embroidery. I'd always wanted to. But I doubted I had the eye for true artistry.

Far too soon after that I was getting out of my car at the waterfront, staring out at the Bay. San Francisco was a pleasant fuzz of glowing fog in the distance; the bridges were bright jewels strung across black.

The water at night was both beautiful and treacherous. I could hear it, not quite a siren's song, but seductive nonetheless. It made me long for flight, literally, so that I could dive like the sea birds, down into the water in a column of air bubbles, then rise up again, breaking the surface, rocketing upward, shedding all traces of sea as I flew.

Keith's voice startled me.

"I thought that was you."

I turned. "Hi, Keith."

"Hi, yourself. Uh. I didn't make you uncomfortable the other night, did I? With the text messages?"

"Of course not."

"Oh good." He was facing the Bay now, features in shadow. "I didn't mean to. I get a little goofy after a few beers."

"Not at all," I said. "Honestly. It's rare anyone texts me. If I sounded stilted or odd, it's probably due to lack of practice."

I caught the flash of teeth.

"You didn't sound odd. Or at least, no more than usual. We should go inside, it's freezing."

We joined Josh just outside the door and went in, exchanging the sorts of pleasantries I find mostly intolerable, though I didn't mind small talk with the two of them as much as I did with other people.

"So tell us more about Cary Grant," Josh said over an appetizer platter that managed to be both fancy and not merely decorative.

"What would you like to know?"

"Anything. Everything."

Keith shrugged. "Why you like him so much."

"Oh." I'd been prepared with a biography and highlights of his roles. This was different. I sipped my water for a moment, thinking about it, contemplating how sound was different in nicer restaurants. Thicker carpets, maybe?

Cary Grant.

"The story goes that when I was four years old my parents bought me a suit. We were holding the grand reopening after renovating the theater and they wanted me to look nice, so there I was, four, in my suit and tie. And they said after that I didn't want to take off my suit. I wanted to wear it all the time because I looked like a movie star."

I blushed, but neither of them seemed inclined to mock my younger self.

"My grandfather told me I looked like Archie Leach, which of course I didn't understand, so one of my parents, I don't remember which one—I don't really remember any of this, of course; it's all family history—told me about how a boy named Archie Leach invented a persona for himself to play, and spent the rest of his life playing it."

"And his persona was Cary Grant," Josh said.

"Exactly. I thought it was such a cool idea to play a character all the time, just like actors in movies." I paused. "I don't remember it the way I remember things now. But my parents bought me more shirts and clip-on ties, and I knew that every time I put one on I felt different, better, happier. I could look down at myself and feel—" I couldn't explain it. I floundered for a word, but none sprang to mind.

"Invincible?" Keith asked.

"Invincible," I repeated in relief. "Yes. I could be this other me, who was stronger and faster and smarter, as long as I had on my suit. Which of course is silly, but I think it helped me get through school. We wore uniforms four days a week, and on Fridays, when the rest of the student body was in the rattiest clothes they could find, I wore a suit."

"I don't think it's silly at all." Josh raised his glass. "To invincibility."

We toasted. They exchanged a look I couldn't read, which I pretended not to notice.

"I understand that. Like a lot." Keith toyed with his utensils. "I wish I'd figured it out when I was that young, though. By the time I knew how to feel safe I was already . . . weak, I think. I already felt so exposed."

"If your parents had been more like the Rheingolds, that might have helped," Josh murmured.

"Yeah. Well."

I wasn't going to ask, but after a moment Keith offered an explanation anyway.

"My folks are not the most supportive people on earth."

Josh snorted.

"They're not the least supportive people. I think Merin's parents might win that one. But they don't really like who I've become. Or I guess they didn't like who I was all along, but now we can all choose polite civility over a relationship."

Keith was the quintessential all-American boy: pale, blond, blue-eyed; ambitious; well-spoken.

"How could they not like you?" I asked. "How could anyone not like you?"

"Pretty easily. My dad wanted a football star."

"Your dad wanted someone he could bully," Josh countered. "Who'd then bully other people and confirm his worldview."

"Regardless. Whatever he wanted, it wasn't me."

"But you're so . . . good." I bit down on my tongue to stop it from talking.

Josh's fingers slid over Keith's where he gripped his water glass. "You really are."

"God, I'm so embarrassed. Can we talk about anything else now?"

"How embarrassed?" Josh half turned, pinning Keith with a dark gaze.

Another look that had nothing to do with me, but that I could practically feel in the air.

"Josh," Keith murmured.

"Now would be a good time to—"

Keith shook his head.

"All right. Saturday, then. In private." Josh met my eyes. "You don't mind hosting us for dinner after the movie Saturday, do you?"

Saturday, then. In private.

I shook my head. "Not at all. My apartment is next door to the theater, above the little gift shop."

"A short commute, huh?" His smile grew more casual and the slight tension between them faded.

"Very short. We've owned the building for years, but after my grandparents died we didn't use the apartment. I moved in when I turned eighteen."

"Definitely looking forward to seeing it. Do you have movie posters everywhere?"

"No, not really. Though I do have Hitchcock bookends."

"I can totally see his face as bookends."

We moved on to other topics, but I didn't forget that moment, and I didn't forget the word *private*, which could cover anything at all, and now I was intensely curious as to how Josh was using it. Apparently I'd find out. Or perhaps I wouldn't. Keith had seemed far less certain.

I could admit a small twinge of envy at the way they worked together, at the way they frequently spoke in "we's" and "us's." At the way that Keith expressed hesitation and Josh picked up on it, immediately, no questions asked.

Despite never having fallen in love with anyone, I could recognize it when I saw it. Not like the movies, though perhaps they'd had that sweeping initial phase as well. This was so much grittier, the kind of love that came with arguments and dishes left unwashed and promises neglected. I'd never seen them fight, but I didn't need to; in every thought left unspoken I could feel the history of their love driven all the way down to bedrock, through both loose soil and granite.

We said good-bye huddled up against the Volvo, a sharp breeze cutting through my jacket.

"We'll see you Saturday!" Keith called, cheeks pink with cold. He reached for my hand, but this time, this time he pulled me into a hug.

I bit down on my lip, aware that most roads now led to appalling awkwardness. I'd never been good at handling casual physical interactions. "Thank you so much for dinner. You really didn't have to."

"We wanted to." Josh hugged me as well, and it was the first time I realized that he hid muscle under his neat, informal clothes. "Good night, Cam!"

They turned away, walking close enough to one another that their arms brushed.

It was time to get in my car, where it would be warmer, where the wind couldn't penetrate. But I watched them just a moment longer.

I'd made friends before. But none had ever taken me out to the San Marcos Grill. And very few of them hugged me. What a profound and somewhat delightful surprise. And I hadn't even made it awkward.

CHAPTER 7

My apartment has always been a place of blessed solitude. I've fancied myself a monk sometimes, though there's nothing austere about it. Only in the way my steps are the only steps I hear, my movements in the kitchen the only disruptive force in an orderly environment. If something is out of place, it is so because I left it that way.

It was left vacant too long before I moved in, so we ended up getting rid of everything that had belonged to my grandparents, and starting fresh. New carpeting in the bedroom, polished floors in the rest of the house, pristine paint. Curtains that my mom made, which echoed the heavy curtains of a theater, but these were in a deep purple, almost blue.

"Indigo," she'd said to me, kissing my cheek. "Many things at once, just like you, love." I could hear her voice when I looked at those curtains.

Pride of place was taken in the living room by my sofa, lush red velvet that brought to mind the throne of a king. And comfortable— neither too soft nor too firm.

I felt ridiculous cleaning my house Saturday morning. First, because it was already clean. And second because I was cleaning enthusiastically, as if I expected them to spend the night. I'd cleaned my shower, changed my sheets. All things I do in the natural flow of cleaning, I assured myself, if with less anticipation. I rarely had company. It made sense that I was paying special attention today.

I made up the dining room table with three settings from the matched dishes Mom had bought me the day I moved in. I tended to use sentimental favorites from my parents' house, but for tonight

I went formal. I did a fresh load of laundry so the cloth napkins wouldn't be dusty. I changed my dish towels to the nice, not-fraying black ones that hardly absorbed water.

The last thing I wanted to do, with the prospect of hosting dinner with Josh and Keith, was spend the next few hours at the theater. I resented the intrusion of the film festival into my Saturday, though of course I'd only met them because of it.

My intro for *To Catch a Thief* was probably rushed or dull. My facial expression was probably neutral.

I wasn't thinking about the film. I was thinking about later, when I would bring Josh and Keith upstairs, to my home, where we would eat whatever they brought for dinner.

It would likely be take-out Chinese, and I'd set out my best dishes. Cloth napkins! What had I been thinking? So foolish.

The movie played, but I hardly watched.

The reception afterward progressed. They were getting longer each week, and slightly smaller; the collection of people who kept coming were beginning to build themselves a little community of old-movie fans right there in the lobby of the theater, which was exactly what I'd been hoping they'd do. But that night I just wanted everyone to leave so that I could lock up and escort my friends— new friends—up to my apartment, where we would eat burritos, or maybe pizza, or no, Chinese was still most likely, on my perfect matching dishes with my fresh, clean napkins to hand.

"We need to go out for a minute," Keith murmured, voice low. "We'll be right back, probably before everyone finishes off the grape juice."

I was startled, but tried to hide it. "Of course."

I tried to distract myself by sitting down with a few of the old-timers who didn't require I speak. Listening to them made me miss my parents, and my grandparents, though I didn't remember them well.

Presences. They were the exact same height, my grandparents. My father's parents. My grandfather had babysat me when I was a baby, and he'd always teased my grandmother that she despised infants. She'd always said the same thing back to him, some joke I no longer remember.

I paid very little attention to the people sitting near me. When everyone began leaving I was relieved, but slightly worried. What would Josh and Keith do if they arrived and the theater was all shut down? Call, probably. It wasn't a big deal. But I had pictured it as the three of us walking the stairs at the same time, the camera pulling back, getting all of us in the frame. Instead it was me, by myself, unlocking the door, walking into my clean, empty apartment. Hanging my coat.

Standing there, uncertainly.

My phone rang. Keith.

"Hi, we just got here, sorry. I so didn't think it would take this long. You're the door on the right side of the Rhein?"

"That's me. I'll come down and let you in."

"Thanks, Cam."

The nickname, this time from Keith. I glanced once more around my apartment (was it a flat? I'd always wanted to know what the difference was between an *apartment* and a *flat*), decided it was pristine, chided myself for stalling, and finally went down the dark staircase to the ground floor.

They stood outside the door. Holding Chinese food containers.

Keith slipped past me. "Sorry. We called in the order, but they were closing so we had to go fast."

"It's entirely all right." I felt myself start to slip into detachment, and fought to stay present. Chinese on my dishes. They'd think I was a fool for setting everything up like that, of course. It would be awkward and we'd all pretend it wasn't. They'd probably imagined us hanging out in a comfy living room, with a movie on the television.

I didn't have a television. I had a monitor set up with a cable I could plug into my laptop when I wished to watch something. I could do that. I couldn't believe I hadn't thought of it.

With a growing sense of dread and disillusionment, I led them up the stairs and, with only the slightest hesitation, into the apartment.

"Oh damn," Josh said. "This place is perfectly you. I love it."

"I love this couch." Keith ran a hand along the rounded wood scrollwork at the top edge. "I would so rock this, except it'd clash with all Josh's minimalist stuff."

"I'm not into minimalism, I just like clean lines."

Keith laughed. "That's kind of what minimalism is, right? Oh, you have a dining room table."

My shame on display; now they would, in a flummoxed-but-polite sort of way, realize I had completely gone in the wrong direction for this dinner.

They didn't.

They set the food on the table and turned to look at me, where I stood, frozen, right inside the front door.

"You haven't lit the candles yet?" Josh asked. "May I?"

I'd put out my mother's old silver candle holders on a whim, thinking they'd like the story of the wedding gift, and how once during an argument my parents had been so serious about divorcing that they'd begun dividing their possessions and snagged on the candlesticks. Dad had demanded they split them evenly, and Mom had told him he was an idiot, that there was no use having only two candle holders for an entire table.

"I'll light them." It bought me a minute to turn away, rustle for a lighter in the kitchen, compose myself.

"This is really nice, Cameron," Keith said. "Thank you. Thanks for letting us come over."

I forced my voice to be relaxed, casual. "Of course. Though there's a terrible imbalance. You've now bought me dinner twice."

"You did a nice thing for QYP. We appreciate it."

Josh cleared his throat. "Among other things we'll get to in a little while. We're not here tonight because of the center. And we didn't buy you dinner for any reason other than we wanted to."

It couldn't stand. I'd be thinking about how ridiculous I was all night. I turned back to them, lighter in hand, prepared to fall on my sword. Or, as it happened, my good china. "I apologize if I—if all this seems terribly formal. It's really the only method I have for entertaining besides standing in the kitchen, eating over the counter."

"Aw, Cam, this is perfect," Josh said. "You have no idea how perfect."

He wasn't making fun of me. He was serious. I glanced at Keith, who nodded, blushing faintly. "You'll see," he added. "Let's eat something."

Serving take-away Chinese on good dishes seemed suddenly less ludicrous. The restaurant was a few blocks away, and I ate there often enough to find its food comforting and familiar, which steadied my nerves some. We talked some about the movie. I asked after Merin, who had apparently decided to go back to his parents' house after spending the summer with various friends. But that topic seemed to make Josh angry and Keith sad, so we steered away.

"That was damn good." Josh pushed away from the table a little, surveying our empty containers and plates. "We forgot dessert."

Keith shook his head. "God, I doubt I could eat dessert. I'm stuffed. What about you, Cam?"

"I'm stuffed too. Thank you again, both of you. That was delicious." I began to gather our garbage. Keith rose to take our dishes to the sink.

Josh remained seated, clearly deep in thought.

Since I wasn't sure what else to do, I returned to my own seat while Keith was still in the kitchen. Josh looked at me, somewhat unnervingly, and I could only blink back at him.

He glanced over at the sink. "Keith."

"I know. I'm coming. I just started freaking out."

"Babe. Don't freak out."

"I'm trying not to."

Clearly I didn't know whatever they were talking about, so I arranged my expression into something suitably bland and waited.

"I'm totally blaming you if this fucks everything up," Keith mumbled, taking his seat again.

Rectangular table; I sat on one short end, and they sat across from each other closest to me, leaving part of the table empty. I wasn't sure which one of them I should be looking at, so instead I studied the candles and kept both of them at the edges of my vision.

After a hesitation, Josh said, "No, you're right. This is pretty hard. Which is why we did it drunk last time."

"Don't remind me about last time."

"Sorry." Josh cleared his throat. "Okay. It's fine. So, Cam, uh, we wanted to talk to you. And if anything I say makes you uncomfortable or you want to end the discussion, you can tell us, and we'll talk about something else. It's important that you understand your comfort is really important. At all stages."

I raised my eyebrows a little, hoping I appeared detached and intrigued, ignoring my heart, which had kicked up into a jig.

He shifted in his chair and cleared his throat again. "And, uh, so, yeah. Man. Seriously, this was so much easier when I was drunk."

"We want you to play with us," Keith said. "In a kinky way. You don't have to have sex with us, like that's not really what we're asking. But we like you, and trust you, and you seem to like us, and I feel safe with you, and I have no idea how to stop talking now that I've started except please don't laugh." He swallowed, Adam's apple jumping in his throat. "Please."

"I'm not laughing." I could say that much. With all the certainty in the world. Nothing here was funny. *We want you to play with us. In a kinky way.*

I forced myself to inhale. Then exhale. The candles flickered, then stilled.

Josh laughed. Then covered his mouth. "Oh shit. Sorry. Keith's right."

Keith threw a cloth napkin at him. "Oh my god, you're freaking out! You said you wouldn't freak out!"

"Only a little, I swear." He closed his eyes and took a few deep breaths. "I'm back."

"Ha. I love that you're the one who's wigging right now."

"Hush, babe. I'm not wigging." Josh leaned his forearms on the table, looking at me. "We're kinky. Keith likes to be dominated and I *love* dominating him. He's always wanted to have two guys at once—"

"What, I'm the only one?"

"*We've* always wanted to include a third guy," Josh continued in the next breath, "but the one time we tried backfired on us pretty hard."

Keith shuddered. "So embarrassing. And we didn't even get to the embarrassing stuff."

"How did it backfire?" I asked, and my voice sounded totally and completely normal. I was impressed. They probably couldn't tell my brain was rapidly trying to reconcile this conversation with my projections about dinner and failing. And my heart, my heart was pounding.

Everything was still in color. These were the kinds of anticipatory nerves I never felt. No dread attached. No feelings of inadequacy.

"We were drunk," Keith said. "Really drunk. We tried to make it into kind of a joke so we wouldn't scare away the guy we were hitting on, but he freaked."

Josh shook his head. "And he was a stranger. We thought it would be easier if we picked someone up and proposed a scene, like it'd be less risk, but it turns out asking strangers if they want to have a kinky three-way isn't exactly simple as A-B-C."

"Surely you picked the wrong stranger," I said.

He grinned. "Right?"

Keith wasn't smiling. He sat rigidly in his chair as if braced for a blow. "You can tell us if you're not interested."

"Don't put him on the spot, babe. Give him a minute."

"I really need this resolved. Also, I'm sweating through my clothes right now."

Silence. It was my turn to speak, on the spot or not. "I'm a little shocked. But not— I'm not laughing at you. And I . . . have no idea what we're really talking about, but I like both of you very much." There. That sounded neutral. Somewhat.

Keith exhaled. "Okay. He's not kicking us out, Josh."

"I never thought he would. You worry too much."

"Last time the guy ran for the door like we were going to kill him."

"This is nothing like last time. Though I could seriously use a drink."

"I have wine," I offered.

They looked at each other.

"I'm not saying we get sloshed." Keith shrugged. "But we already decided we're not doing anything tonight, and as long as we're just talking . . ."

"Wine would be really welcome," Josh said.

"Red okay?"

"Sure."

I brought down a bottle of pinot noir, relatively local vintage (Carneros region, which I mentally placed in Napa, or possibly Sonoma), and three glasses.

"Thanks." Keith took his as if it were Communion wine and he were praying.

Josh nodded, holding my gaze until I sat down again. "On a scale of totally calm to freaking out, where are you right now?"

"Somewhere in the middle. I'm not freaking out. I'm also not entirely sure what we're discussing."

"Right. Keith?"

"Yeah. Uh. I'm going to drink and you're going to talk."

"Got it." Josh didn't even sip his wine. "Sometimes I tie Keith to the bed and whip him. Or I have him bend over for my belt. We have a cane, but we don't use it. He likes paddles, but he's not huge into crops. We use a belt and my hands more than anything."

"Oh my *god*, Josh." Keith rubbed his eyes. "I need way more wine than this."

Josh's gaze remained unrelentingly on me. "He's a little ashamed, but I'm not. If you played with us, you'd have to understand that your role would be to do everything Keith wants exactly how he wants it. Sometimes I push him, and you might see that, but we've been together for a long time, so I can take him places he's not sure he wants to go. But you would do whatever he wants, *exactly* how he wants it."

"Unless you were uncomfortable," Keith added.

"Right, yeah. Obviously not if you were uncomfortable. I forgot that part."

"It's the most important part, though." Keith drained most of his glass and put it down before turning to me. "It's the most important part. If you're uncomfortable—I mean, not because it's weird, but like really uncomfortable—I can't feel safe, and then the scene doesn't work."

Josh nodded. "Everyone needs to feel safe."

They looked at me.

My turn. I took a deep breath, trying to stay calm. I couldn't run any of what they were saying like a sequence of scenes, something I could understand. Right now their words had no context, no pictures. "And the role you'd want me to play is what, exactly?"

"We're not talking about sex," Josh said. "At least, not right now. We'd have you over, and I'd probably demonstrate some things, and have you practice if you've never done it before. And if we all wanted to try it for real, you'd probably get to practice on Keith after that."

Practice on Keith. Josh was the only person sitting at my table who wasn't blushing.

"I see."

"You don't have to," Keith murmured. "I know this is weird, and we totally blindsided you, but you don't have to. Just—will you stay friends with us anyway?"

The candles flickered again, attracting my attention. For a moment I imagined them flickering across many frames, a candlelit montage tying this night to a succession of future nights, other times the three of us would sit around my table. I could hardly believe there was anything they could ever say that would jeopardize our friendship, surely strengthened by this night.

I swallowed. "I didn't say no. I'm not even close to saying no. If—if both of you want this, I'd like to try, though you should be aware I don't have any experience with this sort of thing."

"Oh." Keith exhaled and drained the rest of his wine. "Oh good."

Josh shot him a look across the table, then said, "Can we sit on the couch? I'd like to stretch my legs."

"Of course." I brought the wine down to the living room and took the armchair. It seemed obvious after a moment that Josh didn't really need to stretch his legs; he put both of their glasses on the coffee table, then sat down beside Keith, pulling him until his head was pillowed on one of Josh's thighs.

Josh looked down at him. "Hey. You okay?"

"Yeah. I mean yeah, of course, this is the best outcome. But I got so ready for all the other outcomes that I'm having trouble adjusting." He curled in a little more, and Josh rested a hand on his side. "Thanks, Cam. For not laughing at me."

"Us," Josh murmured.

"I know, but it feels a lot like me. It was definitely me last time."

I couldn't tell, looking at Josh's face, if he agreed or disagreed.

"We thought this would be hard to say to someone we knew, to a friend," Josh explained. "But the flip side is that when you say it to someone who doesn't know you, or care, they don't necessarily take it seriously. We only tried once, and it was over a year ago, but the sting lasted a long time."

Keith shuddered. "You say that like I don't still feel it."

"I'm sorry. That was my fault."

"It was both of our faults, but that doesn't actually help anything."

"Can you tell me more?" I asked, watching the way Josh's fingers dragged over Keith's arm. The way Keith seemed so at home lying beside him. "I don't think I've ever done anything kinky in my whole life."

"I always knew I was into it," Josh said. "Like every now and then there'd be an episode of a TV show that had a dominatrix or something, and I'd watch like there was gonna be a test later, sitting there trying not to let anyone know that I was picturing myself standing over some tied-up man."

"I avoided those episodes." Keith turned, so I could see his face. "Because I knew that was the sort of thing I wanted, and I couldn't let myself think about it. I thought it was weak, you know? I do better now. Josh was right, before. You'd be pretty much at my mercy, Cam." He flashed a smile, not full up with cheekiness, but at least I could see it peeking through.

"I don't object to that." Far from it. My body was thrumming, as if my blood were a rising tide.

His mouth opened, almost a silent "Hah," I considered encouraging.

"We talked about it before we started dating, though," Josh said.

"Yeah, I went over to Josh's place one time and kind of... stumbled onto a flogger he'd left out."

Josh held up his hands. "'Left out' in the sense that it was in my bedroom and you were snooping."

"Maybe a little. Anyway, it completely freaked me out and totally turned me on and I couldn't even put words together to ask him about it."

"Which he didn't need to, because I saw that he'd seen. And I guess I hoped he was interested, though at first I thought the sheltered white boy was disgusted instead."

Keith caressed Josh's knee. "I could never be disgusted by you. Anyway, we started talking, and Josh had done all these things I'd only imagined doing, but he didn't treat them like they were sick and wrong."

"I hadn't done that much stuff. And it wasn't—" Josh paused. "There's stuff you do with people for fun. Like I'd had the flogger out because I'd been with a guy who wanted to try it. But he hadn't been into it that much. We tried it, he shrugged, we fucked, he left. It's a whole different thing when it's not casual."

"Would it be casual with me?" I asked.

Keith shook his head, drawing Josh's attention, making him swallow whatever he was about to say. "It would have been casual with the guy who laughed when he thought we were joking and ran like hell when he realized we were serious. But I don't think casual really does it for me that much."

The room felt heavy all of a sudden. Not oppressive, just dense.

I waved a hand in the direction of the dining table. "If it helps, I don't think I'm all that into casual myself."

"It helps," he said, without any levity at all.

All of this was interesting. But none of it was giving me anything I could sink my teeth into. Nothing I could *see*. "So what . . . what are we really talking about? Can I ask that? I have a— I like to be able to picture things before they happen. It helps when I'm doing something new or different. Not that— I mean, if you didn't want to say—"

"All right, you're never negotiating on your own, Cam." Josh ran his fingers through Keith's hair. "You should always demand specifics if you want them. Especially in the beginning."

"I only meant I didn't want to impose—"

"We don't do the same thing all the time, but your role would be to defer to me, and obey Keith, though sometimes you'll do that through me."

"But we're not into, like, silent, unchallenged dominance," Keith added. "Like at all. We talk about everything new a lot. The first time you come over—if you want to—we might just talk and look at stuff, if that's what worked for us. And Josh was right, before. He, uh, he sometimes pushes me more than I think I want to be pushed, but that's not what we're asking from you."

I had so many questions. But I didn't know if I could ask them. Or even if I wanted to, really. I hated feeling interrogated, and the volume of questions I had seemed to lend itself to interrogation.

"Get a load of Cam right now," Josh said, voice low. "He's gonna explode if he doesn't start talking."

"I think we freaked him out."

"I am not freaked out," I said (sounding freaked out). "I'm really not. But you two— I've been— For the last few weeks I've been telling myself that you're—that you're nice and polite. That I shouldn't read anything into it. And now we're having this conversation, which is so unexpected to me that I have no rehearsed way of coping."

They stared at me. Then Josh said, "Shit."

"I told you we were being weird!"

"But— I thought we were— I mean, okay, dinner was a little much, but everything else was—" He broke off. "God, we're such fucking cockteases."

I opened my mouth to disagree, but Keith spoke before I could.

"Sorry, Cam. Just, we think you're so fucking sexy that even though we were trying not to be overly flirtatious, we probably failed."

My heart stuttered. I replayed his words, but it had only been a moment ago. I was sexy? Since when?

"Ha. Okay, us being teases might be worth Cam looking shocked," Josh said. "You still with us, man?"

"I . . ." I what? "Um."

Keith sat up. "Oh my god. Cameron. You really didn't know. Holy shit. Hey, it's okay. Don't, like, hyperventilate or anything."

My breathing was fine. I was shocked, but my breathing was fine.

"Cam."

I looked at Josh.

"We like you a lot. It's not casual for us, either."

Keith studied me a minute, then turned to Josh. "I know we said we wouldn't do anything, but do you think maybe we could show him?"

"You can't stand him being so uncomfortable right now, can you?"

"It's awful. And we can fix it."

Josh reached out, fingers grazing his face. "On your knees, angel."

My entire body froze as Keith slid to the floor in front of Josh's feet, facing him. A second later he began unbuttoning his shirt.

I had no idea what was going on. Josh was watching Keith and I was watching both of them and dear god, Keith was pulling off his dress shirt, then tugging his T-shirt over his head.

My toes curled and my balls pulsed and I ignored my prick entirely except to cross my legs so it wouldn't betray me.

Of course, I liked Keith a great deal, and was attracted to him, and an attractive man stripping his shirt off in my living room wasn't exactly a common event. Never mind that he was also on his knees.

Never mind that his back was covered in pink marks, mostly concentrated at the top, by his shoulders.

I was breathing through my mouth, a little raggedly, staring at Keith's skin. Peripherally I registered Josh's hand in his hair again, and the way Keith pushed into it.

Dear god. He is so beautiful. I mustn't say that or he'll think I'm laughing, but I'm not. So help me, I'm not laughing at all.

"You can touch," Keith whispered. "If you want to."

He was facing away from me, but I glanced up and found Josh's eyes already on mine.

"Touch him, Cam."

It would be rude not to, having been invited. I shifted forward, leaning over my legs, giving up on having them crossed, and hoping they'd be too polite to mention how obviously aroused I was.

Reaching out seemed incredibly difficult, but pressing my fingertips to Keith's skin was the most natural thing in the world.

He was hot and he breathed deeply, and I might have been imagining it, but he seemed to push into my fingers as he had Josh's hand. Blood and breath and bone, under a tight sheath marked thickly with pink.

"How did you do this?" I asked, my tone library-ish, as if I was afraid to disturb us.

"A flogger and a single-tail whip. I can show you how to use them."

My fingers, still pressed to Keith's back, trembled. "You'd trust me to do this? You don't mind that it hurts?"

This time he definitely pressed back. "I like it. It's almost like Josh gives me something that is pain, and I take it into myself, and play with it, and make it into something else. Like, figuratively. It's not suffering. It's just pain."

"It looks like kind of a lot of pain from here."

"Oh, no. Those are love taps, mainly. He went so fucking slowly I kind of wanted to cry." After a pause, he added, "In a good way."

"I can show you how to do that, too," Josh said. "That's where we'd start."

"So I would—I would cause you pain, because you wanted to take it and transform it into pleasure?"

"Sometimes pleasure, sometimes satisfaction, sometimes sex. Sort of depends. Sometimes it's for Josh, because he likes hurting me."

I looked up, raising my eyebrows, waiting for Josh to rephrase.

Instead, he shrugged. "Yeah. I do. I like it when he begs me to stop and I keep going because he trusts me to not take it too far."

"I trust you *to* take it too far," Keith said. "There's a difference."

"Good point. Are you cold?"

"Cam's warm. You can use your whole hand, you know. I won't break."

I flattened my hand against him and he sighed. "No, I can see that you are . . . strong. Incredibly strong."

"I knew this was a good idea," Josh said. "I knew you'd get it."

I couldn't say whether I got anything except that Keith was beautiful and Josh was tender and I found myself wanting to get lost inside them, just for a moment. I pulled away, marveling at the loss of his heat. "You want me to make your back look like that?"

"I like it." He reached for his T-shirt and sat back on the couch. After a second, he grabbed his wine. "I like it. And I always— It was always kind of a fantasy of mine that there would be two guys with me, focused on me. That I'd sort of be the center of the world. That's totally self-absorbed, right?"

"I always thought sex was a pretty self-absorbed thing. Even when you're pleasing someone else, you're pleasing yourself."

They glanced at each other.

Josh took a sip of Keith's wine and handed it back to him. "So right now we're only talking about a scene, you know, to see how it goes. We're not ruling out sex, but one thing at a time."

"Is that all right?" Keith asked.

"Oh. Of course." Right, yes. I'd taken it too far, despite the fact that they'd been clear from the start. I covered the miserable blush by fumbling to refill our glasses, and would have followed it up by saying something ridiculous, about the weather maybe, if Josh hadn't touched my hand, a brief touch, the way I'd seen him do with Keith out in public.

"Listen, we think you're hot as hell or we wouldn't be here. But sex is a whole other dimension and we're trying to take it slowly this time. And Keith is the one who's more vulnerable, so we—you and I—have to make sure every step is on totally solid ground before we go forward."

"Hey," Keith murmured.

"Babe, come on. You know what I'm saying."

Keith leaned forward and took my hands. "It's, like, limiting our risk. We're starting out with a really simple plan, but we've already built in scalable expansion, and as long as we pay close attention to our returns in the meantime, there's no reason we can't get there."

Josh fanned himself. "You're so sexy when you talk business."

"The twisted thing is he's not joking." Keith squeezed. I belatedly squeezed back. "You can think about everything. You're totally not obligated to answer right now. Or ever. If you want to pretend this never happened, we will totally play along."

"I don't want to do that. I'm not sure I can do any of this, but I'd like to try." Which was true, even though it frightened me to think about. And turned me on.

"Are you going to Scream Night at Club Fred's on Friday?" Josh asked.

"I imagine I'll end up there. I arranged the schedule so I would have the opportunity."

"Good. Then we'll see you there. And if you want, you can come home with us after. And Cam, we can do this slowly. Keith and I aren't in a hurry."

"Hey, you can come on the Ghost Tour with us! We're doing that before going to Scream Night."

"Sorry, I'm working until nine. But I can commit to going to Fred's."

"Good. Then we'll see you there." Keith smiled and squeezed my hands again before letting them go. He looked younger in just a T-shirt, as if I'd scratched the surface of put-together QYP-cofounder Keith and found a teenager with bright eyes and warm smiles underneath. "Thanks for not kicking us out."

"I wouldn't have. Thank you for dinner."

"Sure thing."

As if they knew we couldn't leave it there, they started talking about the Ghost Tour, and all their memories of years past. Josh had gone as a child. Keith's parents hadn't been into it, but when he was ten he'd gone with a babysitter (who'd been secretly visiting her tour guide boyfriend; Keith confided he'd watched them kiss and been confused by how much more intriguing he found the boyfriend than the babysitter). I had gone with my parents every year. They loved the drama of walking the cemetery at night, knowing that volunteers in creepy costumes might be lurking behind every grave and around every mausoleum.

Once we'd established conversational baselines again, all of us relaxed. We drained the wine, laughed a lot, and the two of them touched more frequently, ending up with Keith half in Josh's lap, talking about some fundraising debacle early in QYP's history, during which someone had taken Keith for an at-risk youth brought by Josh for demonstration purposes.

"And he hasn't left the house without a tie since!" Josh finished the story, poking his boyfriend in the side.

"I don't wear a tie to the gym," Keith said primly.

Both of them dissolved into giggles. After a second, I joined them.

CHAPTER

Of course I tried very hard not to obsess over Friday night, and of course I mostly failed. I couldn't get the image of Keith's back out of my mind, or his soft whisper inviting me to touch him, or Josh's voice calling him "angel" in a tone I couldn't reference except that it reminded me of my father speaking to my mother when they didn't know I was just around the corner. He'd called her "my lilac" for reasons they never explained to me, and only when they thought they were alone.

I didn't want to parse that one too deeply, actually. But it had clearly been a private nickname, a sweet word exchanged between them with meanings that stretched deep into the ground like roots, all the way back through their lives.

Like "angel" in Josh's voice, which he'd allowed me to hear. He would not have said that in front of the stranger they'd attempted to seduce (if that's what it had been). Not that I was in competition with some stranger they hadn't even liked, obviously, but if I had been, I'd've won.

Maybe it was creepy to associate that moment with my parents, but I found it cemented something about Josh and Keith for me, some quality of permanence they exuded, which I found hopelessly attractive.

Thus, my thoughts ran after each other in endless circles as I contemplated what Friday would bring. The idea of actually holding a whip in my hand, of hitting Keith with it, was disturbing—up to a point. Past which it sounded intriguing and almost painfully intimate. The kind of intimacy I didn't dare hope would lead to more than what it was.

The other thing that occasionally intruded, pushing thoughts of Josh and Keith aside, was the notion of Scream Night. Even if Club Fred's decided at the last moment to cancel it, even if Fred's decided to close, there was a very real possibility that someone would die this week, and with no way to address it, or prevent it, we were essentially playing a waiting game.

Zane had come to a mid-day family showing of *Inside Out* with a woman I knew to be Mildred—though I didn't know her well—and Mildred's son, James, whom I saw more frequently with Obie and Emerson. They'd made it through half of the movie before bringing James out to crawl around like a small madman.

"I can't decide if I want to stay home or not," Zane said. "Not that I'm worried for myself, but that morning after Honey died, when we'd all seen her the night before . . ." She shook her head. "That was awful. More awful than just remembering her at knitting or something."

Mildred rattled some kind of toy for James and he zoomed across the carpet to grab it. "I know Obie's planning to be there, though I don't know if he'll drag Emerson or not. I worry for Obe a little. If someone asked for his help, even knowing there's a serial killer out there, he'd try to help. I think I'll tell them to go together or not at all."

"Yeah. I might get a ride with Jaq and Hannah. It's all about safety in numbers. You, Cameron?"

I swallowed. "I think I'll be there. I believe I'm meeting up with Josh and Keith."

"The QYP boys, nice. I like them. They're clever, and I like the way they're heading with their business." She nudged Mildred lightly. "You should go down to the center with me one day. I've been thinking of maybe knitting them blankets and donating them."

"Do they have childcare?" Mildred asked dryly.

"That's brilliant! I bet they'd find a way to do childcare if there was a need for it."

We talked awhile longer (yes, Zane was going on the Ghost Tour, and yes, she was bringing Baby James, whether his mother wanted to go or not, and yes, she'd already asked Ed when he was working so she could snag him for a tour guide). They disappeared back into the movie for the last twenty minutes and left with the rest of the families, and I wondered at my brain slotting them into that role. I had no reason to believe they were together; undoubtedly I was only turning people into couples because I had the idea on my mind lately.

The day progressed, the evening, the night. Everything seemed so perfectly ordinary. That's always what they say, isn't it? Dramatic events are rarely preceded by a foreboding omen we recognize at the time, and that Wednesday morning's news hadn't been preceded by anything even approaching a warning. Later we'd be no more wise, considering it, than we were in the moment.

Late Tuesday night another murder occurred. The first not on a Friday. The first not after a theme night. It could have almost been unconnected, except for the method, and the victim.

My phone rang and rang and rang. I squinted in the darkness of my bedroom and picked it up, finally, grumbling "Hello" without looking at the number.

"Cam, it's me. Ed."

I sat up. "Are you all right?" Because no one called before 6 a.m. unless they weren't all right.

"I'm fine, Alisha's fine, but I have to ask you something. Do you know Anderson Philpott?"

"Sure. At least, a little. Why?"

"He's dead. He's dead like the others, Cam, and there's something else, too."

Philpott was dead?

"He was *Togg*. Philpott was freaking *Togg*, Cam, can you believe that?"

"*Togg*? The website guy? With the blog everyone reads?" Everyone but me, though I stopped by maybe once a week to scan through his headlines to see if I'd missed anything. He'd been doing a number on La Vista PD lately, for not catching this killer.

Oh. God.

I rubbed my temple, grateful for the lack of light in the room. No colors. "Are you saying the same—the same person killed him as killed the others?"

"I know. It doesn't make sense, it's the wrong day, there was no theme night, but maybe things were heating up for him and he couldn't cope with it, so he had to change up his MO. I don't know." A burst of static hit the line, and I winced. "Sorry, it's really windy out here."

Out here. "Are you at the waterfront?"

"Yeah. Shit. I—I saw him. Togg. Philpott. I saw his body. He was so messed up, Cam. More than Honey. His legs—his legs were so—" He cleared his throat. "They said it looked like he fought back, that whoever killed him is probably pretty messed up, too."

"Do you need a ride home or anything?" I asked, since he sounded awful.

"No. I'm going to stay here and see what happens."

"How do they know Philpott is Togg?"

"They looked at his phone. He was logged in to his site, and after that all they had to do was call the host to get a billing name and address. Which matched. He's freaking *Togg.*" He sounded shocked, but also almost excited. As if the reality of another murder hadn't quite penetrated the fascinating reveal of Philpott's secret identity.

I hadn't known Philpott well, but I knew he stayed a little detached from people, and that he liked to get into long discussions about politics and social change. Maybe it had been obvious he was Togg all along, but we'd all built up Togg to be someone who couldn't have a beer at Club Fred's and talk about books, or Hitchcock.

Notorious. It was his favorite Hitchcock/Grant collaboration. He'd said he would come see it. And now he was dead.

I swallowed, throat tight, mouth dry. "You okay, Ed?"

"I'm okay. I mean, this is fucking terrible, and I can't believe he's dead twice over, but I'm okay. This is a crappy time for Alisha to have started the new job, though, or I would have gone over to her place and just sat there for a little while."

"Well, feel free to come to the theater later if you want to."

"I'll think about it. But you know, now that Togg's dead? There's no one to report on his murder. He was always the first person to get information up. I want to make sure we have something on the *Times-Record* site before the end of the day. It's the least I can do."

I nodded, then realized I was on the phone and said, "I understand."

"Will you come to Fred's later? I think we'll probably be doing something, though we might only be sitting around weeping into our beers."

"I'm closing tonight," I said, somewhat relieved.

"Oh. Okay. You don't go out after closing, do you?"

"Rarely." It wasn't that it was late. It had more to do with the steady rhythms of my life, which necessitated going home after closing the theater. I could go out, of course. I just didn't plan to.

"All right. Well, I'll talk to you at some point."

"I should be at Scream Night." I paused. "Do you think—if whoever they are killed last night, do you think they'll do it again on Friday?"

"No. They could, but I doubt it. I think they're feeling the heat right now and this is how they're avoiding getting caught. Plus, they'd be all banged up. Detective Green said Philpott definitely got some hits in, because his knuckles were bloody."

"All right. I'll be on the lookout for anyone who looks like they were recently in a fight."

"Yeah. Well, I'll see you, then. Bye, Cam."

"Bye, Ed."

I hung up my phone and disabled the alarm, which was set to go off in half an hour. I was up.

Anderson Philpott, whom I knew casually, was dead. Togg, the blogger who kept all of La Vista's crimes against queer people in the public eye—who kept the pressure on the La Vista PD when they seemed inclined to forget those crimes, or worse, when they treated them as jokes—was dead. I lay in bed and stared at the ceiling, wondering if Philpott's alter ego had ever weighed on him. Cary Grant had spent most of his life, on- and off-screen, playing Cary Grant. Philpott had balanced the intense rage of Togg with the milder persona he had at the bar—a guy you thought was decent and polite, if a little passionate at times, but with a good sense of humor.

Not that it mattered now. Both parts of him were dead. I got up and started my day.

My phone dinged at 3 p.m.

Keith: *Oh my god, Philpott/Togg.*

Keith: *Oh my god, Philpott is Togg.*

Keith: *I can't even.*

Keith: . . .

Cameron: *I know. It's awful.*

Keith: *Josh loves that site. I can't take it most of the time, but he'd sit there in the morning reading the most offensive comments out to me and laughing.*

Keith: *This sucks.*

Cameron: *I know.*

I thought they might stop by the theater, but they didn't. I thought I should text to check in later, but in the end I wasn't sure it would be welcome, so I didn't.

Sometime after I'd gone upstairs, when I was sitting on the couch with a cup of tea reading my favorite Cary Grant biography—which I knew so well it was the adult equivalent of a child's security blanket—my phone dinged again.

Keith: *Club Fred's is depressing as hell right now.*

Keith: *Seriously, we saw him here last week.*

Keith: *Like, at this same table. We sat here, with Philpott, and processed our feelings about straight people who come here looking around like it's a zoo.*

Keith: *(He said sometimes he can't tell if the scared people are straight or in the closet. Which: point.)*

Keith: *I know I barely knew him, but I'm still sad. And we didn't start our day with a new post on his website, which . . .*

Keith: *It's so stupid, but we've always done that. And now we never will again. Like, I get it's not bad like it would be if we'd been good friends with him, but it still makes me sad.*

Cameron: *I think that makes sense.*

It did. That was true. I sat for a long moment, debating what to say next.

Cameron: *When my grandmother died, my grandfather didn't cry for five days. That's how long it took him to run out of bread. When he ran out of bread he started crying and my parents had to call in paramedics to sedate him.*

Cameron: *He kept saying, "We're out of bread, we're out of bread."*

Cameron: *Obviously he was really grieving her. Not worried about bread.*

Cameron: *Not that that's the same as Philpott, but sometimes your brain gets sad about relatively minor things in order to not get sad about the really big things.*

Keith: *I think that is totally true. Exactly.*

Keith: *Because really it's fucking scary that we sat here last week with a super smart guy, who was fit, and strong, and he still got killed. That's so fucking scary and wrong.*

Cameron: *It really is.*

Cameron: *How's Josh?*

Keith: *Doing his thing. Being the rock.*

Keith: *I used to be kind of annoyed by it, like why can't he ever be the asshole who breaks down?*

Keith: *Then I realized that putting up a front was sort of his way of breaking down, of kind of working through whatever was happening.*

Keith: *So now I feel better. Most of the time.*

Keith: *:-P*

Cameron: *You know I have no idea what that means, right?*

Keith: *I'm sticking my tongue out at you.*

Keith: *. . . That sounds less dirty when you don't spell it out.*

Cameron: *:-P*

Keith: *Hahaha, you got it, Cam!*

Keith: *I just told J that I'm teaching you text smileys. He said, "Oh no."*

Cameron: *:-P to him too, then.*

Cameron: *That's the only one I know.*

Keith: *You can do the basic smile face. :-)*

Keith: *And this is a wink: ;-)*

Cameron: *;-)*

Keith: *Are you coming on to me, Cam? ;-)*

I laughed, and blushed.

Cameron: *Is there one for laughing?*

Keith: *XD*

Keith: *Or :-D*

Cameron: *:-D*

Keith: *You're growing up so fast!*
Cameron: *:-P*
Keith: *XD*
Keith: *Okay, we're taking off. Have a good night, Cam.*
Cameron: *Good night.*
Keith: *J says good night too.*
Cameron: *Good night to Josh as well.*
Keith: *<3*

I stared at that one for a long moment, trying to figure it out. A handlebar mustache? But what did inverted eyebrows mean? No, those couldn't be eyebrows.

A horn blared outside and I glanced up for a second, waiting to see if the crunch of metal would follow. It didn't. When I looked back down at the screen with fresh eyes, I realized what <3 meant.

A heart. Keith had texted me a heart. I flushed and put away my phone.

CHAPTER 9

T rue to his intentions, Ed got the news about Philpott up on the *Times-Record* site, and posted updates. He told me when he stopped by on Thursday that his editor had given him carte blanche to write short posts for the site, always pending approval before posting.

By Friday it seemed clear that most, if not all, of Ed's stories were approved.

It wasn't as dramatic as Togg's site—at no point did Ed seem inclined to start a fistfight, and the comments were permanently disabled—but his articles were the most up-to-date local news the *Times-Record* had ever published online. He said he still had the same workload as before and everything beyond that was on his own time, but he didn't seem upset about it.

Somehow Philpott's death had done more for Ed's job in three days than the year or two before had managed. If there was some sort of afterlife, and souls really could monitor the things happening back on earth, I thought Philpott would be pretty satisfied with that.

I donned one of Great-grandfather's old circus costumes for Scream Night (he'd been passing through the Bay Area when he met my great-grandmother, whose dream of having a movie theater— with sound—fit perfectly in with Great-grandfather's notions of exhibitionist entertainment), but apparently, despite its authenticity, my costume failed to impress.

Zane slapped me on the shoulder as I took the stool beside hers at the bar. "Hey, Cameron came as Cameron Rheingold."

"Actually, I came as Harold Rheingold." I tugged at my lapels. "This is a vintage suit. My great-grandfather wore it when he was a juggler in the circus."

"A juggler? Count on a Rheingold to have been in the circus." She straightened my tie. "Still, it looks an awful lot like you, Cam."

"I think he was going for Bobby May, actually."

She blinked.

"He was a juggler. Bobby May. Probably America's best juggler."

"Uh-huh."

I sighed. "Never mind."

Tom walked over with my Scotch and a smile. I waited until he turned away to ask Zane why he looked happier than anyone else in Club Fred's.

"Oh, that's easy. Not that he's not upset about Philpott, but he has an alibi for Tuesday night. The cops were here first thing Wednesday asking around, but not only does Tom have an alibi, no one else saw Philpott here either." She shook her head. "It's still not real to me that he's dead. I always went days without seeing him. Part of me expects to find him at a table inciting one of those marathon debates of his any minute now. Jaq's taking it pretty hard, though."

"They were friends?"

"Not really. But she was his senior mentor when he was a freshman at the high school, so they knew each other for a long time. And they always kind of tried to out-think one another, you know? So it's not so much they were friends as they . . . had a role. Played a role, in each other's lives." She shrugged. "Like Honey. I used to go to knitting with her. She wasn't a close friend or anything, but every time I go to knitting, I miss her. Anyway."

"I understand."

"I think there's going to be a memorial service, if you're interested. His parents are having a small funeral, but Ed got a bee in his bonnet about the community not being able to grieve, so I think he's arranging a thing."

"I'll ask him."

She patted my shoulder again. "I'm gonna go drown my sorrows in the long, gorgeous legs of Mz Prz. Have a good one, boy."

"You too, Zane."

I pulled out my phone and started reading. I'd finished *Rebecca* with the usual sense of lingering unease and moved on to a mystery Alisha had told me to read, about a detective solving murders at a fashion show somewhere in England. The writing was excellent, and I appreciated the immersive quality of the book. A quarter of the way through I still hadn't solved it, which meant it would either reach a terrible conclusion with a heretofore unknown character being the killer, or it would impress me by being someone I'd already rejected. I looked forward to finding out.

I was somewhat lost in the story when two hands clamped down on my shoulders, startling me.

"Sorry!" Keith slid onto Zane's abandoned stool, and Josh the stool on my other side. "Didn't mean to scare you."

"Oh no, it's fine. Good book is all."

"I have no idea how you read in here. It's so loud."

"I guess I hadn't noticed."

He smiled. I turned toward Josh, to be inclusive, but he was grinning as if the idea of feeling excluded had never occurred to him.

"I admire your concentration," he said.

I narrowed my eyes. "What does that mean?"

"Nothing. Exactly what I said. Hey, what about Philpott? Crazy, right? Man, I read his blog every morning with my coffee."

"That's what Keith said."

"Ha, yeah." His eyes slipped to the side. "I liked his site more than Keith. I mean, I didn't always agree with him, but I really liked seeing what he'd say. He had this way of forming arguments that made me think about them differently. His whole lecture on trans politics and how harmful it would be to try to separate 'trans' from 'queer' as if somehow binary queer people shouldn't be saddled with nonbinary queer people—I was up for nights mulling that whole thing over."

"Literally," Keith mumbled. "*Nights.*"

"Dude made me think. But I wish I'd known it was Philpott all along. I would have liked to have told him I really thought about that after reading his stuff."

Keith nudged his shoulder. "You did."

Both of us looked over.

"I'm serious. One night we were sitting here with Philpott and I think Obie and some other people, and you asked him if he ever read Togg's site because it had blown your mind. So you told him, Josh. Even if you didn't know it."

"He was here when I said that?"

"Yeah."

"What'd he say?"

Keith smiled. "He told you he thought Togg was full of hot air, but he'd see if he could find the article you were talking about."

"Oh man. Shit. That just made me more sad. But I guess I'm glad he knew I thought his alter ego was cool." He shook his head. "Listen, what do you guys think about getting out of here? It's not really the vibe I thought it was going to be."

"Sounds good to me," Keith said. "Cam? You're, uh, coming over, right? I mean, no pressure or anything."

I put away my phone. "That was my intention."

"Is that why you only had one drink?" Josh asked.

"I always only have one drink. It's more sentimental than anything. Scotch was my dad's drink, and Humphrey Bogart's."

"Your dad stole his favorite drink from Bogie?"

"He did."

Keith nudged me. "And you stole yours from your dad. Aw. Come on. Do you want me to send you the address? Or ride along?"

"You should ride along," Josh said. "Road work at LVCC screwed up all the maps."

"Good point."

I hadn't prepared for this. I hadn't prepared for them to part with a brief kiss, for Josh to wave, for Keith to follow me to the Volvo.

I hadn't prepared to start the car with him beside me. When was the last time I'd had someone in my car? I sometimes gave the high school kids rides home after closing the theater. That must have been it. Impersonal, friendly, a wave and a "Thanks, Cameron!" at the curb.

Keith exhaled, loudly, a rush of breath that was faintly white in the cold air. "You are making me so nervous right now. You're okay, right?"

"Sorry. And yes, I'm fine. This is unexpected, and I . . . don't cope well with unexpected."

He turned so he was sitting half against the door, looking at me. "Oh, see, that's like so tempting. Now I just want to throw all kinds of unexpected at you. I bet I could make it good. Like, I'm pretty sure I could help you with the coping."

"Maybe. But I wouldn't be able to see the color of your eyes, or the shade of your skin. Everything shifts to black and white when things change too drastically from how I imagined they would be."

"Seriously? I've never heard of that."

"It might not happen to other people. I don't think it's physiological. It's more of a defense mechanism. My brain turns life into an old film reel when it's too overwhelming to deal with in color."

"Wow. Oh, left here, sorry. Get in the right-hand left turn lane. So wait, how often does that happen?"

"Not often. Because I try to limit unpredictable events." I considered it. "The last time was the night the film series began."

"Because of your index cards."

I nodded, relieved when the light changed so he wouldn't expect me to look over. "I visualized a lot of different ways that night could go, but I never imagined I'd trip and fall on my own stage. I should have numbered the index cards."

"What you said was good. I'm sure your notes were good, too, but the way you stood up there and told us about how *An Affair to Remember* demonstrated the radical notion that two rich people might love each other so much they'd get jobs? That was really cool. We laughed at that, Cam. And your teleprompter joke."

"Oh. I'm glad."

"Me too." He gestured to the other lane. "Right up here. So if you start losing color tonight, let us know, all right? It's important. Will you tell us if that happens?"

"I don't— It's not— It really isn't a big deal—"

"I think it kind of is. Josh will want to surprise you, because that's one of the ways he gets off, but he'll want to know if it's too much. And if you have this sort of defensive slide into old-movie mode, we need to know. Okay, so this is where we detour. Make the next right, then we'll go up three intersections and take a left at the light so we can avoid the nonprotected left across traffic. It'll make sense when you see it."

Josh had said it was all about Keith. That it was our job to make him feel safe. The word *safe* in the context of whatever they had planned intrigued me. I hadn't thought too deeply about it the other night—surely anything that caused the marks I'd seen would include as a concept danger, and therefore safety—but I was beginning to wonder if he meant something else.

My world dropped into silver and black when I felt unsafe, regardless of how objectively safe I was. That was what Keith wanted to know, the honesty he was requesting. I could give it to him, I thought. I could take a breath and say "I'm losing color," and he would know what that meant.

I wished that the night would pass without my ever having to say that, but if it should happen, I hoped I'd be courageous enough to share the truth with two men who were courageous enough to share their truths with me.

Their apartment was a small one-bedroom in an apartment block I decided had probably been built sometime in the eighties. Everything still worked, but was dated, though it looked so much like the two of them that I liked it immediately.

A comfortable leather couch, black side tables, black coffee table (Josh's minimalism). A bookcase overflowing with books stacked every which way, a kitchen with appliances littering the limited counter space and a few dishes in the sink.

"We totally meant to clean, sorry," Keith said.

"And by 'we,' Keith means 'Josh.'"

"Hey, I can clean!"

"We know that you *could*, babe, but you don't."

"You're so rude."

"Did you Ghost Tour?" I asked, still looking around.

"We so did." Eyes alight, Keith grinned. "It was great. Well, it was the usual cheesy stuff, but we had fun."

Josh kissed Keith's cheek. "We did. At one point Keith got scared and clung to me, I'm just saying."

"I did not *cling*—"

It suddenly hit me that they were nervous. As nervous as I was, maybe more. I'd been thinking about this like I was the one who risked something because I had no idea what we were doing, but standing there, in the living room, surrounded by little pieces of their lives, I realized that they were risking so much more than I was.

I turned, mustering age and bearing and a little bit of Cary Grant. "Please don't be nervous." Only it wasn't an entreaty, it was an order, with a polite *please* on the front of it.

Keith giggled and thudded his head into Josh's chest. "I am so . . . freaking . . . nervous. Oh my god."

"Don't be." I looked at Josh, whose hands had begun running up and down Keith's back. "I forbid it. We will have fun, and you will laugh at how bad I am at whatever you have in mind, and I will try not to let the world go gray."

Keith lifted his head. "Yeah, don't. So when Cam freaks out he loses color. Like, in his vision. I told him he has to let us know if that's happening."

"Definitely. Let us know how you feel about everything, okay? That's the only way this works. And, in retrospect, probably why it works better if you're friends with people, not strangers."

I nodded.

"Uh, okay, so let's go in the bedroom, because that's where everything is, but we're still not going to do anything yet." Keith hesitated, then extracted himself from Josh and took my hand. "Come on."

Their bedroom was also very them. The dark comforter was probably Josh's influence, but the string of white fairy lights over the headboard said Keith to me.

He flicked on the overhead light and went to the closet. "All right, I'm gonna pretend I'm not Nervous Nellie. So, uh, yeah, okay, here's stuff." He dragged a big box—or maybe it was a trunk—into the room and flipped the lid open.

I stared from a safe distance away, mouth dry. There was more stuff in there than I'd expected. Some of it looked medieval.

"How do you feel about me touching you?" Josh asked, suddenly close beside me. He put a tentative hand on my shoulder, and I couldn't help going a little stiff, so he withdrew.

"Oh— No— I mean yes—" I forced myself to take a breath "I don't mind being touched. I might be . . . out of practice. Sorry."

He turned me, keeping a firm grip on both of my shoulders until I was facing him. "I want to respect your boundaries, but I'm not sure where they are. Is this okay?" His hands squeezed.

"Yes," I murmured, dropping my eyes.

"What's happening right now in your head?"

"Sorry, I— Nothing. Only that this is new and I am not accustomed to a lot of—" I gestured. "People don't stand this close to me."

"We noticed," he said.

"And if you don't want us to stand this close to you, it's cool," Keith added.

"It's not that. I mean, I do want . . . this. Whatever you're offering. I do." I reached up, putting my hands over Josh's. You'd think a broad, strong man like him would have big, thick hands, but he didn't. Josh had the hands of a musician, someone used to doing technical things with them, trusting them to know the next note, the next chord. "I do. But I'm not used to it."

"Then we're all doing things we aren't used to. Let's start with paddles. Keith loves his paddles."

"I really do."

What followed was something like an instructional social club, the mores of which I learned as we went. Despite their history, there were moments when Josh clarified his intentions, or requested permission, or took things somewhat slowly with Keith, and I couldn't tell if they were doing it for my benefit or if this was the way f things between them.

Then again, probably like any couple, certain evenings had certain ods, and tonight's mood was slow and steady.

At first Josh demonstrated everything on the bed. Then he led items to me, and I felt them, turning them over in my hands. gave me space to do this while they sorted out their trunk of laughing to themselves. I sat beside them, taking whatever nded me, considering paddles and different kinds of whips, kinds of hides that went into them. Floggers and wrist cuffs cuffs and crops, and a collection of things Josh referred to as sensation" while Keith pretended to shudder.

A small wheel with spikes on it, meant to be rolled over skin. Three objects of varying shapes that I realized only after accidentally turning one on were vibrators. Not everything was recognizable; some had tines or bristles or feathers.

"What do you do with all this?" I finally asked.

Josh grinned. "I restrain Keith, blindfold him, and do whatever I want. Want to watch?"

"Ugh, you're a pig." Keith smiled and scooted over next to me. "Give me your arm."

I did, and shivered a little as he unbuttoned the cuff and rolled my sleeve up to my elbow.

"Wartenberg pinwheel, technically." He ran the wheel over my forearm and I jumped. "Now imagine that on your dick."

"No, thank you."

"I'm gonna do it again."

The feeling of it was simultaneously prickly and uncomfortable and intrusive. I allowed him to keep my forearm, but I was close to pulling it away.

"See?" He looked right at me. "It's wild, right? Letting me make you feel something you don't want to feel."

He put the wheel down and picked up the thing that looked like a feather duster with very few feathers, brushing it over the same stretch of skin. I shivered. "Am I imagining that I can feel that more than I would have been able to before? My skin feels more . . . awake."

"Exactly." He put the duster down and dragged his fingernails across my arm, and this feeling was bright, as if I could see the paths they left. "Crazy, right?"

"Yes. Crazy."

"Crazy hot," Josh said. "If you want to feel any of this stuff on you, Cam, we can do that."

I surveyed the whips and paddles and straps and everything else. "Maybe. But I don't want to be restrained at any point."

"Me neither. But Keith is like . . . amazing."

"Shut up."

Josh tugged him close. "You are amazing. You know I think that. Completely amazing."

"You're cracked."

I'd never seen them kiss like that, intensely, as if nothing existed but this kiss, as if no one existed but the two of them, bodies held by some tension that was only partly about their arms around each other.

"Should we show him the paddle?" Keith whispered into the silence that followed their parting.

"Hell yes. You good?"

"I think so. I mean, a little weird, but solid."

"You want to tell Cam?"

"Yeah. Okay."

I realized I was staring at them, and perhaps I should have been pretending not to notice that kiss, or the way they molded into one another, or the way even after they separated, each of them seemed to remain attuned to the other.

"Hey." Keith offered me a hand. "Check it out. I'm gonna lean over the bed and Josh is going to paddle my ass. That should be fun, right?"

"Are you still nervous?" I asked.

"Oh my god, I'm like lightheaded with it."

"Can I do anything to help?"

He hesitated. "Maybe. Will you hold my hands? You don't have to hold me down, but will you hold on to my hands? I always had this thought, in my head, of maybe having someone to hold on to while—you know."

"Sure. Of course. Where do I—"

"Here."

They positioned me on the upper half of the bed, and Keith bent over the foot of it, reaching both hands over his head. I clasped them in my own and he murmured something I thought was "Thank you."

Josh had stood off to the side, watching, waiting for us to settle in. Now he lifted the paddle he was using to show me—wooden, rectangular—and advanced on Keith.

"Babe."

"Yeah."

"I'm pulling these down, okay?"

Keith didn't say anything for a long moment, and Josh stayed very still. Then: "Yeah, okay."

Obviously partial nudity might be involved, which I knew intellectually, but seeing Josh actually tug Keith's slacks down and run his hand over the skin he'd just exposed was an entirely different thing.

Keith's fingers twitched in mine.

"Don't hump the bed," Josh ordered, grinning.

"Shut up."

Smack.

Keith's fingers tightened, painfully, then released.

But Josh was still grinning, and he reached out for another caress. "So rude."

"Uh . . ." Keith shifted slightly, maybe pushing into Josh's hand, maybe evading it. "If you weren't here I'd call Josh 'master' and try to make him uncomfortable. I'll . . . try not to do that right now."

Smack.

Keith inhaled, loudly, and exhaled. "This is, uh, an interesting experiment in sensation and psychology right now."

"Yeah, babe?"

"Yeah. I feel way more exposed right now than I do when I'm actually naked."

I realized I'd stopped breathing, as if I'd taken the hit myself. Or as if I was bracing for the next one. I forced my fingers to loosen on Keith's. If anyone should have a death grip, it was probably him.

Josh ran the paddle over his skin, rubbing it, and Keith kind of wiggled after a minute of this, like it wasn't enough. "You want to start? We could do more of what we're doing, just playing around."

"I want to take off my shirt. Actually, it's sort of the last thing I want, but I'm obsessing over it, so I probably should so I can be part of the scene."

"Do it."

Keith squeezed my fingers one last time and released. He slid backward, kneeling on the floor, to unbutton and peel out of his shirts, which he tossed into the corner.

"This is what I'm talking about," Josh mumbled, picking them up and dropping them into the basket in the closet.

"I can't exactly move freely at the moment."

"You say that like if you could, you would have done something else. Back over the bed, babe. You don't mind Cam seeing you, right?"

"No. I mean no, it's fucking hot. I just feel kind of shy."

This time Josh's voice was harder. "Over the bed, babe."

Keith slid up over the bed, all bare skin now, slacks still caught at his thighs. His back was no longer pink, as it had been at my apartment; now it was pale, freckled, incredibly soft looking.

I salivated, gazing over his skin, wondering if I would ever slake that particular thirst. The thirst of wanting to taste him, to know what he felt like on my tongue, and what he sounded like when he was at someone else's mercy.

"You can touch him," Josh said. "Like last time. He and I have talked a lot about it. He wants you to touch him, Cam."

I moved in a little closer, and instead of touching Keith's back, I found myself pressing my fingers to the back of his neck.

"That's nice," he whispered.

It was strange, touching Keith under Josh's gaze, but it wasn't as awkward as I would have thought. His presence made me, if anything, bolder than I would have been on my own. I pushed up into Keith's hair, gently, and he sighed again. Then I let my fingertips drag all the way down, tracing his spine until I could no longer reach.

"You have freckles," I said.

"Yeah, you do." Josh sat down on Keith's other side, and now both of us were drawing invisible pictures on his skin, lines and swirls. I connected his freckles like they were constellations, reading meaning into the pictures.

I'd always been intrigued by the sensual, but rarely had I found a partner with whom to indulge my interests. Dating profiles are not set up for "I want to spend hours learning the landscape of your skin until I can walk it with my fingertips in the dark," but that was far closer to what I wanted than a blowjob that only existed for the sake of being a blowjob.

This was just Keith's back, and I had so much more to map.

Josh tickled his ribs along the side and Keith squirmed. "This is why I tie him down. So ticklish."

"You are not torture-tickling me tonight, so forget it."

"No, I'm not. I'll save that for tomorrow."

"You wouldn't really?" I asked.

"He totally would. It's the worst, Cam. It's fucking horrible."

"So . . . why?"

Josh's nails made a slow path up Keith's side again, making him giggle. "Because I like to push him and he likes to live up to my expectations."

Which sounded fine, if somewhat one-sided. "Does he push you?"

"Are you kidding?" He leaned forward and kissed Keith's spine. "I love this idea, of having another person, but it's fucking hard, too. This is how he pushes me and how I live up to his expectations."

"Josh took it kind of hard last time. I mean, both of us took it hard, but I just felt more embarrassed than I'd ever been in my entire life. Josh felt *responsible*."

"I was supposed to make it safe for you and I fucked up."

"It wasn't unsafe. It was just embarrassing."

I returned to my earlier position at his neck. "Is this embarrassing?"

He shifted. "A little, but not in a bad way. Like, there's embarrassing that you know will be embarrassing forever, like it'll live in your memory as this humiliating *thing* that you'll never really get over. This isn't that."

I considered it, parsing my own memories for the ones with claws. "Okay. I think I understand. What's this, then?"

"This is like . . . early. This is the awkward thing that happens in the beginning, before everything starts to feel normal."

"You think this will feel normal at some point?" I trailed a path down to his shoulder.

"That's how it goes. I mean, I think that's how it goes."

"Not that we expect you to commit to some kind of long-term thing with us if you don't want to," Josh said.

Keith turned to look at me. "You do want to, though. I mean, not like I can read minds, but everything about you says that's what you want. You want the security of having something consistent."

"I don't usually have that, so I guess I wouldn't know." Except I did know, and he was right. He was inescapably right.

"So right now I'm kinda shy because you've never seen me naked, and next time I'll be less shy." He drew my hand to hold it against his cheek for a moment. "Next time, Cam. Okay? You can count on that. Even if tonight went badly, we could try it again. We really like you."

"And tonight's not going badly," Josh said. "Ha. All along I thought you'd scare if we talked like this could happen more than once. If I'd known you wanted to hear that, we would have started with it."

I felt far more naked than Keith was, but I was still making constellations on his skin. "I'm not good at new things. If we do it again, I'll be able to visualize it, I'll be able to feel the space better, that's all. The first time I do something is excruciating because I can't imagine how it will go."

"But do you still see colors?"

I looked down into Keith's eyes. "Blue. Very blue. Clear and deep, like water you see near the equator, blue all the way down to the ocean floor."

His lashes fluttered. "Thanks, Cam."

Josh surprised me by tilting my chin up. "Yours are hazel with little flecks of gold, like you've got buried treasure right below the surface. I'm really glad you're here."

I swallowed. "Me too."

"Good. Now let's play with Keith. I want to show you how to use the paddle. You don't have to try it tonight if you don't want to, but you should hold it, swing it, maybe against your palm so you can feel the impact. I get it about needing to visualize things. This way you'll have the tactile to go along with it. Cool?"

"Cool." More than cool. Incredible.

By the end of the evening I'd held everything they liked using, and taken some experimental swings against the bed (with Keith well out of the way). He'd pulled up his slacks but left his shirt off, and I had grown brave enough to touch him even when it wasn't necessary. Sometimes I touched his arm when I asked him how a certain thing felt. Josh demonstrated the safe places for the whip or flogger to fall, and I showed him with my hands on Keith's skin that I understood, taking all of it in on a mental film reel so I could replay it later, study up.

I had felt their buckling restraints, and Keith had giggled, slipping one over my wrist so I could see that it didn't hurt.

"Now I haff you right vhere I vant you, Mr. Rheingold," he said in what I supposed might be a terrible Russian accent, though I hadn't ruled out anything Eastern European. "Now ve vill do vhatever ve like to your body."

Even though it was one cuff around one wrist—and thus decorative, not restricting—I still felt a trace of its power.

Josh laughed. "You are never getting an acting job, babe. That was *horrible*."

"I know! I'm like the worst. Every time I do an accent it comes off, like, racist or something." He unbuckled the cuff and the moment passed and I smiled—at their antics, at Keith attempting more bad accents, at the fact that I was here with them, and they seemed to accept me, somehow.

There was a sweetness to that first night. A soothing kind of air to their bedroom, where we played, and explored our ideas, and enjoyed one another. We didn't do anything more risqué than those first few smacks with the paddle. Josh demonstrated using the bed, just as he expected me to practice. But there was an intimacy between us, and when I left, rather later than I had expected (after we'd eaten a meal of leftover macaroni and cheese, but the good kind, baked with a crisp crust on top), I felt strangely full, almost buoyant.

Sometime later, Keith texted.

Keith: *You home safe?*

Cameron: *I am. Thank you for dinner and an informative evening.*

Keith: *You'll have to come again soon, Cam.*

Cameron: *That would be nice. Good night. (And to Josh.)*

Keith: *Good night back (from both of us).*

I went to sleep more sated and satisfied than I'd felt in months. Perhaps longer.

CHAPTER 10

I was in a strange mood Saturday. Contemplative, quiet, wishing I could be alone with my thoughts. It was almost impossible to drag myself into my clothes, face the front door, the stairs, the exterior door, where I hesitated, almost tempted to find someone to cover my shift. At lunch I'd found myself absently glancing at Togg's site, which of course had no new updates, and it spoiled the rest of the afternoon for me.

Permanency. No new updates ever. Because the man behind the site was dead.

On a normal night I might have been able to kick the dark edge to my mood, except that night's movie was *Suspicion*, and thinking about Hitchcock made me think about Philpott, whose favorite Hitch/Grant collaboration had been *Notorious*. I wondered what he'd thought of *Suspicion*, which predated *Notorious* by five years, and was a thematically different role for Grant.

None of it should have ended up in my speech, but I found myself standing at my podium explaining that I'd decided to dedicate this showing to Anderson Philpott, who'd liked both Alfred Hitchcock and Cary Grant, but who, I felt certain, would have preferred the original ending of *Suspicion* to the one they invented to save Grant's image.

"Come see me afterward if you want to know how the film was supposed to end before the studio decided against it," I said. "Enjoy."

It had either been the perfect thing to say or a terrible thing to say; more people stayed and I ended up doing a sort of impromptu lecture in the lobby. Even the kids closing concessions seemed distracted by my rambling about the ways the film was different than the novel, the studio's considerations for Cary Grant's image (he was still under contract to them at the time), and the somewhat muddy facts of who actually made the call to change the ending.

So many people stayed to chat that I only got to see Keith and Josh for a moment as they were saying good-bye. Keith leaned in and whispered, "I'll text you."

Did he mean later that night? Later that week? I couldn't ask, of course, so I nodded and smiled and turned back to whomever I was talking to.

Ed lingered to tell me he was touched by my dedicating the movie to Philpott. Obie and Emerson stood to the side eating the last of their popcorn until I had a second. When they approached, I saw why.

"This has been a shitty week, but I got a lot of work done." Obie handed me the tie he was holding.

It looked black, but up close it was more indigo. Little lights flashed in from the edges, as if it were a catwalk.

"It's not super on the nose, but it reminded me of you anyway."

Clearly silk. Like all of Obie's work, it looked like something from a fancy department store, not something he'd put together in his living room. I loosened the tie I was wearing and blessed whatever instinct I'd had earlier to wear purple.

"Oh, you don't have to—"

"He knows he doesn't have to," Emerson said. "He wants to try it on. And anyway, I don't know dick about color, but I bet it'll look great with that shirt."

I nodded. "Exactly."

It did. I could tell by glancing down, though I looked forward to getting in front of a mirror.

"What do I owe you? This is fantastic, Obie."

"Oh, nothing. That's stress tie-making there. I'm glad to be able to give some away."

"You shouldn't be giving them away."

Emerson offered a grunt in agreement. "This is what we keep telling him. He has a PayPal thing on his site, FYI."

Obie elbowed him.

"Thank you," I told Emerson, making a mental note to transfer money into the account later. "Did you guys like the movie?"

"I liked the movie," Obie said. "*He* wants to go home and see if the original ending is available online anywhere."

"Of course, you'd have to know which of the supposed original endings you were looking for," I said. "But good luck."

I found Hugh looking at the *White Christmas* poster and almost didn't say hello, which would have been rude, since he'd clearly lingered to talk to me.

"It suits you, you know. Talking to people."

I rolled my eyes. Neither of us had siblings, but our families had known one another for a long time. He'd always been a little older, a little more detached and interesting. As a kid, I'd followed him around like a puppy whenever he was in the theater. When I was a teenager I'd wanted to talk like him, weirdly archaic inflections and cadences.

"I don't know how it can possibly suit me when I hate it so much."

He smiled, turning away from the poster. "Genetics, possibly. You're sounding more comfortable than you did a few weeks ago."

"I must be doing all right. I'm not as exhausted afterward."

"Good."

He didn't speak again, but he kept looking at me.

"You really think I'm good at this?"

"Absolutely. Not a doubt in my mind, Cameron. It seems as if you spent thirty years getting to know yourself, and now that you do, you're ready to take your place."

"And my place is the theater in this analysis?"

"It's wherever you want it to be. Whether or not that's the theater is a question you have to ask yourself." He tapped the frame of the poster. "I came that year, you know. First time since Mom died. Your mom gave me a huge hug and told me how happy she was to see me, and if I ever needed anything to call. And your dad made a show of shaking my hand, but he couldn't help himself, so he hugged me too."

"Did he cry?"

"He was a bit teary. You had the night off, if I recall correctly. You were reportedly at home juggling and muttering to yourself about what movies were best for spring."

"Juggling is good for thinking," I said.

"The car accident was three weeks later, wasn't it?"

"Right after Christmas, yeah." I sucked in a breath, and he reached out to put a hand on my shoulder. "I'm glad you said it directly. Leaving it unsaid is worse."

"I can generally be counted upon to say things. You look good, Cameron. This is your domain, and you are certainly the heir to both of your parents."

"Thanks. You coming back again next week?"

"You'll be showing *The Philadelphia Story*?"

"No, next week is *Monkey Business*. *The Philadelphia Story* is the following week."

"Ah. In that case, I'll be back in two weeks."

"I'll see you then, Hugh. Say hello to your husband for me."

He smiled. "I will."

He was right. That was the kind of thing my parents would say. They'd always remembered to ask after husbands and wives and children. They'd always remembered to ask Mildred about her aunt, not her parents. They'd always remembered to ask Obie what he was painting or drawing or making. I'd never heard them slip up and ask after someone who had died (a fear I constantly had).

This was the fifth week of the film series, and while it hadn't doubled movie attendance by any means, I could honestly say I was more comfortable now making small talk. I recognized more people, even on days that weren't Saturday. For all those years I'd thought that maybe the rest of my family had a gift, a knack, for knowing people, that it was a skill I didn't have, but now I had to wonder if by hiding in the safety of the ticket booth, I'd never tested myself. Sure, I knew our once-a-week regulars, but there were other people, too, who came frequently enough that it wasn't odd if I was a bit more familiar with them.

After all the stories people told me about moments my parents made them feel important just by looking them in the eye and saying, "How's your grandma?" or "I heard you got a new car," you'd think it wouldn't have taken me so long to realize that *that* was the way to keep the theater alive. The film series was only a vehicle to do the other thing.

Armed with this stunning realization, I lingered, resentment-free, with my stragglers, and actually enjoyed small talk without trying to make it into anything else.

CHAPTER 11

Cameron: *Probably. But I'd rather not.*

Keith: *Josh says I'm not allowed to kill people, even if they deserve it.*

Cameron: *Who are you trying not to kill?*

Keith: *Merin's parents. But they SO deserve it.*

Keith: *Not joking.*

Keith: *They're fucking horrible.*

Keith: *And we said Merin could stay with us, but the parents said no. Just to be dicks.*

Keith: *Oh. Josh says he thinks they were being homophobes. More than dicks. Or maybe they were being homophobic dicks.*

Keith: *They already said Merin can't work here anymore, but we're all ignoring that. They can't do anything about it since M is eighteen.*

Cameron: *Why doesn't Merin move out?*

Keith: *Because. I think maybe douche bag asshole parents still feel more parenty to M than, you know, supportive people with boundaries.*

Keith: *M says to wait until graduation. I had to walk away. M&J are still talking.*

Cameron: *You all right?*

Keith: *Fine. I'm making sandwiches. Well. I will be, when I'm done venting at you.*

Keith: *Sorry.*

Cameron: *No need to apologize. I don't mind being vented at.*

Cameron: *I'm off at eight. Do you want me to bring dinner over to the center?*

Keith: *That sounds amazing. I'll see you then.*

I'd intended to pick up pizza or something, but I was in the grocery store for almond milk, to which I had an unfortunate addiction, and ended up collecting a sort of picnic of foods: French bread, grapes, two types of cheese, olives, and salami. I gathered roasted red pepper hummus and a bag of precut broccoli and cauliflower, then hesitated over an avocado and rejected it because it wasn't nearly ripe enough to eat right away. I threw in chips and salsa at the last second and handed over my single cloth bag at checkout (which was almost not up to the job; I'd really only gone in for almond milk and bananas).

Of course, by the time I made it to the Harbor District, I'd decided I should probably go down the street and pick up something to order at one of the trendy little bistros on the far side of Water Street, where the city had been repainting and rebuilding and reinvigorating the neighborhood. But I didn't feel like braving the lights and cocktail dresses, so I carefully picked up my bag and made my way into the center.

Merin was sweeping the floor of the kitchen when I settled everything on the counter.

"Dinner?"

"They fed me already." After a second I heard the broom stop moving. "What'd you bring?"

"I honestly don't know. I just started putting things in my basket and now I guess we'll find out if any of it's dinner."

"You went to the store hungry, didn't you?"

"In my defense, I only went in for bananas and almond milk."

"What's wrong with regular milk?"

I unloaded everything except the almond milk. "Nothing, if you like it. But at some point I realized it was basically the same thing as breast milk, except for cows, and it grossed me out, so I never drank it again."

Merin's eyes widened. "Oh *sick*. That's disgusting."

"What's disgusting?" Josh asked, coming out from the office. "Oh damn. Look at all this."

"Drinking breast milk is disgusting."

"Um." Josh picked through the groceries. "Is breast milk on the menu? Because if so, I pass."

"I have almond milk, so no."

Merin, face still twisted, shook his head. "Jesus. I can't believe I never thought about it like that. You totally ruined milk for me." He shot me one last disgusted glance and went back to sweeping. (It couldn't be convenient to go around all day every day with a big, bulky parka on. But if the goal was to hide any semblance of a body beneath it, I had to admit it was doing its job.)

"You want a ride home tonight?" Josh asked him.

"Nah. Might as well put it off as long as possible. Plus, I'll pass Sammy's on the way. If he's up, maybe I'll go in and screw up milk for him." He dumped the dustbin. "I'm saying bye to Keith."

Josh waved, already opening the chips. "This is a feast."

Even the way he opened a bag of chips was graceful, controlled. I fought a flush and made myself look away. "It's not that much. I probably should have picked up something easy, but I was in the grocery store already and some of this started to sound good."

"I'm definitely not complaining. Let me grab a cutting board and some knives and stuff."

Between us, we had the food organized and mid-prep by the time Keith and Merin came back out from the office. Merin suffered to be hugged at the door and mumbled, "Lock up behind me" as he pulled the big slider shut. Keith locked it.

"Should I not be thinking of Merin as 'he'?" I asked. "Merin reads as 'he' to me."

"Merin *should* read as 'he,'" Josh said.

"But when we offered—" Keith began.

"We offered, and it sounded like a favor, so Merin said no. But Cam's not doing a favor, it's an organic thing."

Keith sighed, leaning against the counter. "It's fucking complicated. But I guess I don't think it hurts anything if you use 'he' since that's totally what Merin secretly wants. If he just fucking told us that, we could help."

"Babe, we can't help everything. But you're right. Maybe we start doing it subtly and let Merin get used to it. I mean, at this point I have to correct myself *not* to say 'he.'"

"Or tell Jaq to stop saying 'she' all the time. Seriously."

"She's trying. She said it's hard because when she's got Merin in class she can't switch pronouns from what everyone else is using."

"Why not?" I asked.

Josh's jaw tightened. "Because Merin would kill her."

The words were so blatant they took my breath away. "I'm not sure I understand."

"Sorry." He glanced over, toward the door, then back at me. "I think the problem is that the second he asks for it, the second he admits it's important, it exposes too much that he can't take back."

"And it's too revealing," Keith added. "Asking for what you need always feels way too revealing. Or maybe I'm, like, projecting or something. Anyway." He reached out for a grape. "Yum. I love every single thing I'm looking at right now. Except green olives. Yuck."

"More for Cam and me." Josh opened the jar. "Mm, delicious olives. You know what I should do? I should make you hold olives in various locations on your body until I feel like eating them off your skin."

It was so unexpected, on the heels of such a serious subject, that the resulting full-body flush I experienced felt like an acute medical condition.

Keith responded by smacking his arm. "Twisted bastard."

"I really am."

After a moment, apparently realizing that I'd gone perfectly still, like a statue in the wake of Medusa, both of them looked at me.

"This one time," Keith said, "he wrote a business letter on my chest with chocolate syrup."

"Ha, yeah, that was hot. Keith had a crush on the dude I was writing to."

"I did not."

"You did too. You liked his mustache."

Keith hit him again. "It was a *handlebar mustache*. I mean, how often do you see that in the wild, right? Plus, he was cool."

"He was cool. Here, try some salami."

"And that's *not* a sex joke?" Keith took the slice, pairing it with cheese and a disc of bread I'd just sawn off the loaf. "Oh my god. We are kings right now. This is so delicious."

"It really is." Josh and I traded and I added a couple of olives to my sandwich.

The salt of the olives, the creaminess of the cheese, the bite of the salami. I'd done good. I chewed slowly, trying to enjoy every bit of it.

Keith moaned. "This is amazing. Why do we never think to eat like this?"

"Well, if I plugged this into my app, it'd probably tell me it has about a thousand grams of fat in it." Josh took another bite. "Mm. Worth it, though."

"Like you need to worry about fat," Keith mumbled, reaching for another slice of bread. "Maybe I should eat like this all the time. It'd make me buff."

"If you lifted weights," I mused. "Though this isn't particularly high in protein, I don't think."

Keith raised his eyebrows. "Do you lift weights?"

"I don't—I'm out of the habit. But in the past I've actually done a little bit of weight lifting."

"Josh does."

Josh obediently posed with his arms out and upraised, one still holding a hummus-dipped piece of cauliflower. "Three times a week, no excuses."

"And he runs, too." Keith smiled at his boyfriend. "Hottie."

"You're only with me for my looks."

"I think we've pretty much proved that isn't true."

We continued with our snacks, sharing stories from the week. They didn't fill me in further on the Merin situation, and I didn't ask. When we'd made mincemeat of the food, Keith shook the crumbs off his hands and proposed a drive to the pier.

"You know it's about to be freezing out there, right?" Josh asked.

"I know. We'll bring coats. I just want to take a walk and like . . . *feel* something right now."

Josh glanced at me.

I shrugged. "I don't have a coat."

"We have extras, as long as you don't mind wearing a donated coat."

I didn't mind a donated coat.

We took the Volvo, which was bigger than Keith's Golf.

"You know you're serious about someone when you give up your car because he drives everywhere," Josh said from the backseat.

"Remember I tried to talk you out of it? Then we needed to pay rent."

"We mostly had rent money. And my parents *would* have fed us . . ."

"Yeah." Keith looked in my direction, which I noted as I headed northwest on Water Street. "Josh's parents are amazing. I mean, you met them. You can kind of feel how awesome they are."

"I liked them."

"They offered to buy his car from us and let him still use it, but neither of us felt comfortable with that."

"I was a little comfortable with it," Josh said.

"You were not. You just got to play the moderate one because I was so against it. If I'd said we should think about it, you totally would have said no."

Josh laughed. "You're so right. That's exactly what it was. Anyway, I don't have a car now, which is weird but also kind of nice."

"Is it?"

"Yeah. No insurance, no gas, no car trouble."

"You still split all those things for my car!"

"Yeah, but it's kind of like babysitting, you know? You can take care of a kid without *having* a kid. I like your car, but it's not my responsibility, and that works for me."

"Are you saying I baby my car?" Keith teased.

"When's the last time you got the oil changed in that poor thing, anyway?"

Did they want kids? I could have asked, except it was such a prying question, and it didn't seem like the right time. I could picture the two of them as parents. Good parents. Caring and firm at all the right moments, understanding, generous, principled, forgiving.

Suddenly I wanted them to have kids, for my own reasons, because if I remained friends with them I could benefit from the proximity of children without having them myself. Exactly as Josh had said.

I wondered if we would remain friends long enough for children to be relevant. It seemed foolish to proceed thinking we would, since I'd only known them for a few weeks, but in realistic terms every friendship begins with a few weeks. These could be the first few weeks of many, many years. Likewise, they could be the first few weeks of a scant couple of months, after which I'd see them when they went to the movies if we remained on good terms. At some point they'd adopt, or maybe find a surrogate, and then I'd see them every now and again at the family movies on Sundays, as their brood got older.

I'd remember all their names, of course. If Josh and Keith had children, no matter how far apart we drifted, I could never forget their kids' names. Perhaps someday I would be taking their tickets in the booth and telling them that I'd met their fathers after a viewing of *An Affair to Remember*. Then again, that might be a bit on point, and it really wouldn't do to blush while saying *an affair* to the children of men I'd had something of an affair with.

"Do you get the impression Cam is deep in thought right now?" Josh whispered loudly.

"Seriously. He's thinking so hard that if we concentrate we might be able to hear what he's thinking about."

I really doubt it. I cleared my throat. "We're here."

"Saved by the parking lot, old boy." Josh offered a companionable clap to my shoulder as I pulled us into a space near the break in the bushes that led to the pier.

"You can tell us all about it later," Keith said. "Does everyone have a coat?"

Excellent fathers. They would bring their kids here, too. Everyone in La Vista brought their kids to the pier, or to toddle along the waterfront. The picture of them again overwhelmed me: Josh older, but still strong, still thick through the shoulders without seeming oversized; Keith older, with slightly longer hair and no tie, having aged out of the insecurity of youth. They'd adopted, I saw in this projected future summer day. Little mixed-race kids, probably a sibling set. Two boys and a girl.

I swallowed, banishing the vision for the inky black water and biting wind of the present.

We didn't speak immediately. I was still considering many domino futures, each of which seemed to tip into the next, providing ever more images. When Keith spoke up, it was clear he was thinking of something else entirely.

"How is it possible that Philpott let himself be lured out here? He was so smart. And aware. It makes no sense to me. There's no way he goes to the waterfront with a stranger when he probably knows more about this killer than the cops do."

"It wouldn't have been a stranger," I said.

"That's another thing. How hard is it to run all the credit card receipts for all the theme nights and cross-check who was there, you know? They can't have that many solid suspects, and they still can't figure out who's doing this?"

"Ed says that Fredi has a lot of cash customers." I paused. "Though I take your point. What's the use of connecting all the murders if it doesn't help stop them from happening?"

"It's not just that," Josh said. "Aside from the fact that some people pay cash, and even aside from the fact that this person doesn't necessarily have to be drinking in order to be at—or around—Club Fred's on theme nights, we were there on almost all those nights, Keith. I bet a lot of people were. They've been popular, you know? So it's probably not that short a list anyway."

"We weren't there for the first one. Were we?"

Josh slipped his hand in Keith's. "Babe. It was your birthday."

"No way. The first murder was a few weeks later."

"Drag Night, remember? We held your twenty-first at Drag Night. That's when the first murder happened."

Keith stopped walking. "Shit. Seriously?"

I was stuck on something else. "Keith, you're twenty-one?"

"Um, yeah, guilty as charged." He shot me a look that was partially bashful and partially defiant. "How old are you?"

"Thirty-two."

"Oh."

We stared at each other until Josh started laughing.

"Oh man, your faces right now. Damn, that's funny. Don't worry about it, Cam. I fell for him when he was eighteen and looked about fifteen, so I get it."

"Josh is only twenty-four," Keith mumbled.

"Yeah, but Cam couldn't actually have fathered me, so I feel like it's way less awkward."

"Oh, shut up. Jerk."

"I couldn't have fathered you," I said to Keith, offering him my arm. He took it, after a beat, like he'd never walked arm in arm with a gentleman before. (Kids today.) "For one, I was eleven when you were born, so it's biologically unlikely. But more importantly, I didn't have sex with anyone until I was sixteen, and I didn't have sex with a girl until I was twenty, so I can say with absolute certainty that you are not my son."

"Dodged a bullet there," Josh said helpfully.

I glared at him.

He grinned and took Keith's other arm.

Keith wasn't as willing to surrender to levity. "It's just—if it could happen to Philpott, who I would have said there's no way, at all, that he could get killed by this person . . . If it could happen to him, it could happen to anyone."

"Not us. We're always together."

"But Cam isn't."

"Nothing is going to happen to me," I said. "Please don't worry about it."

"I think we should worry. All of us should worry. Philpott sat with us, what, a month ago, and laid out exactly who's most likely to be the killer. Which means they walked *right up to him* and, even though he should have known, he didn't."

"Babe, maybe he was wrong. He was laying out the statistical likelihood. This person may be an exception."

"They're already an exception for motive, aren't they?" I gestured with the hand not locked around Keith's. "Different genders, races, ages, backgrounds. Club Fred's was the only thing they had in common."

"And being queer. Except for that boy, though he probably wasn't straight, since he was at Fred's."

"I bought him a drink," I said. The wind picked up, sending chills rushing down my back. "Steven. Seemed like a nice kid."

Josh looked over. "Oh shit, Cam. You knew him?"

"No, no. He sat down next to me because Zane was making a big deal of it being his birthday. So I bought him a happy birthday drink." I thought about the boy, who'd apparently been Keith's age, but where Keith wore his years with a sense of gravity, Steven Costello had worn his with a sort of furtive wariness, as if he'd expected the world to hurt him.

I shivered again.

"You think he was a closet case?"

"Probably. Judging by the fact that his parents didn't even tell the police that he was gay, or that he might be at Club Fred's. I assume if they knew, it wasn't an accepted thing."

"He got killed on his birthday. And someone else got killed on mine. It's like . . . it could have been the other way around, you know?"

Josh stepped in front of Keith and cupped his face. "No. It couldn't have. Because you have me. Neither one of us is going to die, Keith, you hear me?"

"We don't know. Maybe this guy, Steven, was an easier target than I am, but Philpott was way harder. You and I aren't together every hour of every day. I go to classes and stuff. Plus, how do we know this killer hasn't been to the center? We talk to strangers all day long, Josh. Both of us do."

The wind picked up again, blowing spray over the pier, misting us. Suddenly I realized where we were. I had no idea where along the waterfront the bodies had been found, but I watched the darkness and small pools of yellow lights, strung just far enough apart to be less than helpful. What would I do if someone jumped out at us? Beat them with my borrowed Raiders jacket?

No one would be dumb enough to attack three of us, though. Even if they could take down Philpott. I flashed to Ed talking about how hard he'd fought back and said a silent prayer for his soul, hoping that whatever happened after death was either peaceful or nothing at all. Philpott certainly deserved peace.

"Let's go back to the car," I said, nudging them. "Come on."

We started walking back. This time the two of them held hands and I walked off to the side.

Keith hunched a little in his coat, protecting himself from the wind. "It's not like I'm super worried we're the next victims, but we *could* be, and that's fucking scary."

"We take all the precautions we can take short of staying in the house all the time," Josh said.

"I know we do. Sorry I'm such a downer."

Josh kissed the side of his face. "You aren't."

We escaped the wind and closed our doors tightly against the outside.

I started the car and turned on the heat.

"They must have known Philpott enough to trick him." Josh reached up and locked both of our doors, then both doors in the back. "That's the only thing I can think of. I mean, he was a smart dude, but if I'd wanted to lure him to the waterfront, all I would have had to say is, 'Hey, let's go check it out, see if we can find any clues.' If he trusted someone—or at least thought they couldn't get the drop on him—he would have gone."

"At 1 a.m.?"

"It wasn't a theme night. He probably figured it was safe."

"And he had an ego," I added.

"Yeah. He wouldn't have seen himself as a victim at all. It probably wouldn't have occurred to him."

I could see the pale reflection of Keith's face in the windshield, brow furrowed, lips pursed.

He gave a quick, violent head shake. "It just makes me so angry that I'm afraid to hang out at Club Fred's and that I'm afraid it'll be someone I love next. There's a next, you know? Unless they catch this person, whoever they are, someone else will get killed, probably someone we know, and that's . . . It doesn't make any sense to me that this is the world we live in."

Josh leaned forward. "It's the world we live in all the time. It's just that you aren't used to being so aware of it."

"Is that supposed to make it better? Because it makes it worse."

"No. I don't think there's much 'better' to work with here, babe."

I glanced into the mirror and Josh looked back. He was right. There wasn't a whole lot of good you could project onto this situation.

Enough.

"Will both of you stay after the movie on Saturday? I mean, if you're coming to it. I could get something for dinner."

"Sounds good to me," Josh said.

"Me too. I really am sorry I'm being so morose."

I wished I could reach out to him, but I didn't know how. "I don't mind morose. And if neither of you objects, I think I'll make a casserole."

"Keith loves a casserole."

"I really do. There's something so warm and comforting about them, you know?"

I knew. That was why I was thinking about casseroles. "Consider it a date." Then, in embarrassment, I glanced at the mirror again.

Josh, of course, was smiling. "Oh hell yes, it's a date. Keith, we gotta plan something to thank our host."

"I'm good with that."

I dropped them off at the center, with the Raiders jacket, and told them to keep the snacks.

"We'll see you on Saturday!" Keith called.

I waved and pulled away, reflecting on how much emptier my car felt in the wake of their departure. I drove alone all the time, but it had never felt this hollow.

After a second of deliberation, and feeling quite ridiculous, I hit the automatic locks. Obviously the killer wasn't walking around pulling victims out of their Volvos, but still.

What would they plan for Saturday? I gave in to the little edge of excitement and allowed myself to dream.

CHAPTER 12

They waited throughout the reception in the lobby after *Monkey Business*, and I locked the doors and ignored the curious looks of my staff as I ushered Josh and Keith to the little step-down lounge.

"I hope you don't mind waiting."

"This is awesome," Keith said. "I told you, I always wanted to work here."

"Well, if your current job doesn't work out, you can give me a call. It should only be a couple of minutes."

"We're good. We are totally good."

The Rhein had always trained staff to prioritize customer service above all else—with a close-second emphasis on cleanliness. Film series nights had a slightly different rhythm than the rest of our closing shifts: the theater would be swept long before the lobby cleared out, and concessions would also be entirely ready for closing. I could hear both vacuums running, and I wiped down the refreshments table with a cloth from a clean sanitizer bucket. I double-checked the booth and let the ushers leave, finishing up the vacuuming myself.

I forgot, for a few minutes, that Keith and Josh were there. I suppose when I'd pictured it, they sat talking, or maybe looked at movie posters. I never imagined that they would sit there for twenty-five minutes . . . watching me.

Once the vacuum was safely stashed away and the platters dried and put up until next week, I let the last of the staff out and crossed the lobby toward Keith and Josh, trying to figure out what was so riveting about watching me close the movie theater.

"I apologize for the wait."

"God, don't. It was totally worthwhile. I like it when you walk, Cam." Keith giggled. "That sounds really stupid, but it's true."

Josh nodded. "Seriously. You walk like you're going somewhere important."

"How do other people walk?"

They glanced at each other.

"Like they don't know they're doing it," Josh said. "Like they're not paying attention. You walk deliberately."

"Oh." Did I? Surely no more deliberately than most people.

"You move deliberately in general," he added. "It's one of the reasons we thought we could approach you. Because you value intention."

I stood in my lobby, which smelled of popcorn and the powdered deodorizer we sprinkled on the carpets before vacuuming (with an undercurrent of dust I could never fully get rid of, no matter how deeply I cleaned), and realized that no one had ever paid attention to me the way the two men sitting on the sofa did. No one had ever found me interesting enough to consider me like this, or to trust me the way that they trusted me. It was humbling.

"Thank you," I murmured.

They got to their feet.

"I think we kind of embarrassed Cam," Keith said.

"Yeah, but in a good-for-him way."

I herded them to the alcove with the alarm in it and turned out the lights. "We'll have a minute to get outside once I set this."

Keith bounced a little on his feet. "Oh my god, we're in the Rhein with the lights off right now. So freaking cool!"

"One minute. And if we don't get out, then we have to stay here until the security people arrive so I can explain that it was an accident."

He zipped his lips and assumed what must have been an "I'm ready to run for the door" expression. Josh nodded, studying the alarm panel.

"Here we go."

I set the alarm, and it beeped at us as we went out through the left front door. I locked it quickly, then went to the other door to make sure it was locked as well.

My ears picked up the last of the alarm beeps. It was set.

"I feel so privileged, being inside the Rhein at closing. Like, seriously, that was sort of a dream come true. Thanks, Cam."

"Of course. Don't mention it."

This time all three of us went upstairs at the same time, and I'd already set the table, but I wasn't worried they'd find it absurd. Without the pressure of all of my projections about how the night would go, I could actually relax a little.

"I think it'll take about thirty minutes for the casserole. It's cooked, but the last time I made one, I didn't reheat it long enough and ended up with a cold, mushy center."

Josh flashed one of his toothy smiles. "You got impatient?"

"I did. Not tonight. I refuse to serve you guys cold and mushy."

"Appreciated." He finished lighting the candles (he hadn't asked permission, which thrilled me a little, as if taking the liberty had meaning beyond convenience). "I know what I want to do with the next thirty minutes. Is there a timer?"

"It's set."

He nodded. "Keith."

"Hmm? Wow, Cam, you have a crazy version of *Lord of the Rings* over here. In, like, a case."

"We have thirty minutes before dinner," Josh said, enunciating each word.

Keith turned. "Oh. Um."

"I think the couch will work to show Cam what we didn't show him last time. You ready?"

This was unexpected. Thirty minutes—I figured we'd make small talk, or even serious talk, but I didn't figure on whatever was happening now, or Josh's voice dropping a register.

"Okay. I mean, I thought we'd probably wait until after dinner. Um."

Josh pointed at the floor in front of his feet, and Keith, with a split-second glance at me, went to stand there. "It's so much more fun when I surprise you, though." He put his hands on Keith's shoulders. "Babe, yes or no?"

"Yes. I'm still worried about all the same stuff, but yes."

"Cam's going to think what I think."

Keith rolled his eyes. "You think I'm hot and amazing."

"You *are* hot and amazing. How much time left now, Cam?"

I'd almost forgotten I was there. I fought a sense of discombobulation and sighted the timer. "Twenty-five minutes, forty-three seconds."

"I'm going to spank you for the next twenty-five minutes and Cam's gonna watch, babe. You're not allowed to come."

The words replayed in my head after a hiccup during which I couldn't take in sound: *I'm going to spank you for the next twenty-five minutes and Cam's gonna watch.*

"Oh my god," Keith whispered. "Okay."

"I want your jeans all the way off. Keep the jock on. Is that okay for you?"

"I said it was."

"I know. I'm asking again."

"I'm fucking scared, but yeah, that's how I want to do it. As long as it's okay with Cam."

"I'll check in with him for a minute. Backwards on the couch. And be quick so I have all the time I want." Then he kissed Keith, and what began as a press of lips against lips became something deeper, without ever moving beyond a little play of tongues. Josh commanded intimacy as if he was born to it, with no need for drama or pageantry.

When he turned to me, as Keith obeyed orders, I caught my breath. I was attracted to the man who could smile and shake hands and sit with Merin at a table, containing all of his fear and sadness without doing more than leaning a bit forward. But the man who ordered Keith to disrobe without blinking, whose effortless self-possession made him the focal point of the room—he was riveting. I was riveted.

"Follow my lead. Say 'red' if you need what we're doing to stop or 'yellow' if you want to pause." His hand waved in front of his eyes. "And tell me if the black-and-white thing happens. And Cam?"

I gulped. "Yes?"

"Thanks for making us feel safe. This is crazy hot right now, and he's wanted it for years."

"Oh. Yes, of course. Anytime."

He flashed the cheeky grin. "I'll definitely hold you to that. I want you to start by standing right there, on the far side of the coffee table.

I may ask you to come closer, or touch, and if you don't want to, say 'yellow' and we'll move on. Got it?"

"I have it."

"Sweet. I gotta get to beating some ass over here. Babe, I don't know how I always forget how fucking pale you are, but I do. Look at your skin. Mm."

And oh—*oh*—Keith, skin from the waist down save for his socks, was bent over the back of the sofa with his knees pressing into the red velvet seat. His thighs were squeezed tightly together and the jockstrap perfectly framed his ass.

Good lord, there was a nearly naked man in my apartment. My heart was pounding. My cock was fighting its containment. I adjusted myself before walking over to the spot Josh had indicated, and stood there, breathing fast, simultaneously wanting it to begin and wanting to draw out the bliss of anticipation.

Josh knelt beside Keith, one hand on his upper back, pushing his head to the top of the sofa. The other hand smoothed over his legs and thighs, up and down. I held my breath as it went higher, over the plump globes of butt cheeks. He tugged on a strap and let it snap back into place. Then he did it again.

"I could tease you for hours. I almost want to tie you up and make you wait while we eat, tease you the whole time."

Keith's back rose and fell. He buried his eyes in his arm.

"Babe, you can talk. Do what we usually do. That's what we should be showing him. Not you trying to pretend like this isn't moving you at all."

"'M not. I just—I just—" The rhythmic rise and fall lulled me. He was breathing so fast. "It's harder than I thought, Josh."

"Bummer for you. My thing is way easier. I thought it'd feel weird doing this in front of someone, but it doesn't feel weird doing it in front of Cam." He pulled back and smacked one side of Keith's ass. "Feels pretty good, actually." Then the other one.

"Oh god," Keith whispered, pushing back. "It's not enough time."

"I know."

If you'd told me I could watch twenty solid minutes of one man spanking another, I would have told you that sounded boring. That I wasn't interested, and I didn't find spanking the least bit sexy. I would have pictured it as an arm raising up, then coming down, then raising up, then coming down. I wouldn't have known how much variety there could be within the word *spank*, or how many times Josh would pause to rub over the skin he made pink and red, how many times he would lick his fingers and draw symbols on Keith's skin, making him writhe.

How many times his thumbs peeled apart Keith's cheeks so he could blow warm air over him.

If you'd told me about all that, I would have imagined a sweet, sensual spanking. Something that didn't contain more than perhaps a brief sting, immediately soothed by a lover's hand. But this wasn't that, either. Josh's blows rained down on Keith, and Keith's legs strained, holding him up. After a while, he began to flinch away, even though it was clear he wasn't really resisting. From light slaps to meaty thuds, I could sometimes tell by the sound how hard the impact had been. Or by Keith's grunts.

Josh began with smacks in a wide area, all over Keith's cheeks, his thighs. But as they kept going, he tightened the impact zone until he was nailing the same spots again and again, intensity rising, only broken when he let Keith breathe while he brushed his palm over the deeper-looking marks.

He glanced up. The timer. Both of us could see it from where we were. Only Keith, eyes still buried, had no idea how much longer this would continue.

Two minutes twenty-nine seconds. Twenty-eight. Twenty-seven.

This time there was no break. This time Josh's arm, yes, raised and lowered, and he bent over to marshal more force, and I breathed shallowly, as if I were running and couldn't suck in enough air to suit my lungs, not quite gasping at the same sound, again and again, *thwap, thwap, thwap, thwap*.

I was desperate for it to stop. Keith was beginning to thrash a little, and Josh flattened his forearm across Keith's upper back, keeping him down, never stopping in the constant blows.

The timer went off.

Josh stopped, and Keith launched into him, tumbling them over on the sofa. I thought he was laughing at first, but a minute later I realized he was sobbing, pummeling Josh's chest with soft fists, his ass red and undoubtedly sore, waving in the air.

"Baby," Josh said. "Angel."

Keith stilled.

"You are so fucking beautiful. You have no idea how hot you are."

"Shut up. Josh . . ."

It should have been a moment only for them. I should have eased away, gone to check the casserole. But I found my legs moving me closer, lowering so I could sit on the edge of the coffee table beside them.

The center of Keith's back felt safe. In between the protective grip of both of Josh's hands. I pressed my palm over the loose shirt, and Keith inhaled deeply.

I had no idea what I should say, but I needed to try. I needed to let them know I was there with them, that I'd borne witness. "Thank you so much. Did you want me to pull him off you? Because it was a near thing at the end there."

Josh's lips turned up in a soft, tired smile.

"No," Keith mumbled. "No, he was good, I just didn't realize we were going that far tonight, and it wasn't—it's a lot more intense than it usually is. That's totally not Josh at his most extreme."

"Really?"

"Oh god. Cam." He sniffled and pushed up to sit with his legs over Josh's, still pinning him. "That wasn't even a taste of Josh at his most extreme."

The timer in the kitchen went off again.

"I'm so messed up now." Keith slugged Josh in the arm. "You messed me up before we started dinner."

"I knew you thought we were waiting, so I kind of had to. C'mere."

Keith sighed, and allowed himself to be pulled to Josh's chest. "Thanks."

"You know I'm good for it."

"I know you're good for me. Did we totally freak Cam out?"

"I am not freaked out," I said, affronted.

Josh laughed. "Nah. He was solid. He couldn't stop looking at how beautiful you were."

"Shut it with the bullshit."

"It's not bullshit," I protested. "It's not bullshit at all. You are. And I was serious before. If you ever want me to pull Josh off because he's taking it too far, let me know, okay? I was *so* uncomfortable at the end."

Keith turned his head so he could look at me. "Aw, Cam. That was a baby spanking because we only had a few minutes. It wasn't nearly extreme enough for me."

"But don't worry." Josh's smile acquired a slightly predatory edge. "We'll be gentle and lead you in slowly."

They weren't kidding. I could see that. But it was hard to accept that something I thought was severe wasn't even scratching the surface of what they did.

"And that was only my hand," Josh added. "We change it up a lot more than that when we're really going down deep."

"But I— You don't need me to do that. To go that . . . deep. Right?"

Both of them shook their heads.

"We don't even need to do it with you, if you don't want us to. No worries, Cam." The timer went off for a third time, and Keith levered himself up, tugging his pants back on. "Can I help with dinner?"

"Shouldn't you be on a swooning couch somewhere?"

"Oh, a swooning couch! We should get a swooning couch, Josh!"

"Yeah, okay. We'll run right over to Ikea's swooning-couch section and pick one up."

"Hey, that's not a bad idea. Ikea should totally have a swooning-couch section." Keith walked into my kitchen as if he was perfectly used to it, as if he spent time there frequently, and grabbed an oven mitt out of the drawer beside the oven.

"Cam."

I looked at Josh.

"You're good, right?" He held up a hand. "Really think about it for a minute, don't just answer."

It didn't take long. Yes, I'd been shocked, but I wasn't out of my depth by any means. And although I'd tried not to be aroused, there was that, too.

"I'm good. I'm honored. That you invited me in. That you trust me." I glanced up over his head at Keith. "That he does. Thank you, Josh."

"All the thanks are on our side. I could have gone easier on him, but he was right: that was a fraction of us in a typical scene. I had to know you could roll with it. It's not the kind of thing you can come out and ask a guy, you know?"

"I'm starting to work that out."

"We have dinner!" Keith called. "Also, we need one of these. Josh, Cam's got a digital thermometer. I've been telling you how much we need one, and we so totally do."

Josh groaned and got to his feet. "Don't encourage Keith about kitchen appliances. He doesn't cook and yet he wants all this stuff."

"The tuna drainer isn't about cooking, it's about making tuna sandwiches. Or tuna salad. Tuna noodle casserole!" Keith covered his mouth with the hand that still had on my old *Goonies* oven mitt. "Sorry I'm goofy."

Josh rolled his eyes. "You hear anyone complaining? You want me to bring the plates up, or do you want to bring the casserole down?"

Now both of them were acting at home in my kitchen. I decided I liked it.

"Cam, do you have a trivet or something? Or no, I think we should serve ourselves, then foil the casserole and leave it in the oven with the heat low in case we want seconds."

"Sounds good to me." Josh gathered our dinner plates from the table, and I opened a bottle of wine.

Dinner was excellent. I didn't eat cheese much, but I'd bought some fancy cheddar for the casserole, along with ham, red peppers, and figs. It was my first experiment with fruit in a savory casserole, but it ended up surprisingly delicious.

This time when they left, each of them kissed me on the cheek. I felt the lingering impression of their lips until I drifted off to sleep.

CHAPTER 13

Keith: *Come to Club Fred's with us tonight?*

Cameron: *I'm off at eight.*

Keith: *We'll pick you up. We can't be out too late, but we kind of feel like we want to give Fredi some money since it's not her fault some asshole chose her place to stalk people.*

Keith: *You good for an early night?*

Keith: *If not, we can meet there and you can stay later.*

Cameron: *Early night sounds fine.*

Keith: *We'll be there nine fifteen-ish. I'll text and you can come down.*

Cameron: *Sounds good.*

Keith: *See you then! Yay! Club Fred's date!*

Cameron: *:-) (Did I use that right? It's a happy face, isn't it?)*

Keith: *:-o*

Cameron: *Why are you yelling at me?*

Keith: *It's an excited face. :-P*

Cameron: *Oh. In that case: :-o*

Keith: *;-)*

Cameron: *:-)*

Keith: *Josh is laughing at both of us now. See you in a few hours, Cam!*

Cameron: *See you soon.*

I finished at work, went upstairs, and grabbed my camel hair coat (possibly overkill, but it was chilly, and you never knew where you'd have to park to get to Club Fred's; Steerage was notorious for having no parking). I waited for a while in the apartment, but even after I went back to the theater, I still had about half an hour before they were supposed to pick me up, so I went and fired up the secondary computer in the corner of the ticket booth, keeping well out of the clerk's way.

No one liked being in the booth with me, a fact I used to take personally until my dad pointed out that it probably felt like close supervision to the rest of the staff. I'd never thought much about us owning the theater and other people only working there. We'd had a core group of employees for most of my childhood, whom I'd considered family; I must have been sixteen or seventeen before I realized that newer employees deferred to me in a way that wasn't solely because I knew the workings of the theater inside and out.

I made myself as small as possible and turned all the way toward the little alcove where the extra computer was tucked. The booth was eight and a half feet long, but felt smaller when you were sharing it with another person.

Since technically the Cary Grant Film Festival was a promotion, I needed to be able to analyze it to see if it had been successful. It was exactly half over, and so far I couldn't see any patterns emerging. Attendance on Saturday nights had naturally spiked over the last six weeks, but I needed the habit of going to the theater to spread out over the rest of the week, even in small ways. We were seating a slightly higher average in the beginning of the week—Mondays and Tuesdays had always been our slowest days, though Wednesdays were usually steady—but that could be explained by the recent cold weather, or the stresses of the incoming holiday season, or any number of other things I couldn't account for without digging into last year's sales.

I was still staring at my numbers when I got a text from Keith to say they had arrived. Before I could text back, Iliana, who'd been selling tickets, said, "Um, Cameron? I think there are people here trying to get your attention."

Keith was grinning and waving from the far side of the windows. I waved back and glanced over Iliana's shoulder at the monitor. The movie had begun and everything looked harmonious.

"You can go ahead and start the closing stuff," I told her.

"Thanks." She offered a little smile. "They seem nice."

"They are. Thanks, Iliana. If you need anything, call me."

"Sure. We won't, though. Have a good night."

"You too."

I let her out and Josh and Keith in. "I need to shut down my computer and I'll be ready to go. You can wait here, or if you want to cram in, you can—"

"Oh my god, we can go in the *ticket booth*? Pinch me, Josh."

"Don't tempt me." Despite the attempt to play it cool, Josh looked kind of excited, too.

"It's not that big a deal. It's just the ticket booth."

"*Just* the ticket booth?" Keith shook his head. "You have no appreciation for the total awesomeness of this moment, none. Can we go in the booth? Please, Cam?"

I opened the door with a flourish and gestured them in. Keith was the more boggle-eyed, but Josh was definitely restraining a grin, which I still didn't understand. "It's really just—"

"You hush. Don't let the ticket booth hear you talk about it like that. Oh man. This is so cool. It's like being inside a legend!"

I closed the door and stood against it. Keith touched everything: discarded misprint tickets, torn stubs for the last show, schedules for movies, work schedules, phone lists for distributors. His fingers traced the edges of the little awards in the window, which I supposed he'd only ever seen from the other side. Best Movie Theater for most of the eighties and nineties, though I only kept up the last ten years of awards. These days they called us the Best Independent Theater so we wouldn't have to compete with IMAX up at the Cinema 18.

"Hey, do you mind if I look at this?" Josh sat down at the secondary computer. "We don't have a decent accounting program and we need one."

"It won't be much help, then. The system is really just cobbled together Microsoft Access databases. I know I need to replace it with something, but I'm always worried that there's so much going on in the background I'll export all the wrong things."

"Wow. Well, I'm impressed. Keith, look at this. Look at these reports."

Keith pulled himself away from reading many years of notes gouged into the crumbling sheet rock beneath the counter (my parents' handwriting was down there somewhere; I'd show him if I thought about it later).

"Check this out." Josh indicated the screen. "Ticket sales by day of the week, right, Cam?"

I nodded.

"Oh my *god*. This is hot." Keith leaned in close and started navigating around, occasionally giving soft grunts of approval.

I raised my eyebrows at Josh, who surrendered the chair.

"He's so good at this stuff. I wish I could look at a spreadsheet and understand half the stuff Keith does."

"Is this your projections, Cam? Oh, no, I see. This is showing me last year. Do you have projections?"

"Projections? No. Do you think I should?"

He swiveled in the chair and gave me a *look*. (Josh whistled low.) "How will you know if you're meeting your goals if you don't have any goals?"

"Well. I guess I . . . assumed that as long as I could pay the bills, I was meeting my goals?"

"But how much is the Cary Grant Film Festival costing you? You have to know that in order to know if you're breaking even."

"You mean how much am I paying per film?"

"The overhead on the film, the food, the drinks. Did you add staff hours to cover the receptions after each movie?"

"I have an extra person on. Or no, I have the ushers stay later."

His eyes narrowed. "You didn't even cost it out, did you? You did it on a whim."

"It wasn't a *whim*—"

He swiveled back to the computer, and I shut my mouth.

Josh whistled again. "Give him a minute. Wait for it."

"The film series runs until when?" Keith asked.

I had the distinct impression I was being interrogated. "December seventeenth."

"Right before Christmas."

"I thought if I could get people in the habit of seeing movies on Saturday nights, you know, then maybe they'd be in the habit of seeing movies more—"

"My point is that you're building a habit right up until the holidays, which will interrupt the habit you just spent you-have-no-clue-how-much-money building. What's your plan for January?"

I cast a helpless glance at Josh. "I'm not sure. Should I have a plan?"

Keith sighed loudly. "Please at least tell me you keep your receipts from all the food."

"Of course I keep my receipts."

"Can I have them? Only for the film series supplies. I want to see exactly how much you're paying for those receptions."

"Well, I—I mean, I buy all the food at the same time. Rather, it all comes in the delivery. I don't have it separated out—"

Josh began massaging Keith's shoulders. "It's okay, babe. It's okay. Cam doesn't know. He's not trying to hurt you with his indifference toward business basics. He just doesn't know." He shot me a covert smile.

Even Josh smiling didn't ease the sensation that I'd been extremely dense about the whole thing. "I can see what you're saying. I guess I didn't think about it that way. I wanted to do something new, and this seemed like fun, and it seemed like maybe the kind of thing I could make into an opportunity. I don't remember my parents talking about how they made those kinds of decisions."

Keith waved at the screen. "It's all here. I can show you. This goes back to 1994, though they clearly migrated everything in the late nineties, because I can't manipulate the numbers before that. But I'm looking at how whoever made this database thought, Cam. And they used projections."

"My mom." I moved in closer. "It was never good enough, but she worked on it for years."

"I can see that. This is amazing. I don't have any idea how she's making some of these reports do what they're doing. Man, I wish she could explain it to me. I bet that'd be fucking sweet."

"Hey," Josh murmured, squeezing his shoulders.

"Huh? Oh shit. Oh my god—" Keith turned to look at me with a stricken expression on his face. "Sorry. Cam, I'm so sorry, I'm such a thoughtless jerk."

"It's okay." I watched the screen, where Keith's cursor bounced between sheets and reports and graphs. "What are we looking at?"

"In 2001, your folks had some kind of event in March, and again in May, and again in July. Each time they did it, they made more money because your mom kept tweaking little things. Look, she made notes. They started movies at different times, they tried two-for-one ticket sales, they had a promotional week pass it looks like, though I'm not sure she tested it completely. There's a note here, 'OBWT big repeat,' whatever that means."

"*O Brother, Where Art Thou*," I said. "People would come five times to see it, they'd sing along and call out the lines. We were going to run a two-week pass next, for that and *Gladiator*. Except we were supposed to start it in the second week in September."

"Why didn't you?"

"Because that's when the World Trade Center came down." I brushed my thumb across my mother's notes, as if I could almost see them in her handwriting, my mind superimposing her scrawl on the screen. "The week pass was ten dollars with unlimited viewings, so people liked it. We usually show at least two movies per week, so even if you only went once to each movie, it was worth buying a pass. And we make most of our money off the concessions anyway."

"I think you should try that again. The passes. Maybe in January."

"Or pair it with another film series," Josh said. "Fifteen dollars for unlimited movies, hook people by inviting them every Saturday so they feel like they're getting one movie free."

"Fifteen dollars *promotional pricing*, though. You're not going to make money off that in the long run, but if you start with it, if you get people talking about how much fun they're having at the Rhein, that's when you up the price."

Josh nodded. "And maybe more stuff for kids and families. How many people grew up coming here, you know? When they have kids, they're gonna want to bring them to the Rhein, to keep up the tradition."

I swallowed and backed away, suddenly overwhelmed. "Yes. Yes, I can— That all makes sense—"

"Hold up," Josh said. He stepped toward me. Eight and a half feet and three adult men.

I froze.

"Cam, hold up." His hands, warm from Keith's skin, descended on my shoulders. Beyond Josh was the glass of the booth, and beyond the glass was the nighttime traffic on Mooney, headlights flaring as they passed. "Let's head to Club Fred's, okay? We'll buy you a drink."

Keith turned back to the computer. "I'll send you a marketing plan next week."

"He will, too."

I stared into Josh's eyes, trying to figure out how to express that I couldn't talk about this anymore, that I couldn't look at Mom's notes, or think about the summer I was eighteen, immediately stained sepia by the morning in September when we woke up to reports of planes crashing into buildings. Had I loved the movies we'd had then so much? Or had it only seemed like it later, when everything was up in the air and simple pleasures had to be earned back?

"I'm sorry," I said. "This is all really helpful."

"It's too much. And we blindsided you. Keith will write something up and then you can come down to the center and we'll hash it out, okay?"

"You don't have to do that—"

He squeezed my shoulders. I'd seen him do it to Keith, who sometimes didn't seem to notice. I noticed. I tensed and immediately tried to relax because I didn't want him to think I didn't like the feel of his weight, the comfort of his touch.

"We know we don't have to," Keith said over his shoulder. "We want to. We love the Rhein, too."

"And you aren't so bad, either. Let us help, Cam. Please. But tonight let us buy you a drink." Josh released me. "Come on. Shut down the computer, okay?"

Keith regretfully offered me the chair. "I wish I had Access so I could look at this all the time. I'd just put it up and like stare at it. This database is art."

"You're a huge nerd, babe."

"Don't be jealous."

I shut everything down, hit the lights, locked the door, and waved to Iliana and the rest of the crew. All mechanical things my body did while my mind attempted to process the heavy feeling of Josh's hands on my shoulders.

And whether it would be possible to feel it again.

CHAPTER 14

The Philadelphia Story was the highest-attended film of the series since *An Affair to Remember*. Mr. and Mrs. Walker came again, and bought the family dinner package, which meant they got to sit in the first few rows, outfitted with little tables between sets of seats. I could see them from where I stood at the entry to the long hall back to the lobby, and I didn't linger there for the entire movie staring, or anything, but for the first time I felt a sense of . . . propriety over Josh and Keith. Almost as if Josh's surely casual shoulder-squeeze had translated into a deeper feeling of belonging.

I cautioned myself against it, of course. They had each other. Clearly they enjoyed my company, but that was nothing to what they'd already established, the relationship that pre-existed our friendship.

Still, I liked having them in the theater. I liked that they kissed my cheek, even as they were escorting Josh's parents out after a few minutes' socializing at the reception. They were now known to be friends of mine, and that was a pleasantly homey sensation.

Mildred and Emerson had come to this showing. I said hello to them, intrigued by the configuration but not quite sure I was at liberty to ask about it. Obie was the extrovert in that household; the most I managed was, "And where's Obie tonight?"

"Babysitting," Mildred said.

Emerson grunted. "I was supposed to be watching James with him, but he told me I was in a rotten mood and we'd all be better off if I went to the movies. I'm not in a rotten mood, Mildred, am I?"

"No more rotten than you usually are."

He made a face at her. She smirked.

"God, I love that movie," she said. "And that pool. I really want that pool."

"You should build it for us," he replied. "I'd like an extra-large changing room, please. Wheelchair accessible."

She hit him. "The movie was great, Cameron. I'm really glad you started doing this. And I'll be back for *Arsenic and Old Lace*. I love that one."

"I look forward to seeing you," I said, and it wasn't a lie, but it wasn't deeply meaningful. It was small talk, or chitchat. It was the kind of thing people said to other people, and I meant it exactly the way people usually meant it.

And really . . . it was liberating. To not be limited to saying only things that I felt intensely. Was this how other people lived all the time? They offered these surface phrases like tissues to be used and discarded?

"Thanks for coming," I told them, implicitly excusing myself to continue making the rounds. Did I have any trivia about *The Philadelphia Story*? Sure. That scene where drunken Jimmy Stewart hiccups wasn't scripted that way; if you watched closely, you could see Cary Grant trying desperately not to laugh.

I felt slightly more buoyant the rest of the night, as if by freeing myself from the shackles of emotional depth, I'd floated to the top of social interactions, and now I could rest there, treading water, neither meaning anything too much, nor too little.

Sometime later, when people were still milling about, I slipped into the ticket booth for a moment and texted Keith.

Cameron: *I've had an epiphany. I think I know how to make small talk now.*

Cameron: *:-)*

I promised myself I wouldn't stand there staring at my phone when Keith could be busy, or with Josh's folks, or any number of other things, none of which was waiting for me to text him.

But this was Keith. He'd probably grown up with cell phones. He was much more suited to their constant demands than I was.

Keith: *Happy dance!*

Keith: *That's great, Cam.*

Keith: *Small talk is super helpful, though sometimes it's also super annoying.*

Keith: *:-o*

This, though, was whole new territory, and even as I carefully typed the angle bracket and the three, I didn't know if I'd go through with it.

Then I did.

Cameron: *<3*

Cameron: *Thanks.*

Keith: *Anytime. And <3 right back at you.*

I quickly texted *Good night* and put away my phone.

The lobby crowd drifted away, staying a little bit later than last week. Keith was right: reception creep was going to affect my labor costs if people lingered on past midnight. But I was internally jubilant as I showed people out and told them I'd see them next week. I'd been afraid to talk like that before, as if I was somehow presuming, as if my casual "see you next week" to people I'd seen every Saturday for a month and a half was somehow intrusive.

But not a single person acted like it. They waved, and smiled, and called back, "You too!" or "Hope it's another good one!" They were *glad* I presumed. They wanted to belong, and watching Cary Grant on Saturday nights, staying for light snacks and fruit juice after, made them feel exactly that.

Keith was right about everything. Now that I'd made this, I'd be a fool to let it fizzle. But what could I follow with in January? *Not* another twelve weeks; even if it costed out worthwhile, it was exhausting, and we were still only halfway through.

I considered having speakers come down, but I couldn't think of anyone interesting, local, and willing. Maybe the young woman who'd written and directed a film and had her opening at the Rhein had something new. Or, barring that, perhaps she'd like to screen her old film again.

A film series of local filmmakers, now that would be interesting. That would be the kind of thing I could sell a "series" ticket for, and include a little Q&A after. It was a great idea. I wondered what Keith and Josh would think of it.

Of course, that would take much more than a few weeks to plan. Maybe for February. Perhaps I could simply order up some other old favorites for the Saturday nights in January. And seriously look at what I was paying for food and labor to see if it made sense to continue having receptions. The theater was hardly in dire straits. I was willing to invest in a sense of community if that was what it would take.

And for the first time, I was beginning to feel like I could do it. I could make the Rhein my parents' dream again. On that note, I said good night to the staff, finished closing up, and went home.

Gunga Din's audience didn't compare to the crowd we'd hosted for *The Philadelphia Story*, but a disproportionate number of people stayed for refreshments after. My new skills at small talk were challenged by the sheer volume of discussion, and how frequently I found myself apologizing for the controversial nature of the film. I'd chosen to show it because my father had always loved it, and I'd led my introduction by noting the incredibly problematic portrayal of the Indian people. But showing it had been a misstep, and I regretted it even as I sat in the theater watching it. As a child, I hadn't noticed how offensive it was; as an adult I blushed in the dark and couldn't believe I'd made a sentimental choice to publicize an incredibly, unavoidably racist film.

I avoided leaving the apartment for most of Sunday, texting back and forth with Keith, enjoying the peace and quiet. But by evening I was unusually restless, and decided to head to Club Fred's. I nearly didn't text Ed, but at the last moment, I did. Just to let him know I'd be there in case he and Alisha were out, or bored, or interested.

I hadn't seen him much lately. He'd come to a few movies with Alisha, or I'd seen them at Club Fred's, but since the two of them got together—or maybe since things with the serial killer started getting more intense—he hadn't been in close contact.

Ed's friendship had been a gift in my life right when I needed one. He'd come to interview me about an independent film opening I'd hosted at the theater, and he'd been back soon after for something else, and somehow we'd become friends. I'd told him a little about my parents dying; he'd told me about his parents and their refusal to accept that he was trans. Small, significant confidences, built up over time.

Halfway through my Scotch (I'd finished the mystery at the fashion show and was continuing to read the rest of the author's books—in order, this time), someone hugged me from behind.

"Cam!" Alisha's hair draped over my shoulder and brushed the screen of my phone, turning pages. "Oh my god, faux pas! Sorry! I lost your place!"

"It's okay. Hey, Alisha."

"Hey, how are you?"

"Good." I gave Ed a more controlled sort of hug. "I didn't know if I'd see you guys tonight."

"It's the first time you've ever texted me, I mean without me texting you first." He shrugged in that unassuming way he had, which had changed in the last few months as the testosterone took hold in his system.

"Plus, there's the whole man-crush thing," Alisha added.

I raised my eyebrows. "Pardon me, the what?"

She laughed. "Wait, you didn't know— Ed, he doesn't know—"

Ed elbowed her. "Ixnay on the— Shush. Tom, can I get a beer? Alisha will have a slice of lemon and a shot of reproach."

Tom, all six feet of him, chuckled as he pulled the pint. "Beer, Alisha?"

"Tom, you get man-crushes, right? I don't mean about guys you want to have sex with, I mean guys you want to *be*. You know the type. The way they move, the way they lean, you just want to— Oof!"

"I detest you," Ed muttered, blushing.

"Sure thing." Tom pushed their beers across the counter and accepted Alisha's money. "For me it's all in how they talk. I always wish I was more, y'know, articulate."

"Exactly. For me it's all in the bearing. A woman who can walk in the room and command all eyes on her without even speaking? Mm. Lady-crush."

"Oh, like you *don't* want to have sex with women like that."

"Well, no, but like, usually they're straight or my boss or running for office or married to the president or something, you know? So it's not a real have-sex-with-them thing. That's just a sort of corollary to how much I want to be them when I grow up."

"I'm through with this topic now." Ed waved the hand not on his beer. "How's the Rhein?"

I was not through with this topic. And I could only come to one conclusion about why we were discussing it in the first place. I made my voice light and nudged him. "You have a *man-crush* on me?"

"Everyone can shut up."

"That's very flattering, Ed. And the theater's good, I think. I've been talking to Keith Whelan—you know, half of the QYP team—about continuing promotions and things like that. He wants me to do projections and track my spending for events better, which I think is probably exceptional advice. And he can make sense of Mom's databases, which is a bonus."

"That's really great." Ed, apparently sensing we were done messing with him, took the stool next to mine. "So I heard kind of a funny rumor about the QYP guys."

"Oh yeah?" I'd never been inside the rumor loops deeply enough to feel the flow of them, but I'd never heard of anything good coming out of rumors.

"Totally my cue." Alisha kissed my cheek, then kissed Ed far less casually. "Dancing now."

"I'll be out there when I'm done with my beer. Good?"

"Gorgeous." She spun around, and the scarf wrapped around her hair trailed softly in the air after her as she walked off.

"Don't you want to hear the funny rumor?"

I focused on Ed and braced for whatever the grapevine had invented about Josh and Keith. "What?"

"I heard"—he made a design in the condensation on the side of his glass—"that the QYP guys have been seeing a lot of movies at the Rhein lately. And that sometimes they stay after and accompany the owner to his apartment. I told you it was funny."

Every bit of moisture in my mouth dried up. "Where did you hear that?"

He grinned. "So not revealing my top secret sources. Obviously I'm willing to believe that you and them are just friends, if that's what you tell me is true."

"I hate the phrase 'just friends.' What does that mean about friendship, that we're so quick to dismiss it?"

"What does it mean about you and the QYP guys that you haven't dismissed it at all?"

I glanced around, but no one was near us and if Tom could hear, he'd take it to his grave. "We aren't 'just' anything. We are friends. Please don't say more about this. It's up to them what they want to share with people."

Ed turned fully toward me. "Oh my god. There's something going on between you and the QYP guys. I had no idea, Cam. I was really only playing."

"I know. And it's fine. But I—" I had no idea how to explain. Or how much. "It is a—a casual thing, but I don't want to make anything difficult for anyone."

"I won't say anything, obviously, but you—" He paused, as if he had to be careful about his phrasing. "You don't do 'casual,' do you?"

"Not historically. But that's what they need." Or at least, it seemed like it was what they'd asked me for in the beginning. Though of course, they didn't like the word *casual* much either. And I couldn't reconcile the way Josh had put his hands on my shoulders the other night to calm me down with a sense of "casual" that included Alisha's flippant cheek-kiss.

"What do you need?" Ed asked. "I'm serious. Casual or not, it's not just about them."

"Nothing. I don't need anything. And I like both of them very much, so any effort you can make to ensure that no rumors spread, I'd appreciate."

"Sure, Cam. Of course."

"Thank you."

After a moment, Ed added, "They seem like good guys."

"They are."

"Well, good, then. Anyway, tell me more about the theater. How's the film festival going? I keep running announcements on the *Times-Record's* social media for them, but maybe I should talk to Keith about how I can help more. I feel like there are a lot of people in La Vista who'd love to support the Rhein. We just have to give them simple ways to do it."

We retreated into the easy familiarity of our usual conversations, and I resolved to at least broach the subject of what Josh and Keith wanted me to say, should anyone ask me about them. Clearly I could lie. I was willing to, if that's what they wanted. (Or at least to deflect, which was far more my style.) But we should have anticipated that in a community as small as ours, with a healthy vein of gossip, people would talk.

If I'd wanted to be ironic, I could have shown *People Will Talk*. But the plot of that one had always bothered me, and it wasn't Cary Grant's greatest work, so I'd decided it went in the no pile. Before my brain could distract itself with a lecture on his best and worst films (and considering that the world was starting to look a little gray), I texted Keith and asked if I could come over after I left Club Fred's.

His answer, of course, was yes.

Both of them were in pajama-type clothes. Josh in long cotton lounge pants and a T-shirt, both blue. Keith had on a black-and-white striped matching set, which he told me had been a joke gift from Josh.

"Prison motif, you know. Though I kind of like them." He stroked down the arm of his shirt. "I usually get super cheap pj's, but these are really nice."

"Only the best, babe. Or, you know, the stuff you get at the slightly higher-quality discount store."

I felt a little strange, standing there in my usual suit, while they were clearly ready for bed. "I hope I didn't disturb you. I know it's late."

"We're old, but we're not *that* old." Keith tugged my hand so I'd follow him to the sofa.

"Twenty-one *is* ancient," I agreed.

"What's up? Not that something has to be up for you to spontaneously visit us, but I bet something is."

To my surprise, Josh took a seat on my other side, sandwiching me between them. We were not all equally distributed. Keith had sat himself somewhat on the line between "his" cushion and "mine," leaving him and me quite close together, especially owing to the fact that he still held my hand.

He still held my hand.

"Ed told me that he heard a rumor that you two have been seeing a lot of movies and spending time with me lately."

"Hell yes we have." Keith grinned. "What, you didn't notice?"

"I wasn't sure what you wanted me to say. Or if—if I should pretend I wasn't aware what he meant. Or perhaps I should have deflected the topic."

He frowned. "What do you mean?"

"Just that . . ." Actually, I didn't know. And nothing I could think of to say really made sense.

Josh shifted, drawing my attention, and his expression was serious. "Is this about our privacy or yours, Cam?"

"I don't really know. I thought it was about yours. But maybe it isn't. I don't think I've ever been the subject of a rumor before, and although Ed meant nothing by it, I can't say I'm that comfortable with the idea." I searched Josh's face for judgment or censure and found none. "I'm sorry. Am I making a big deal out of something that isn't?"

"That depends. Do you want the fact that you spend time with us to be a secret?"

"No. No, not in the least."

"Then what part makes you uncomfortable?"

Keith played a little beat on my palm with his fingertips and it made me want to arch into him; I was hungry for more touch, more sensation.

More Keith, more Josh.

I swallowed. "Forgive me. I'm so sorry. He asked if we were 'just friends' and the baldness of that phrase sent me to strange places in my head."

"It's a stupid phrase, anyway," Keith said. "I have friends, but you're something else entirely, Cam, you know?"

"I suppose I overreacted."

This time Josh moved forward, sliding over to sit on the coffee table, his knees brushing mine. "It's okay. We don't think of you as 'just' anything."

"If you view it objectively, it's more complicated. I only mean that it isn't true that we're having a deep, romantic love affair, which is I think the impression I may have given Ed by the way I reacted to 'just friends.' So if I did, I'm sorry."

Josh's eyes shifted to Keith's, then back. "We haven't broached anything to change our arrangement with you because it's been working, but we're open to expanding things between us."

"Uh, yeah." Keith smoothed a thumb over my palm. "Josh means you can touch me more."

"I—" *Yes.* I remembered Keith's pale skin stretched out under my fingers. My heart beat faster.

"I have some thoughts," Josh said. "Thoughts I think both of you would be into. But no pressure, Cam. And Ed's your friend; you can tell him everything, or nothing, or whatever you want."

Keith's hand squeezed mine. "We totally trust you, or we wouldn't have asked you in the first place. But if you're worried about us, don't be. We knew when we started this that there might be stories, or rumors, or whatever. We can't be worried about that stuff, Cam. If you'd rather only meet us here for your own sake, that's fine, too."

"No, it's not that. It's more that I suppose I wouldn't want anyone to think I was trying to come between you, or that I . . . was making a nuisance of myself."

"No one's going to think those things," Keith said. "For real."

"And if they do, fuck 'em," Josh added. "That's our motto."

"It really is."

"I think you're both very brave." I was humbled by them. They took chances with each other, and unlike me, they didn't feel any need to put up a calm, unthreatening facade for anyone.

"Nah. Plus, why would we want to hide you, Cam? Look at how sexy you are." Keith flattened his other hand all the way down my tie.

I went very still. Except for my pounding heart, and the other location in my anatomy that was registering an increase in blood pressure.

"Damn. We should make Cam uncomfortable more often." Josh waved a hand. "Anyway, do you want to stay for a movie? Or a TV show?"

"Josh just rediscovered the magic of the DVD player," Keith explained.

I wanted to stay. I wanted them to touch me more, even casually, because their casual touches held more gravity than any intimate caress I'd ever felt.

They were waiting for me to answer. "Maybe for a little while."

Keith grinned. "Sweeeeet. You guys choose. I'll make popcorn."

We ended up with a television show called *Project Runway*, which I had no real interest in or understanding of outside the fact that the show's "mentor" was a man called Tim Gunn, whom Keith said I reminded them of.

By the end of three episodes I had a definite man-crush on Mr. Gunn, who carried himself with such precision and such grace that I wanted to watch him walk and talk forever. It was very late by then, but Josh insisted I take the rest of the season one DVDs home with me.

Each of them kissed me good-bye. I felt warm all the way home.

CHAPTER 15

Unknown number: *You up to surprise Keith tonight? He's a little messed up in the head over Thanksgiving.*

Cameron: *Of course.*

Cameron: *Assuming this is Josh. Not so much if it's someone else.*

Unknown number: *Ha-ha, yeah, that'd be creepy as fuck. No, it's me.*

Josh: *You aren't busy?*

Cameron: *I'm redundant at the theater on Sundays. Tell me when to be there, and I will.*

Josh: *Timing's gonna be a thing. I'm aiming for nine, but I don't want you to come up until I text you. Is that cool?*

Josh: *You're my surprise. :-)*

Cameron: *I will plan to be there around nine. And I'll wait for your text.*

Josh: *Solid. This is going to be a little intense, but I think you'll enjoy it. And if you aren't into it, you can let me know.*

Josh: *Cam.*

Josh: *Confirm that if you're not into it, you'll let me know.*

Cameron: *Yes, I will. Though I'm not too worried.*

Josh: *You don't even know. I can't wait. This will be a good reward for putting up with Mr. Grumpy Accountant Guy today.*

Cameron: *. . . Are you talking about Keith?*

Josh: *Don't leave him unsupervised with your books is all I'm saying. I have to because he's my business partner, but man, dude's like the Inquisition.*

Josh: *"Do you have this receipt? WELL, DO YOU?"*

Josh: *He's calling. Probably I used the wrong color highlighter for something. See you later.*

Josh: *Get excited.*

Cameron: *See you later.*

Cameron: *:-o (That's "excited," right?)*

Josh: *Hahaha, yep. Sweet.*

I didn't know what to expect. I sat in the Volvo, trying to meditate on the rain.

Half of the experts were saying we were in for a doozy of a wet season; the other half, predictably, were saying it would be dry and the drought would only get worse. Raindrops. Water. The streetlight exploding into a dozen shards of white and yellow across my windshield with each new wave of rain.

Quarter after the hour.

Maybe Josh had forgotten he'd invited me over? But no. No. It had only been a few hours, and it wasn't the kind of thing Josh would forget. I couldn't imagine what Josh would forget, really, but I knew it wasn't this. It wasn't me.

He wouldn't forget a surprise for Keith.

I was starting to contemplate turning the car back on to run the heater when my phone finally chimed a text message.

Josh: *Sorry. He's a beast. But everything's taken care of.*

Josh: *Are you here? Come up. But be relatively quiet.*

Josh: *He won't hear you, probably, but still.*

Josh: *Text up when you get to the door and I'll buzz you in.*

Cameron: *On my way.*

What did *he won't hear you* mean? Only one way to find out.

He let me in, taking some care with the door, and I hung my coat on the hooks behind it, not sure if I should speak.

"I covered his ears with noise-canceling headphones playing white noise." He wasn't whispering, but his voice was lower than usual. "We're probably fine to talk, but this scene pretty much hinges on him giving up all control."

I blinked, not sure at all what that meant.

Josh smiled, took my arm, and led me to the door of their bedroom.

My stomach dropped to my knees. My balls tightened. My cock— I shouldn't think about my cock.

Keith was entirely naked, lying in the center of their bed, arms and legs spread widely out to the sides and tied there. A black band covered his eyes. The headphones dwarfed his head, looking more like earmuffs. And the rest of him . . . I shouldn't think about his cock, either.

Josh pulled me away again, to the kitchen, where I stared down at the countertop, the afterimage of Keith's body burned into my mind.

"We have to leave him there for another few minutes, until he feels like it's never going to end. He fought me every fucking step tonight, so he's got a lot of shit to work through before we can start this scene." He set a glass of water in front of me. "Too much?"

"Oh, no. No. Unexpected, but . . . not too much." I forced myself to meet his eyes. "He is so beautiful. I'm sure he'd hate it if I told him that."

"Yeah. I do anyway, but he doesn't like it. He feels like it's feminizing, and I get that, but there's nothing about beauty that is innately female, you know?" He shrugged. "I can call a sunset beautiful because it takes my breath away, and that's not implying it's girly. But if I call him beautiful because he takes my breath away, he gets offended."

"You still do it?"

"Oh hell yeah. Because he knows it's stupid. So you can actually see him lecture himself on how beautiful isn't feminine, and how feminine isn't bad, and how just because I see him as one doesn't mean I see him as the other, but even if I did, that wouldn't be a slight— basically, it's a whole one-hour drama, played out on Keith's face."

I glanced back at the bedroom. I could see a corner of the bed and a side table, but not Keith. "He is breathtaking. That's how I feel looking at him. I hope that's all right."

"Cam, hey." This time Josh's firm hand grazed my jaw, turning my head toward his. "This isn't a thing where we need you to think of us exactly the same way. You'll have different relationships with both of us because we're different people. Man, I guess we should have gone over all this, but listen, you feel whatever you feel for Keith. I don't even think I'm capable of jealousy, and if I were, it wouldn't be for a guy who looks at him as sweetly as you do. I could never want him to have less of that, you know what I mean?"

I had almost a decade on Josh, but he managed to make me feel young and safe. "Thank you."

"You're so welcome. I'm glad you could come tonight." The hand disappeared and he picked up my glass of water, offering it to me again. "We're going over to Keith's folks' place for Thanksgiving. Or his dad and stepmom's, but his mom and stepdad will also be there. It's going to be a clusterfuck, but we always do Thanksgiving with his family and Christmas with mine."

"Why will it be a clusterfuck?" The word tripped off my tongue. I didn't know when I'd ever have an excuse to use it again, but I liked it.

"His dad is a macho douche bag, who's probably the reason he hates being called 'beautiful.' His mom's super micromanaging. His stepdad is the kind of guy who chuckles at things that aren't funny and doesn't have any read for when to let the joke go. His stepmom's actually totally cool. Last year she took us aside and told us if we were slipping out the back door to go to Taco Bell and we left her there, she'd never forgive us. But he's been dreading it since the plans were made and it's still four days away, so I had to do something." He checked his watch. "Every minute feels like about three minutes to me. To him, every minute probably feels like ten. Especially when he's all messed up in his head like this."

"Messed up in what sense?"

Josh leaned against the counter. "It's a mental game. He knows I'd never restrain him and leave him. Never. But he was a dick all day, which means right now he's feeling guilty and ashamed and a little like I'm punishing him, even though I'm not. We don't do that kind of thing."

"So what are you doing?"

"Taking away his control, his agency. Because every instinct he has is telling him the only way he'll survive this week is if he controls everything, if he grasps for every scrap of decision and bites off all ambiguity. And Keith's not built for acting like a jerk; he feels so bad, so fast. He doesn't even enjoy it."

I nodded. "So giving that up to you helps."

"Giving it up? Ha. I had to fight him so hard tonight, man."
Another glance at his watch. "But it'll be worth it when he realizes
you're here. And I guess it helps, as a sort of one-to-one ratio of needing
control and handing it over. But it's more, I don't know, personal than
that. When we got together, he never let himself act out, for anything.
He never bit my head off, he never snapped at anyone. He held it all
inside. So now he lets it out more, and this is another way of doing
that. Of choosing to externalize anxiety differently than spending
eight hours poring over the books and griping at me for misfiling
things."

"Even if the choices are all yours, not his?"

"Hell, Cam, all the choices are Keith's. Always. Yeah, it looks like
I'm doing *to* him, but I'm just his instrument. And anyway, that's not
what we're doing tonight. Tonight's all about sensation and surprise."

"So no paddles?"

"Fuck that. Paddles, whips, clothespins, ice cubes, whatever we
want. But it's not about endurance." He paused. "When it's about
enduring, he goes to a place in his head that digs in and locks down.
He knows he can get through it. Maybe it's really hard, but he knows
all he has to do is wait it out. Tonight's a whole different game, so
we'll get to him a different way. And it's time. Christ. That was exactly
twenty minutes and it felt like a fucking *hour*. He must be losing his
mind."

"What are we doing?" I felt suddenly nervous. First-date nervous,
as if I might trip over my feet or spill my coffee.

"Sensation." He wiggled his fingers at me. "We might not need
anything else at all. Come on. It's a really awful feeling, not knowing
when someone's coming back for you."

"Then why make him feel that?"

"Because tonight he needed it. He needed to find a way to
surrender to it before we even started, and it had to come from him,
not me. Come on."

I followed him back to the bedroom, where Keith twitched a
little, though it wasn't cold. Josh turned to me, made a gesture I didn't
understand. After a moment I offered my hands and he smiled, rolling
up one of my cuffs, then the other.

It was a shockingly intimate thing, Josh's fingers brushing over the sensitive skin of my forearms, the insides of my elbows.

He'd said we could speak, but I found myself only mouthing *Thank you*. He nodded and motioned me over to the opposite side of the bed.

I didn't think we'd made any sounds, but perhaps Keith could feel us moving around. He tugged against the restraints, first each hand, then each foot.

Chest rising and falling, licking his lips—Keith looked more frightened than I was prepared to see, and neither Josh nor I moved until he whispered, "Josh?"

Josh pressed two fingers to Keith's lips, and he subsided back into a more relaxed position.

"Sorry. Knew it was you, but started to freak out anyway."

Josh's fingers traced his upper lip, then his lower lip.

"I love you too," Keith murmured.

The moment felt far too private to witness, so I stood there, frozen, hoping no one noticed me.

Josh slid his fingers into Keith's mouth and Keith sucked them.

Arousal twisted into my guts, spiraling down to my cock, my balls, tying me into a knot of need and desire. No matter how I tried to tell myself to back off, I couldn't. Josh's fingers, dark and brown against the pink of Keith's lips, didn't stay in one place; he plunged them in and pulled them out, a clear parody of sex, but there was nothing tawdry about it, nothing even dominant. Keith sucked harder, lifting his head until Josh pressed him back down again.

This time the play was more bald: Josh, holding him down, fucking his mouth with two fingers. Keith, sucking hungrily, almost whimpering.

"Good boy," Josh said softly, though Keith couldn't hear him. The hand holding Keith's head down caressed him, fingers sliding into his hair. "So good." He glanced up at me. "Your turn. Do something very light."

"I should—" *Touch him?* But yes, obviously.

"It's gonna startle the hell out of him. We've never done this before, so I might pull off his headphones to tell him it's you, but I'd rather not, if I can keep him safe without doing that."

Safety, yes. I leaned over, staring down into Keith's blindfolded face. He'd be able to feel both of Josh's hands; he'd know immediately that something was off when he felt mine.

I knew what to do. What I'd want if I were in his place, full of question marks. I cupped his cheek lightly with my palm, letting my fingertips rest just in front of his ear.

He thrashed and I stepped back. Josh muttered "damn it" and reconfigured, framing Keith's face with his hands and kissing him deeply.

Keith calmed immediately, breathing fast. "I'm okay. I'm okay. Sorry. That's gotta be Cam. I can't believe you fucking—"

Josh kissed him again.

"Yeah. Yeah, sorry."

"We tried with a gag once," Josh said, still keeping his voice low. "But I couldn't take it. I needed him able to talk." He offered a rueful smile. "He trusts me so much. I take a lot of strength from that. But I still worry."

"I'm sure that makes you a good fit for this."

"Yeah." His thumbs brushed over Keith's lips, then traced the bottom line of the blindfold. "Come over here, Cam."

I moved in again, heart having settled down a bit since Keith's short-lived attempt to escape.

"Will you kiss him? I think it would make him feel better to know for sure it's you."

I didn't know what to say. Except: "Yes, of course." I leaned low, touching his cheek, kissing him—lightly, chastely, briefly—on the lips.

Keith sighed. "Hey, Cam."

Since that seemed to want a response, I kissed him again, and stood back up.

"Good," Josh said. "Now we get to play. But look at him. You saw all the tension when we walked in, right? The way his muscles were so rigid he was practically shaking?" Josh dragged one finger down the palest, softest part of Keith's arm, making him tug against the buckles holding him down. "Now he wants this more than he wanted to fight it."

I mirrored what he did on the other arm, and I could hardly keep my voice even enough to speak when Keith's body responded.

I'd managed not to look too closely, but now his arousal was obvious. "I thought fighting was part of the point. Or why do you need these?" I indicated the restraints.

"No, those are for Keith. And it's different for everyone. Some people have to fight all the way through. If he was gonna tie me down, I'd be that guy, the one who'd basically have to be beaten into shape. But he and I don't take our clothes off until he's way past that kind of fighting." He bent over and breathed across Keith's cock, which bobbed in response.

"Ahhh." Josh did it again and Keith's hands fisted.

"Poor Keith." I certainly wasn't going to mimic *that*, so instead I traced a line over Keith's clavicle, then followed his sternum down to the center of his body.

"Good. That's perfect, Cam. That's exactly what he needs."

Feeling especially daring, I circled a nipple, then the other, then abandoned both of them to return to his arm. This time I gave him a rough, slightly awkward hand massage, and it only belatedly occurred to me that I was projecting my attention on his hand to prevent it going elsewhere.

Josh took up the same thing on the other side and again, Keith sighed, relaxing into the bed.

"Let's do his feet next," Josh said.

I agreed.

We didn't use ice cubes, or whips, or anything else. We used our hands, mostly, though I hadn't been aware how many different sensations you could make with only your hands, but Josh's creativity was boundless. He'd use his knuckles on Keith's toes, or his nipples, or his lips. He'd pinch and twist with abandon, until Keith's thighs and belly were marked in red. He slapped and smacked, the sounds making me jump even when I expected them.

I tried to follow along, to experiment, to be brave, like they were. It wasn't easy to admit to myself that slapping Keith's bound thighs turned me on, or that I liked the way his cock dripped as I did it. I found I could try new things, despite how closely Josh watched me. Or perhaps *because* Josh watched closely. My first attempts at slapping Keith's taut belly were embarrassing. Josh showed me how to commit to it without my hand bouncing back, how to control each strike so it landed where I wanted, with the impact I wanted it to have.

We tickled here and there, infrequently; Josh might hold Keith's foot back so it was bared to him, then lightly play his fingertips across it until Keith writhed and begged him to stop. I realized I could elicit begging from any sensation over his ribs, and I found myself wanting to keep doing it, using my fingernails, my knuckles. Josh, grinning, went to his side of Keith's body and used the stubble on his chin, brushing it over Keith's ribs, only stopping when his painful forced laughter became howls.

I almost didn't repeat the trick. I didn't have the thick, coarse stubble Josh sported at the end of the day. The most I could do was a little bit of fuzz. Still, I balanced myself and bent over, kneeling at his side, and brushed my cheek over his torso.

His cock was right there. Still drooling a little pool onto his belly. When he thrashed again, because even my fuzz was enough to make him arch off the bed, his erection bobbed.

I wanted it in my hand, in my mouth. I wanted Keith's pleasure, after everything we'd put him through.

My cheeks were scalding when I straightened up again, and I couldn't look over at Josh, whose eyes I could feel on me.

"I am completely and totally sure that anything you'd do, he'd want. But we're not going to do it until we talk about it first. Sorry, Cam. Sometimes it feels like all we do is tease you."

"You don't. And I agree. I only . . . got distracted, for a moment."

"I can offer you more distraction. He's desperate for you to watch, you know. Hey."

I took a deep breath and looked up.

"Want to watch me torture an orgasm out of him? It's pretty hot."

"He's okay with that?"

"Oh my god, Cam. It's like the number one fantasy of his since we met you. That's . . . probably not something I needed to share. Damn. Forget I said that. But yeah, explicitly." He raised his eyebrows. "What do you think?"

"Yes. God, yes."

"You can keep doing whatever you want. If you want."

I didn't. I stood beside their bed with my mouth hanging half-open, breathing heavily, while Josh expertly deployed first fingernails (scratching along the bright pink crown of Keith's cock), then more pinching, more twisting, more—yes—torture, squeezing his balls until they were shiny, then flicking them. Making Keith cry out and grunt and hiss and beg.

When Josh finally sucked Keith inside, I sighed in relief. He still controlled it, pinning Keith's hips down, not allowing him enough movement to dictate speed or rhythm or anything else. He gagged, and Keith cried out again, arms pulling hard at the buckles around his wrists. Josh forced himself down and gagged again, and Keith came, one long moan punctuated by gasps.

Josh looked as smug as I'd ever seen him when he pulled up, resting his face against Keith's belly. "Yeah. That was good. You can hit the buckles if you want, Cam. I'm gonna take a breather for a minute here."

The buckles. Right. I could let him loose. For some reason my mind resisted the idea. I'd never lost sight that it was Keith I touched, Keith's breathy sounds I sought with my fingers, but letting him up, actually speaking to him now, seemed harder than it should have been.

Part of me wanted to beg off, walk out, not be available to Keith for whatever he needed now that he'd given up so much. I knew it was wrong, but for a second I thought about leaving as if that were more real than staying.

Of course, I didn't. And I'm not sure Josh would have let me go easily, even if I'd dared bring it up.

I made my fingers work the restraints, first a wrist, then both ankles, then the other wrist. When he remained still, I lifted the headphones off. One more thing after that.

Keith raised his head so I could loosen the blindfold. Then his dark-blue eyes were blinking into mine, a little watery, and he pulled me down for a kiss.

This one was less chaste, but certainly not intrusive.

"Hi, Cam." His voice was a little hoarse. "You okay?"

I swallowed, feeling far more exposed than he looked, naked and spent with his boyfriend still lying on him, watching both of us. "Yes. I didn't expect— I wasn't sure what to expect, but that wasn't it."

"But you're okay?"

"Aftercare," Josh said. "Keith's checking in with you, Cam."

He'd explained aftercare as a concept that I thought only applied to Keith. For a moment I was unable to fully put my feelings into words, but Keith's clear gaze made me brave.

"I'm okay. You were amazing." I glanced at Josh. "You were amazing too. I admire you both."

"Ha. You're terrible." Before I could react, Keith was pulling me toward him, and Josh was hauling himself up, and then all three of us were somehow lying in the bed, Keith's arms connecting us. "That was really good for me. Thanks, guys. Even though it was a totally underhanded thing, surprising me like that."

"Underhanded my ass. You knew something was up all night."

"I did! I so did. And you were such a tool about it, pretending I was making it all up."

They seemed perfectly comfortable with the arrangement, but I felt like I might disrupt something if I took too deep a breath, so I tried not to move. Which lasted for the twenty seconds it took before they caught on.

"Cam's wigging again," Keith said.

"I know. It's all right. Give him a few minutes."

"I'm not *wigging*," I protested. "I'm . . . not used to lying in bed like this. With two other men. While I have all my clothes on."

Keith gasped dramatically. "I think Cam's saying he's totally naked with multiple guys all the time."

Josh laughed.

Since pretending to be invisible was clearly not going to work, I sat up instead, facing them. I touched Keith's arm. "Are you cold?"

"A little."

I reached down and wrestled a blanket out of the pile of linens beside the head of the bed, then draped it as gently as I could over him. "I never knew any of this existed. Or I knew, but not as a real thing, as a thing that could be relevant to me."

"So it wasn't too much for you?" Keith stroked my hand.

"It really wasn't. You can both stop asking me that now."

"We can't."

"Why not?"

"Because you haven't seen it when we really get extreme. You've only seen little bits of it."

As much as I wanted to say *Then show me*, I also knew I owed them more than flippancy, or my greed to understand. I nodded. "When you want to show me more, you can. Tonight wasn't too much, and if something is, I'll tell you."

"You didn't lose color?"

"With you spread out naked and Josh showing me what to do? How could I?"

Keith blushed. "My brain wanted to scare me about that, that you wouldn't like me anymore."

"I— You were stunning. I could never not like you anymore."

"Yeah. I mean, I knew that, but you know. It's not always that easy."

"I know." My gaze slid past the alarm clock on the other (Josh's?) side of the bed. "Ohh, is that time right? Is it really almost one?"

"Damn." Josh stretched. "We gotta be up soon, babe."

"Someday we're taking the day off."

"Today was our day off."

"Okay, someday we're taking two. Like in a row."

"Keep dreamin'." Josh kissed Keith. "I'm gonna take a shower before bed."

"If I'm passed out before you get back, good night."

"Night." When he leaned over Keith toward me, I suppose I knew this would not be a dry kiss on the cheek. But I wasn't quite ready for how warm and right Josh's lips felt, or how much I wanted to kiss him more. "I'm really glad you came over, Cam."

"Me too," I said.

"If you gotta go, you can. Just make sure you lock the knob. I'll get the dead bolt after I'm out."

"Okay."

Another kiss, quicker and over faster. "You're kind of a natural. By the way."

With that cryptic remark, he left the room.

Keith sighed. "God. Tonight was amazing. We should do it again sometime. When I can see."

"I'm not sure I could have if you weren't blindfolded," I admitted. "That made it easier for me. I felt sort of ridiculous."

"Yeah, that should go away the more you practice. And you really should practice. On me. All the time." He smiled, cheeky and sleepy at once. "Thanks, Cam."

"Thanks for trusting me."

"Oh, I do, but mostly I trust Josh. And Josh trusts you, which is like . . . you know, pretty much the best endorsement ever."

"I agree. I really should head home. Good night, Keith."

"Good night."

I stood, straightened my clothes, rolled my shirtsleeves back down. Keith watched from under drooping eyes. I almost didn't kiss him again, but it seemed like I should. "Good night," I whispered, repeating myself as I brushed my lips against his.

"I really like you," he replied, eyes falling shut.

I let myself out and locked the door behind me.

CHAPTER 16

T he Rhein stays open for Thanksgiving. Our normal menu includes turkey sandwiches; for Thanksgiving we also offer a side of cranberry sauce and a side of stuffing (though technically it's dressing, since it's not actually stuffed in anything—an argument correctly belonging to my parents, which my brain nonetheless brings up every year when I'm rewriting the specials board).

Since all of my Thanksgivings have been spent at the theater, I don't miss big family dinners, or whatever other people consider "normal" holiday fare. I've always liked how when I say "Happy Thanksgiving," most guests smile and return the sentiment, and I usually remember to pick up a few rolls of turkey stickers to give out to kids. Handing out stickers was one of my early favorite jobs; I stood next to my dad, who took tickets at the door, and ripped off one sticker for each child who walked in. I liked it because it was giving, not taking.

We ran normal hours, but I closed concessions the second the last film began (we usually stayed open through at least half of it), and let almost everyone go home. My two ushers insisted on staying until the end so I wouldn't have to sweep out the theater alone, but the three of us had the lobby pristine by the time the movie let out.

Most people seemed to understand that it was time for them to leave, though one young man lingered, asking me questions about the film festival while his fellow guests slowly emptied out of my lobby (and the ushers glanced longingly at their watches).

Since "Why don't you come by on Saturday and we can talk more" didn't do the trick, I was beginning to rehearse saying something more direct, like "You don't have to go home, but you can't stay here."

Thankfully, before I needed to resort to that, Ed and Alisha barged into the lobby loaded down with bags, and the young man dodged out.

"*Who* was *that*?" Alisha asked, surveying him from behind.

"No idea." I waved to the ushers and started hitting lights. "If you two are staying, we're going upstairs."

"Seriously, who was that? He totally looked familiar." Ed frowned at Alisha. "Didn't he look familiar?"

"He looked like every other white boy, how could I tell? Anyway, Happy Thanksgiving, Cam!" Alisha gave me a one-armed hug.

"Happy Thanksgiving to you, too."

I shooed the two of them to the alarm alcove and said good night to my loyal ushers, who were happy to escape. I did the locking, alarming, unlocking, relocking routine and was a little relieved to see my pesky guest hadn't decided he had one more question.

They followed me up to the apartment and spread out quite a feast on my coffee table. Alisha sat on the floor while Ed and I took the couch.

I hadn't realized I was hungry until I smelled food. "Where did all this come from?"

"Alisha's folks. This is only a fraction of the leftovers. They actually wanted us to take more."

"Thanks for thinking of me." I piled my plate high. "I think I may have forgotten to eat earlier. I usually catch a sandwich between movies, but I was doing something on the computer and lost track of time."

"Sure."

I glanced at Ed and raised my eyebrows, figuring I didn't have to come out and ask about his family.

He shook his head. "I didn't see them. I called earlier, so at least I got to talk to Abuela, but that's it. Dad's still sticking to his guns."

"He's a damn fool," Alisha muttered. "Anyway, my family really likes you." Dramatic pause. "Because you're a boy."

"I know! And like, I want to be so offended by that, except it makes me happy. Sorry I'm totally ruining your lesbian cred, Alish."

"Right? You so are. Brute!"

They grinned at each other.

Ed had Alisha, which was good, and Keith (for whom this had been, as far as I could tell from sporadic text messages, a horrible day) had Josh. I, in some sense, had all of them. And in another, none.

I did, however, have delicious food. "Ed, were you able to eat anything? Nothing here looks vegan."

"I'm not vegan on national holidays," Ed said breezily. "Like Christmas and Thanksgiving. And the Fourth of July."

Alisha laughed. "What's not vegan about the Fourth of July?"

"You can't have a veggie burger on the Fourth. It's unpatriotic. Though summer holidays are easier because there's usually a few different salads." He picked at the roasted carrots lumped in with the turkey. "I really shouldn't. Every time I eat this stuff I feel more sick than I did the last time."

Alisha mock-swooned, falling backward. "You're going to force me to be a vegan. Vegan for love! It's like a religious conversion!"

They stayed another hour, and despite the fact that I generally dislike drop-ins, even from friends, I was glad they'd stopped by. No pressure to mourn my family, no drama. A lot of laughter. I heard updates about the usual things. Alisha had started assistant-teaching at my elementary school and had some fun stories. ("I'm Catholic *enough*," she explained when I asked. "I mean, I remember some of that stuff, and I make the rest up, just like the Church.") Ed skirted the issue of the Club Fred's killer, only saying that his last conversation with the detective in charge of Philpott's case hadn't gone particularly well. He also said that Fredi's business was down.

"Do you think it'll come back?" I asked.

"Maybe if they catch the guy."

Alisha shook her head. "I don't know. At some point they'll catch the guy, but I'm not sure Club Fred's will ever be the way it was before. It used to feel like the safest place in La Vista, you know? Kind of grungy, completely dated, but you didn't care because it was home. It doesn't feel like that anymore."

"I can't imagine this town without Club Fred's," Ed murmured.

I had to agree. Once a week, I went there and read my book at the bar. Maybe it wasn't much, but it was a hundred percent of my social life outside the theater (and Josh and Keith). Alisha's point was sound, though. It didn't feel the same. And finding out who the killer was wouldn't fix that.

Especially considering the killer was almost certainly one of us.

We managed to bring the conversation back to less dire topics before they went home. They were huge fans of *Project Runway*, and spent at least ten minutes talking about their favorite contestants and their least favorite dresses. Then we packed up the food, exchanged final "Happy Thanksgivings," and said good night.

CHAPTER 17

Q YP had been closed on Thanksgiving Day (somewhat over Keith's objections, as far as I understood it, though he admitted he was mostly only trying to keep the center open so he would have a good excuse not to go to his parents' house). But they reopened with their usual hours Friday and Saturday. I'd meant to go down and bring lunch Friday, but I had one genuinely sick employee and one who I thought was "sick" in the sense that he'd had too much to eat, possibly drink, the night before, and now he couldn't face work.

I texted, but our exchanges went something like this:

Cameron: *How are you?*

Keith: *Fine. You?*

I'd tried little text faces, but either I hadn't been using them right or Keith hadn't felt like playing. He sent me a smile and said he had to go.

It was some relief to see them approach the ticket booth on Saturday night. It was even better, twenty minutes later, to get a text from Josh, asking me back to their place after *Only Angels Have Wings*. I said yes, quickly, and spent the next two and a half hours somewhat desperate for the lobby to clear out so I could see them for real.

I headed over after closing. They'd left with a covert "See you soon" that made me feel oddly elated, and now that I stood in the entryway of their building, waiting to be buzzed up, the buoyant excitement started to turn on me. What if they wanted to see me to tell me it was over? Or what if something awful had happened on Thursday, something they didn't want to discuss at my apartment?

But no, that didn't make sense.

And if they were calling it off, they wouldn't have picked a Saturday night to do it. Daytime, over lunch. Unthreatening, public place, well lit, casual atmosphere. No mistaking that kind of meeting for anything else.

In the time it took me to climb three flights of stairs, I'd managed to gray-out all intense colors. I hadn't completely lost color, only the bright ones.

Keith answered the door, pulled me inside, and buried his face against my neck. I belatedly put my arms around him and looked at Josh.

"Rough couple of days," he said.

I nodded.

Keith's breaths were hot and damp against my skin, but he didn't speak. I didn't move. Josh, though, walked over and kissed me hello, making my heart stutter for a moment.

"That okay?"

Except for the part where my body forgets how to work. "Yes." Because what else could I possibly say? *You kissing me brings color back to the world.*

"Good." He wound his hand into Keith's hair, right at the back of the neck, and tugged lightly. "Keith wants to blow you. Is *that* okay?"

I couldn't believe I'd heard what I thought I'd heard. When I just stared at him, Josh smiled.

"Don't you want to feel his mouth?"

The boldness of it: *his mouth.* Conjuring images of Keith's pink lips wrapped around Josh's fingers, heightening the heat of his breath on my neck. Lips, tongue, oh god.

Josh's other hand tapped my cheek. "I'm pretty sure you're into it, but you have to tell us, Cam. I'm not gonna risk being wrong."

Keith's face against my neck, Josh's hand on my cheek; they must have been able to feel the sudden flush of my body responding to the idea.

"Yes," I whispered, fearing that if I tried to say more my voice would break.

"Sweet. This is going to be so fucking hot. But not yet." He stepped back. "Babe, tell Cam about Thanksgiving."

Keith thumped his head onto my shoulder before straightening. A blush painted his skin. He was excited too.

"First, I hate all holidays and I think they should be totally abolished. Right?" He grabbed my hand, as usual, and pulled me to the sofa. "Fuck the holidays!"

"I do good business at the holidays," I said mildly, as Keith and I sat, blushing, beside one another, pointedly not discussing the subject Josh had already covered and closed.

"Fine. You can have the holidays, but I'm boycotting. Josh? I'm boycotting the holidays!"

"You can't boycott Christmas. Mom would come over here and drag you out kicking and screaming."

Keith's expression softened. "Okay, fine. I'm boycotting all the holidays that I can't spend with your mom and dad."

"And don't forget Gran and Papa and Aunt Rose Marie. And the kids."

"Okay, the whole family. Just not my family."

I shifted my leg against him, not quite daring to reach out. "Do you know Ed Masiello? His dad basically decreed that he wasn't allowed to go back to the house. He'd probably be up for doing Thanksgiving as a group next year. You guys could come down to the Rhein. We have turkey sandwiches with cranberry sauce on the side."

"Aw, see, now I feel shitty, because that's awful, but I'm kind of jealous. My dad enforces that I come to Thanksgiving exclusively so he can disapprove of me in person." He leaned his head back over the top of the sofa to look at Josh, who was pouring something from the stove into mugs. "You gonna tell me that's not what he's doing?"

"Nope. For one, because it wouldn't make a difference, and for two, because I don't think that's right, exactly, but I also don't think your dad is trying to promote happiness and family harmony with his Thanksgiving thing."

"See? When even Josh says he's being a dick, he's clearly being a dick." Josh turned to give Keith a look, and Keith stuck his tongue out, still upside down.

"I'm about to give you something to do with that tongue, boy."

"Yeah, hot." Keith sort of slithered back into the actual seat of the sofa. "It was fine. I have to stop moping about it. Obviously there are way worse things in life than parental disapproval. I guess I just wish we could give up on this whole bullshit thing where we all eat dinner and pretend to like each other once a year when in fact my parents got divorced because there are like three topics on earth they can discuss without fighting, and Ronnie's got half a brain, and Marianne is way too nice for Dad, like I don't even know what she's doing with him, it's ridiculous."

"Maybe he's different when we aren't there," Josh suggested, bringing each of us a mug. "Hot cocoa, with almond milk."

"Really? Almond milk?" I sipped. "Thank you. I mean, assuming you don't always make hot cocoa with almond milk."

"Bought it all for you." He returned to the kitchen for his own mug and sat down on Keith's other side, propping his feet on the table. "This is pretty good."

"So good." Keith slid down even farther, so Josh could put an arm around him. "Mmm."

"You gonna tell Cam what we're doing tonight?"

"You really think I need to?"

"Uh-huh."

"So yeah, okay." Keith sipped his cocoa, looking at me over the rim.

I looked back.

"I like a certain kind of thing when I'm all whiny and annoying."

Josh's arm tightened. "You're not whiny and annoying, Keith."

"I'm whiny and annoying to myself, anyway. But, like, the best way to stop doing this is for Josh to really kind of go at me, which he hasn't done so much when you're here. But you know, it's all good. We're not doing anything we haven't done before."

"With obvious exceptions," Josh said. "I'll talk differently, and I won't explain things as much. But you can still ask questions, and if we're at an okay spot to pause, I'll answer them."

I nodded to both of them. "All right. I think I understand a little. Or maybe not, but I think I can go along with it."

"And same rules apply as always." Keith gestured, long fingers counting off. "You're a part of the scene, so if you want it to stop, say 'red.' If something makes you uncomfortable, say 'yellow.' If you're totally turned on, feel free to jack off—" He giggled. "Okay, I made that last one up."

"So not whiny or annoying." Josh kissed the top of Keith's head. "He's right, you can stop the scene at any time, but it might make you uncomfortable even if you don't want to stop it. If it does, that's okay, Cam. Got it?"

"I think so."

"Good. Now we relax and enjoy ourselves for a little bit."

"Fucking sadist," Keith muttered.

"Oh yeah. You know that's right."

Ah. We were making Keith wait. I now understood the purpose of the hot cocoa, and made certain I didn't finish mine too quickly.

I had needed the warning. Even if I hadn't realized it.

It wasn't the physical. I'd seen Josh use the whip, the flogger, and the paddle. This was more, and harder, and deeper on some level, but I could have handled it.

It was the verbal. I had never imagined Josh could talk like he was talking now, and if I hadn't seen everything that led up to it, if I didn't know how much they both invested in each other, in their relationship, I would have been desperately uncomfortable.

As it was—I certainly didn't feel comfortable.

"You're so fucking weak." Josh brought down the paddle again. "All day long, so weak, like a little fucking baby, like you can't even keep your shit together for long enough to eat dinner. It's pathetic."

Keith reached back, writhing, trying to cover his skin, but Josh pinned his hands and kept going, spitting all sorts of vile words down on him.

I'd retreated until I was standing against the wall with my hands clasped in front of my horrible erection. No matter how disturbing I found it, I couldn't help but be turned on by the sight of Josh's body covering Keith's, forcibly restraining him, hurting him despite his pleas to stop.

It was so terrible, and so arousing, and so damn confusing. And Keith was crying, but I didn't miss the way his fingers gripped Josh's, or the way Josh almost caressed him with the paddle, even as he called him a cocksucker and told him he was filthy and worthless.

How this could be healthy was beyond me, but I knew them to be responsible. And more than that, I knew them to be decent, good men.

It seemed to go on forever. Josh told Keith to hold still and berated him when he failed to, when the whip nipped at his arms, at the tender flesh of his sides. I'd lost all track of safe zones, but I could see that no matter how hard it seemed to me that it hit, on the softest parts of Keith's skin it barely marked him. Those were harder in his head than they were on his body, and I was grateful for the moment of comprehension.

Josh was relentless, coming up with new ways to dig in with his words, covering the same ground with his flogger as he had the paddle and the whip. I was utterly relieved when he released Keith's hands and draped the flogger over their big trunk. He rubbed Keith's entire body, and Keith cried harder, wracking sobs, as if he were falling apart. This time Josh didn't speak.

I wished I wasn't hard, so I could cross my arms, hug myself, do something to feel more stable. As it was, I felt open and exposed.

Josh's motions ended at Keith's neck, where he lingered, fingers digging into skin, a silent massage that seemed to soothe away the last of Keith's tears. He sat back and stood, and when he beckoned me over, I almost couldn't go. I almost couldn't order my legs to move.

Except I could see that he thought I was hesitating, and I wasn't. It was just that my limbs had turned to stone, and if I walked closer, he'd certainly know how much it had turned me on to see what they'd done, and what would he think of me?

I was unable to stop my eyes from grazing over the front of Josh's trousers, and of course I wasn't the only one, of course he was as turned on, if not more. It gave me the push I needed.

Closer, focused on his face, I could see how exhausted he was, how his eyes pulled down at the corners.

"You good?" he asked, voice low and a little hoarse.

"I think so." I nodded at Keith. "You guys?"

Josh's hand smoothed down over Keith's spine. "Yeah. So there's a way I'd like to do this, but I don't want you to feel like a piece of meat between us."

I couldn't imagine complaining about being a piece of meat between them, but I waited.

"Do you mind if I touch you?"

He'd asked before, I thought, though it was hazy now. My mind had protectively fogged over everything but this moment, relegating all of it to a filmstrip overexposed beyond recognition.

In this moment I said, "I don't mind. I think I might enjoy it. Both of you. Sorry, I'm not sure how to do this, and that was—" I glanced at Keith again. "Can I ask if he's okay?"

Josh's smile—still tired, but so incredibly warm, so pleased—made me smile. "Oh, you can do anything you want to him. Right, babe?"

"Ugh."

A light slap to Keith's tenderized thigh. He yelped, but I could tell this was more for show. I knelt beside the bed and brushed the hair from his eyes. "That was so intense. How did you convince Josh to talk like that to you?"

"He kind of invented it, but yeah, once he started up, I made him keep going." He took a slow breath and exhaled. "I gotta tell you a secret, you ready?"

"Of course."

"Don't tell Josh."

I drew an *X* on my heart with my pinky finger. In my peripheral vision, Josh's smile widened.

"That shit is really hard for him, but he'll never admit it. Check in with him later, okay? Like, I can, but he doesn't want me to think it's too much for him or I won't ask him to do it. So you check in with him. Promise?"

"I promise."

Sweaty, red-eyed, disheveled, and yet Keith looked every bit as boyish and wholesome as he ever did. I couldn't reconcile it.

"Now let him get handsy. It's gonna be hot. You know he thinks you're only here because you like me, right?"

I frowned, turning my face up to Josh's.

"It's okay," he said. "You don't have to like us perfectly equally. No obligations."

"You think I like Keith more than you?"

"I think Keith turns you on more than I do, which is different."

I slowly shook my head, marveling, wondering where signals had crossed, and how determined Josh must have been to see that when it was always both of them. "You're wrong. Is that why you keep asking if it's okay if you touch me? Josh, I—" *I want you* seemed so inescapable. *I like you* so juvenile. "I like the idea of you touching me, Joshua."

"Oh god," Keith mumbled. "You should call him that all the time."

"It would lose its impact if I did it all the time." I raised my eyebrows at Josh in challenge.

Now a little of the performance fell away, and I could see more of the exhaustion, more of the caution that must have been a larger feature of those earlier encounters than I knew.

"I have to trust that you'll tell me if you don't like something, Cameron."

"I will."

"And if I get a little—a little bit—" He faltered.

"Forceful?" I suggested.

"I wouldn't even go that far. But it's okay with you if I act like I'm in charge?"

"Josh, you *are*. How could it be anyone else?"

"It gets all twisty," Keith said. "Who's in charge, who's got control. Like the guy who isn't in charge is the one with all the control, kinda, except if you think about it that way too much, it sort of ruins it, so you kind of have to pretend that you aren't— It's easier to say Josh is in charge. As long as you get that, you can end it whenever you like."

"Has it ever struck either of you that all this requires a lot more conversation than other forms of relationships?"

"Oh you have *no idea*, Cam. Seriously." Keith wiggled a little, encouraging Josh's hand to continue its languid path up and down his spine. "But the major thing is, we're about to pretend Josh is the guy calling the shots, and he's gonna make me go down on you, and that's gonna be, like, the things dreams are made of, so I'm totally excited."

Josh's hand slid down his cleft, then under. "You are excited. On your knees, babe."

Josh stood and Keith knelt. I caught my breath and adjusted my trousers again, while I was still low enough so the bed hid my movement.

"Pretty boy," Josh said. "Such a pretty mouth. How long do you think Cam's been fantasizing about this mouth? Awhile, I bet. Maybe a long time. You're gonna take him nice and deep, aren't you, angel?"

Keith leaned into Josh's palm on his cheek, eyelashes fluttering.

"You take my breath away," Josh said, almost too softly for me to hear it. Then he looked at me. "Cam. C'mere."

I stood, maintaining as much dignity as I could, heart keeping up a steadily increasing beat in my chest. Each step brought me closer to them, to the energy of them, like I was on the cusp of something so much greater than myself. Everything was in Technicolor.

"Here." Josh stepped back, drawing me against him. His hands smoothed over my body, and I sucked in my stomach. I wasn't naturally lean like Keith, or gym-lean like Josh. I perpetually carried a little bit of extra weight, hidden beneath vests and suit jackets. But Josh's hands released the buttons of my waistcoat and stole over the shirt beneath it as if he were feeling his way in the dark. Nowhere to hide from his fingers, or Keith's eyes, following them.

"You're shaking." His hands slipped along my sides, and I realized he was hugging me, holding me, his erection hard at my ass. "Here." Josh's hand took one of mine and wound it into Keith's hair. "Let Keith ground you. He's so good."

Keith pressed his face against my leg.

I took a few shuddering breaths. "It's just . . . everything is so bright right now. The lines are blurring."

"Then close your eyes."

It seemed like it was far too simple to work, but I closed my eyes and the darkness was immediately calming, lowering the visual overstimulation, intensifying the heat of Josh's arms around me, the sweet pressure of Keith's head.

"We don't want to creep you out, Cam, but we've been thinking about this for a while." Josh pulled my shirt out of my trousers, and when I was almost overcome again, he paused with both hands on my belt.

My other hand found its way to Keith, and he moaned.

"Yeah, that's good. Real good." My belt undone. The clasp of my trousers. I expected him to go directly to the zipper, but instead his fingers traced the length of me, making me tremble in his arms, making me tighten my grip in Keith's hair.

"Please," Keith murmured.

"I might keep Cam for myself and make you watch," Josh replied, still teasing me through my trousers, and I could feel little jolts as he pushed against me from behind.

I would do anything with them. Anything at all. In the spirit of exploration or affection or the bubble of this moment, in which all things seemed attainable.

I dragged Keith's face against me, and Josh immediately joined in, hand clamping over mine. I kept my eyes closed, but I could feel the tension of his hand directing Keith's head, and Keith reached around to hold my legs, letting us rub him against my body.

Josh laughed roughly. "Oh fuck yes. This is so good. I'm really liking having a partner in crime, babe. You're a genius."

"Thought *I* was your—"

"Suck him through his clothes."

Keith bent to his task, and I had to look now, I had to see it, I had to watch Keith's bright-pink lips and red tongue as they darkened the brown weave of my trousers. If Josh hadn't been so strong behind me, I might have melted right into the floor. The physical sensation was pressure and warmth and perhaps not enough friction, but when paired with the visual I was almost undone.

"Babe, don't make him come, that's fucked up." Josh hauled Keith's head away. Now he unzipped me, and I shuddered as he withdrew my cock and stroked me until I could only control my urge to pump into his hand by holding myself so rigid I shook.

"Hey, boy," Josh murmured.

"Please," I said. "Please. I need to— I have to—"

"He knows, Cam. This is Josh getting off." Keith met my eyes. Then he opened his mouth and oh god, god, Josh rubbed my cock over Keith's lips.

I shattered, losing all ability to keep still. "Please—please—"

"Take him slowly, angel. Draw him out."

"Fuck yeah."

What followed cannot be described in simple words, at least not in English. There are four words for love in Greek, and three in Japanese. I don't know if any language has the ability to express the way two men can slowly take apart a third until he doesn't know his own name or where he is. If you rolled all the words for love and sex and grace together into one, maybe you would have some sense of that night, of how timeless it was, and how eternal, as if it had been happening all along, as if it would continue happening until the end of the world.

I had never experienced pleasure like that: liquid, hot, desperation with an edge sharp enough to cut like a knife. I had never felt so held, so contained, so taken care of. Every sensation was extreme, but when I parsed them, separated them carefully, unwound them, not a single one was more than I'd felt before. It was the symphony of all at once, of Josh's fingers splayed across my belly, of Keith's hair brushing one of my thighs, eventually of fingertips pressing into my darkest, deepest places, of pleasure so high and pure that even after it passed I could still practically hear it, the long tail of a note no one had ever played before.

Later, much later, I rose from their bed, extracting myself from one of Keith's legs. I was unsurprised to discover that Keith was a sprawler, all long limbs, and that he looked younger while asleep, a boy who slept with abandon and no sense of rules.

I dressed and found Josh in the kitchen with a cup of tea. He lifted the kettle when he saw me, testing its weight.

"Still enough if you want a cup."

"I should get home."

He put the kettle down. "You can stay the night, Cam. If you want."

"I half think I'll turn into a pumpkin if I try to stay any longer." I stood there for a long moment. He looked perfectly fine, if still tired. I knew that neither one of us had slept. Keith had dropped off and I had lain beside him. Josh had straightened up, made the bed around us, dimmed the lights.

"I made him a promise," I said finally.

"Consider me checked in with." He sipped his tea and leaned down over the counter. "What about you?"

No answer I could give such a casual question was worthy enough to describe how I felt. "I hope I proved to you that you are not an also-ran."

He offered a rueful smile. "Sorry about that. I was pretty convinced, but I should have listened to him."

"Why didn't you?"

"I guess because if he was wrong, and I'd gotten invested in your—in your interest, it would have hurt to find out we were off base."

Unspoken words shimmered in the air between us, but I couldn't catch all of them, couldn't understand all the threads we were holding or where they led. I stepped forward and he straightened as if to meet me, setting the mug aside.

I touched his jaw and stared into his eyes. "Deep brown like the wood grain on the seats of the theater, strong and enduring. Why aren't you asleep, Josh?"

"Insomnia."

"Is that all?"

He pressed his jaw a little harder into my fingers, and I slid my hand until I cupped his face. "I'm just thinking. You're a hell of a variable, man. I thought I had this all pretty well planned, but you—everything is *more* than I expect with you, Cam."

It wasn't reproach, so I didn't apologize. "Is that a bad thing?"

"Hell no. But it's something to think about." His eyes skimmed to the side, then returned. "Do you believe in God?"

"I'm Catholic."

"Yeah, but do you believe in God?"

Even this didn't feel like an odd direction for the night to go.

"Yes. I mean, I struggle with it, but I pray. I still believe someone—or something—hears my prayers."

He nodded. "After scenes like that I stay up to pray. Keith's an atheist, always has been. I don't really keep secrets from him, but he doesn't ask me about God and I don't tell."

I tilted his head down, kissing his forehead. A benediction, maybe. Or a sign I understood.

Josh let his head fall forward onto my shoulder. "He's right, you know? It's hard for me to say all that, even when it's fun, even when it's hot, it still gets to me later. So I ask Jesus to forgive me. You think that's crazy?"

"Does He forgive you?"

He huffed a laugh. "Yeah. Yeah, He does."

"I don't think it's crazy, Josh. And I think you're brave to do things that scare you."

"I'd do anything for Keith. Sometimes I don't think he gets how much I'd do for him."

But he'd been the one who sent me into the future with instructions to check in. Keith understood more than he'd overtly say, I thought.

"He gets it."

"I'd feel better if he didn't. If I could hide it. Not that—I don't mean that really. But he makes me feel like flying, Cam. How nuts is that?"

I dared to touch the back of his neck. "I think that's called being in love."

"Yeah, I knew I was in love with him like two months after we met. But I thought it would kind of . . . fade. I thought the crazy part of it would lighten up a little. We live together, we run a business, how can he still make me feel so . . . out of control?"

"I don't know." I stroked his neck. "But it seems like he feels the same, and that's something like a miracle."

"Yeah. It really is." He lifted his head and kissed me. "You make everything so much more intense. I have no idea how that works. You sure you don't want to spend the night?"

"I'm sure. Thank you."

"Okay. Good night, Cam."

"Good night."

It was chilly outside. I'd been in a hurry earlier, hadn't grabbed my overcoat. I missed it, walking down the street to my car. A noise from down an alley startled me, and I suddenly realized that despite the cars in the distance, I was alone.

The wind was ice-cold and bit into my skin. I was grateful to reach the safety of my car, and I locked the Volvo's doors once inside, feeling foolish, but willing to accept foolish for the resulting security.

My apartment, also empty, nevertheless welcomed me home. It was a quarter past 4 a.m. when I emerged from a hot shower where I'd discovered all manner of physical souvenirs from the evening, in the form of scratches and spots rough from stubble and a few bruises forming that I felt certain were from teeth. I had no memory of having acquired any of these marks, but I found myself lingering over them affectionately, fingertips tracing the outlines of sensation, wondering how they had happened, and if it would happen again.

Exceedingly grateful I didn't have to open the theater on Sundays, I finally fell asleep.

CHAPTER  18

The following Saturday I showed *Penny Serenade*, a film that garnered Cary Grant an Oscar nomination but is mostly lost on people who only catch the most popular black-and-white movies. (My father, after half a bottle of wine, would call them the *Casablanca* classicists. My mother would laugh and tell him to stop being elitist.)

Penny Serenade is a film about love and grief and the intersections thereof. I find it difficult to watch, a bit like I find du Maurier: it's so good it hurts, making my chest tight and my fists clench.

I wanted to sit beside Josh and Keith, imagined perhaps taking their hands for a moment when I knew what was coming and needed to brace, but in the end they were sitting somewhere in the middle of the theater and I lingered on the edges, unable to commit to a seat.

I stood, watching from the wall along the hallway, back just far enough so that no one could see my anticipatory tears.

For the first few minutes of the reception, I put up a pretty good front of having everything together, until Hugh Reynolds found me and offered me his hand, which I shook and did not let go.

"I purposely came here alone tonight," he said, his other hand coming up to grasp mine. "My husband and our very dear friend are sitting in the house right now waiting for me to call and tell them I'm all right."

"Are you?" I could hear how close the emotion was in my voice, feel it in my throat.

"Do you ever find that sometimes their absence is merely a fact of your life, and at other times it is a needle stuck directly into a nerve, unrelenting no matter how much time has passed?"

I couldn't speak. Hugh's mother had died years before my parents. He was one of the only people whose presence I had been able to tolerate afterward. He'd asked me if I planned to kill myself, and when I'd told him I might, but it'd mean the end of the Rhein so I hadn't decided, he'd acted like that was a reasonable answer. Hugh had never demanded I be okay to save him worry, which enabled me to not be okay, a gift I hadn't fully recognized until years later.

He squeezed my hand and smiled, tears glittering in his eyes. "Forgive me, Cameron. I knew watching that particular movie would do this to me. It's why I asked them to stay home."

"Isn't that backward?"

"I've never been very good at accepting anyone's help. They know this about me. I expect a creative and therapeutic evening upon my return." He leaned over and kissed my cheek. "You shouldn't go home and sit alone in the apartment tonight."

"Oh, really?" I arched an eyebrow at him, and he laughed.

"Do as I say, not as I do. And I'm not going home alone, I came here alone. I have a plan for self-care in place already. And you?"

My plan for self-care was approaching, clearly curious but trying to be respectful. I smiled at them.

"Let me introduce you to a couple of my friends. Hugh, this is Josh and Keith. This is Hugh, whose crazy immigrant grandparents knew my crazy immigrant great-grandparents."

"And resented them for their success," Hugh added. "So good to meet you both. How did you like *Penny Serenade*?"

"Oh my god, I need therapy now," Keith said. "Right when you think everything's great, *bam*, that movie knocks you back down."

"Which is the sign of a good movie," Josh agreed. "But man, you should have given away tissues with the tickets, Cam."

"Seriously!"

Hugh gave the two of them a long look before pivoting toward me, smile quirking up on one side of his lips, just beginning to turn into a smirk. "I see I leave you in good hands."

If I hadn't blushed, I might have been able to ignore the insinuation. But I blushed, and Keith locked an arm through mine. Josh grinned.

"Really excellent to meet you both," Hugh said. "I have to get home. Have a good night."

"You too," I said. "Say hello to the family for me."

His eyes took in Josh and Keith again, then landed back on me. "Of course. I'll bring them to *Notorious*, I think."

"I look forward to it. Good night, Hugh."

When he spoke again, his tone had shifted to something I didn't trust. "Thanks for tonight. I needed a good cry more than I knew." The slightest pause, as if to invite commiseration. When I said nothing, he nodded. "Good night."

The three of us watched him walk out.

Keith immediately turned to me (but didn't release my arm). "Okay, *who* was that? And why was I blushing when I don't even know the guy?"

"You were blushing because Cam was blushing," Josh said. "The real question is, why was Cam blushing?"

"Be quiet, both of you. And an old friend of the family, I told you."

They just looked at me, until I relented, aware as ever of all the people milling around.

"Man-crush," I mumbled.

"Say what?"

"I really should get back to—"

"Ohhh," Keith said. "Man-crush. Friend of the family. I get it. He was older and cooler and you wanted to be him?"

"So much. So, so much. Did you hear him talk? Or maybe you didn't get the full effect. When I was twelve and he was eighteen I basically wanted to follow him around everywhere like a puppy dog."

"Aw, baby Cam had a crush." Keith seemed about to lean forward, then stopped, the movement arrested awkwardly and overcompensated for by a half-step away. "Whoa. Okay. No kissing Cam in public."

"At least, probably not in the lobby of the Rhein," Josh said. "Should we wait until you're free?"

"Yes. Please." I fumbled my keys out and detached the ring with the outer door to my building, and the apartment dead bolt. "Go upstairs whenever you want."

He took the keys, and I may have been making it up, but it certainly felt like our fingers sparked.

Keith gave my shoulders a squeeze. "Now everything I do seems manufactured and bizarre. Like, I almost patted you on the back. Why did I almost do that? Anyway, let's eat some snacks and go make out in Cam's bed."

Josh and I glanced around guiltily at the same moment, and Keith laughed, covering his mouth.

"Okay, no one tell me state secrets. Promise."

"Promise," Josh said. "Let's go, Trouble."

"Sorry, Cam."

But I wasn't sorry. I wasn't sorry they were going upstairs, or that people might know it. I certainly wasn't sorry about whatever impression we'd given off to Hugh that made him look at me the way he had, as if he understood, after meeting Josh and Keith, that I wouldn't be alone.

Obviously we couldn't advertise. But we could be seen to be friends in public. Even close friends. Whatever people wanted to think that meant.

CHAPTER 19

I hadn't been keeping up with my one enforced night out a week since the film festival had begun. At first I'd justified it because Saturday nights had become social events, if not as relaxing as sitting at Fredi's bar with a book and a Scotch.

It didn't hit me until later that the other reason I didn't need those nights was because I spent so much time with Keith and Josh, either at their apartment, or mine, or the theater, or the drop-in center. And when I wasn't with them, Keith and I texted a lot.

Apparently, somewhere along the way, I'd become . . . social. Not like most people, maybe, but my parents would have marveled.

I showed up at Club Fred's on Tuesday armed with a good book on my Kindle app, and planned to make an evening of it. I might even get myself a plate of fries, if I was feeling indulgent. Fries, Scotch, and Bulgakov.

I was lost inside the conflicted, agonized, ultimately weak mind of Pontius Pilate when someone sat beside me.

Alisha.

I pulled myself out of my book and noted that she'd had her hair braided again. "Hello."

"Ed's driving me up a fucking wall right now with this theme-night thing."

Since Alisha and I had never really had a conversation before—unless you counted casual greetings over the years or vague pleasantries exchanged as a side note to conversations involving other people—I wasn't entirely sure how she usually communicated, but I didn't think this was it. "Are you okay? And what theme-night thing?"

"Oh god. You didn't hear? I thought he was proclaiming it from the rooftops." She shook her head ruefully. "Sorry. You know I love him. But he's so obsessed, and then we do something and it eases off for a while, but it always comes back in. Uh, sorry, the thing where Fredi canceled all the theme nights. You really didn't hear that story? I thought everyone was talking about it. But maybe Ed's talking about it enough to save the rest of La Vista the trouble."

"Fredi canceled theme nights?"

Tom, who was standing nearby, side-stepped closer to us. "She said she feels too responsible for everyone's safety," he explained, voice low.

I wondered what it must be like for him, the continued anxiety and threat. He'd been the only suspect the cops had come up with, and despite the fact that they'd cleared him, he still made fewer tips than he used to.

"That's so fucked up," Alisha mumbled. "Like, I get it, but that's fucked up. Fredi shouldn't have to feel responsible for some stupid bullshit guy running around killing people. Plus, Philpott wasn't killed after a theme night. The pattern's already broken."

Tom shrugged, still drying the same glass. "She's pretty upset about it."

What did it look like when Fredi was upset? She was more of a fixture than a person to me; it was like trying to imagine a teacher doing laundry or brushing their teeth. I couldn't picture Fredi in a context that wasn't Club Fred's. I couldn't begin to think how "pretty upset" would manifest in a woman whose demeanor I'd never seen a crack in, whether she was shoving a drunk in a cab or breaking up a fight.

"That fucking *sucks*," Alisha said. "Also, Ed and I were supposed to go out tonight, but that editor he likes called him and now he's off fighting crime or something."

"Fighting crime?" Tom teased.

"Actually, I think the guy's trying to keep an eye on him so he doesn't go over the edge. *Anyway*. Oh my god, Tom, isn't your wedding coming up? And where the hell's Carlos? He's, like, never here anymore."

I listened with partial attention to their conversation (yes, his wedding was in the second week of January, and no, Carlos wasn't around as much these days because he was still too pissed at a lot of the regulars; Tom didn't explain why, but clearly we were meant to infer it was about his arrest and subsequent treatment at work). Canceling theme nights made sense to me. More sense than continuing them did. But whoever was doing this had selected the perfect target, either by cunning or luck. Attacking Club Fred's, the place where the widest swath of queer La Vista felt comfortable, was monstrous—but very, very clever.

Ed had thought all along that we were looking for someone inside the community. I couldn't help but think, sitting there at the bar, that he had to be right. And if he was, the killer, whomever they were, must feel incredibly satisfied with the effects of their work.

I felt a little sick and said good night to them. I probably should have dropped by Josh and Keith's, but I didn't want them to think I felt the need to be with them all the time. I wasn't really willing to admit that to myself, though knowledge of it seeped in through the porous walls of my denial more and more frequently. I settled for going home and texting instead.

Cameron: *Hi.*

Keith: *Hi, Cam! What're you up to?*

Cameron: *Drinking tea. I finished /Project Runway/.*

Keith: *Ha. You text-italicized.*

Keith: *You need season two. Or you can stream, but you can't get the early seasons online.*

Cameron: *I want to watch in order.*

Keith: *Of course you do. You can come over and pick up season two . . .*

Keith: *;-)*

Keith: *WINK WINK.*

Keith: *Just in case the emoticon wasn't clear enough.*

Cameron: *I should have stopped by for it on my way home.*

Keith: *Did you go to CF's?*

Cameron: *Yes. I heard about Fredi canceling theme nights.*

Keith: *I'm bummed. I really liked the theme nights.*

Keith: *And also I'm pissed, because fuck this guy, seriously, fuck this.*

Keith: *But if no one dies on Friday, which was supposed to be Noel Night, then I guess it'll be good that she canceled them.*

Keith: *So basically I feel a lot of different things, and most of them disagree with each other.*

Cameron: *Me too.*

Keith: *Josh said you should come over.*

Keith: *Unless you don't want to.*

I tapped my phone, thinking about their apartment. Were they sitting on the couch right now, maybe with a movie on pause, while Keith texted and Josh looked over his shoulder?

Keith: *We'll take that as a no . . .*

Keith: *Hahaha, J says I'm putting too much pressure on you.*

Keith: *Hello? Cam?*

Cameron: *P-)*

Cameron: *Did I do that right?*

Cameron: *No, wait.*

Cameron: *:-P*

Cameron: *That looks better.*

Cameron: *You aren't putting too much pressure on me.*

Cameron: *You guys are still up?*

Keith: */Obviously./ :-o*

Keith: *You coming over? I mean, the wink, wink was for fun. I wasn't actually implying you can only come over if you, uh, you know, put out.*

Cameron: *. . .*

Cameron: *Did you just say . . .*

Cameron: *. . . "put out"?*

Keith: *Lol. Uh-huh.*

Keith: *Are you coming over?*

Keith: *So I can put on something more comfortable.*

Keith: **ducks flying things**

Keith: *Sorry! I'm like made of horrible innuendo tonight!*

Keith: *I'm just stuffed full of sexual innuendo . . .*

Keith: *Oh my god, I can't stop.*

Keith: *This is Josh. I stole his phone. Tough love, man.*

Cameron: *I'll be over soon. If that's okay.*

Keith: *Then we'll stop texting you so you can drive.*

Cameron: *Good plan. See you soon.*

I went to their apartment, and they had almond milk hot cocoa already made by the time I got there. We watched the first few episodes of season two and Keith teased me about mooning over Tim Gunn. Then he made me promise to stop by QYP so he could set up a marketing plan.

Even when we didn't do anything the least risqué—when it was just the three of us drinking hot cocoa watching television—being with them felt better than being alone. I'd never had a boyfriend whose company I preferred to my own. I'd never felt the least bit lonely, and while companionship was nice at times, I'd never sought it out beyond being available on whatever online service was in vogue.

But this was different in every way.

I left with the DVDs for season two and an erection.

CHAPTER 20

No one died on Friday night. I'm sure I wasn't the only one who checked the online version of the *Times-Record* the second I woke up on Saturday morning, but no new bodies had been found at the waterfront. It was probably too much to hope that it was over, that Philpott had been the last, but it was at least a possibility.

Arsenic and Old Lace pleased my film festival fans. I talked about how little Cary Grant had liked the film, and its delayed release due to the success of the Broadway show. I also repeated the cute, though anecdotal, story about how Jean Adair had once nursed young Archie Leach back to health when he contracted rheumatic fever twenty years before they played aunt and nephew in *Arsenic and Old Lace*.

I didn't use index cards anymore. I thought a little bit about what I wanted to say beforehand, but for the most part I made it up.

Before I knew it, it was Saturday again, the final night of the film festival.

Notorious. Which I'd forced myself not to watch over the last twelve weeks so it would be fresh.

At least half of La Vista seemed to be at the Rhein for *Notorious.* Zane arrived, escorting Mildred and fighting for the right to buy her ticket. ("I can buy my own fucking—" "Oh my god, it's a *date*, you're insufferable—" "It is not!" I hid a smile and wished them a good night.) Josh and Keith bought their tickets and waved at me. I was still watching them when Hugh stepped up to the window. He gave me a look, which I ignored, and smiled at his husband (whose name I couldn't remember) and the guy with them.

Jaq and Hannah ran up to the booth late, but I hadn't shut down yet.

"Are we missing it?" Hannah asked breathlessly. "I love this one."

"You're still golden, but I hope you weren't planning to buy sandwiches."

She shook her head and Jaq groaned. Hannah rolled her eyes. "You can live without sandwiches!"

"No, I can't!"

"You can get *popcorn*, and only if it's already made!"

I waved them inside and called over to concessions as I locked the booth. "Two medium popcorns on the house, please!"

"And Cokes!" Jaq added.

Hannah hit her, laughing. "You're terrible. You should be ashamed of yourself." I heard her say to Bobby, who was getting their drinks, "But could you please make mine an iced tea? Thanks, sugar."

Bobby glanced at me as he handed over the food, but I waved. We could stand the freebies for loyal customers.

I walked into the theater that night thinking about Anderson Philpott telling me he would come for *Notorious*, that it was his favorite Cary Grant film. I hadn't prepared anything special to say, so I told the story of the famous key, which plays a role in the film, being passed from Grant to Bergman, and later to Hitchcock. I got weirdly emotional talking about it and had to clear my throat.

"This is where it would be good to have index cards," I said.

Someone called, "Except when you drop them!"

People laughed. Probably more than actually remembered that moment. I found Josh and Keith in seats toward the front and off to the left, where they enjoyed sitting for proximity to the door. The lights were still up; I could see Keith's foreshortened wave. And the empty seat in between them.

I smiled. "Please enjoy *Notorious*. And be gentle with one another toward the end. I fully encourage you to grab hold of the person sitting beside you when tensions begin to rise." A few more laughs at that. "You will tell yourself that everything comes out all right in the end, but of course, it's Hitchcock. You really never know. I present to you one of the best films in cinema history, and the final film in the series. Please join me in the lobby after to say good-bye—until next time."

If I had planned to retire to the booth, or to climb the steps to my usual row, I couldn't possibly pass up the opportunity to sit in the seat they'd kept for me. I was touched beyond measure.

"Thank you," I whispered, resisting the urge to dab at my eyes as the studio logo filled the screen.

Keith took my hand and tilted his head toward mine. When he spoke, his voice was very low. "I've never seen this one. If I have nightmares, I reserve the right to hold on to you all night."

On my other side, Josh laughed.

It was shockingly hard to declare the reception over. People lingered. Little groups at the sofas in the seating area, in any alcove they could find, talking and laughing and sharing their plates of refreshments.

"You did it." Ed gave me a huge hug. "You did it, Cam. You brought the Rhein back to life."

"That's exactly it!" Alisha agreed. She hugged me, too. "You should take a vacation, Cam. You so earned it."

"Alisha's obsessed with vacations." Ed grinned. "We're, uh, going away for the weekend next week. Like, skipping out on all the Christmas stuff completely."

"We're *escaping*," she said. "Speaking of, it's been fun, but this man owes me a strip tease. I bet him someone would die at the end of the movie."

"I maintain that it's ambiguous—"

"It's totally not ambiguous! Come on, Cam, you're on my side, right?"

I smiled (enigmatically, I hoped). "It sounds like you two have an exciting evening ahead of you. Good night."

They laughed and said good night, though it took them another ten minutes to make it through the lobby.

There really were a lot of people. I recognized many of them from previous movies, some by name, some only by face. The group stayed much later than I expected, and I dismissed as much staff as I dared let leave.

I only saw Hugh and his family as they were leaving. He kissed my cheek and told me he was proud of me, then melted into the night as most people were now doing. It was only right, but part of me mourned the loss of the film festival, as eager as I was for it to be over, for my Saturdays to be my own again.

When only a few people were left, I clapped my hands and told them I looked forward to seeing all of them at the Rhein in the future, but for now we had to close up.

This time I didn't single out Josh and Keith to stay inside, but passed them my apartment keys. They smiled, I smiled, they walked away, and I locked the door behind them. Closing went fast and soon enough I was setting the alarm, walking across the lobby in the dark, letting myself outside.

All so perfectly mundane. That's the genius of filmmakers like Hitchcock, of course. You start with a party, and it's so mundane it seduces you a little. The guy sitting in silhouette in the foreground may be the hero, or he may be the villain. You aren't always sure until the end.

"Sorry," someone said as I was pulling out my phone to text Keith to come downstairs and let me in. "I'm so sorry, I know you're technically off the clock, but would you mind if I asked you one more question?"

"Sure." I'd seen him before, one of the film-festival regulars. I might have talked to him, though I'd talked to so many people. "What can I do for you?"

He smiled. Cute smile. My mind dismissed him as "too young," though he had to be Josh's age at least. My mind had let go of some of the rules when it came to Keith.

"Okay, so, like, I read this story that this movie has the longest onscreen kiss for its time. Is that true or just, like, the internet making stuff up?"

"Yes and no. The Hays Code restricted kisses to three seconds, but Hitchcock skirted the letter of the law, prolonging 'the kiss' by having a phone call interrupt it."

"Oh! In the hotel room, or whatever, right?"

I paused. Anywhere he would have read about the kiss in *Notorious* would have surely told that story. "Exactly," I said, and focused on my phone.

Cameron: *Knock knock.*

Keith: *Omw.*

"Thanks so much for coming to the movie tonight," I said to the young man, walking over to the door to the vestibule. "I'm glad you liked it."

"Oh, I did, like, so much! It was great! And that last scene, wow, he just, like, disappears into the house *never to be seen again*. Right?" He laughed.

"Well, good night."

"I know I'm bothering you, sorry, do you think maybe I could stop by sometime when the theater's open and ask you more questions?"

"Sure," I said, grateful for the out. "Of course, yes, though the internet has a lot of really fun old trivia, if that's what you're after. You can't necessarily be sure it's true, but if you like the stories—" The door opened.

Josh, not Keith. "Hey." He held the door and the three of us stood there for a moment in a strange tableau.

"Well, good-bye!" the excitable stranger said, starting to turn away.

"Good-bye. Thanks again for coming to the movie." I passed Josh in the doorway and began up the stairs.

Keith grabbed me the second I was inside and pushed me toward the sofa. I opened my mouth to say something, but then we were kissing, Keith half kneeling over me, my head against the arm of the sofa, his hand in my hair. I arched up into him, and he smiled against my lips, finally pulling away. "You were so hot up there tonight. I kinda wanted to maul you, but Josh said probably I shouldn't."

Josh laughed, watching us from the doorway like we were the main attraction.

I licked my lips. "I don't object to mauling."

"I only objected to the timing," Josh said. "I mean, the theater seemed a little—"

The next thing we heard was a *thud*, and then everything happened very fast.

Laughter, strange and wrong. "I can't fucking believe that worked. Fuck yeah!"

Josh's body on the ground, crumpled.

Keith's voice, far too loud: "Josh, oh my god—"

And the gun. I'll never forget the gun. It was small, not at all flashy, and even in that moment, when I was staring it, part of my brain wanted to tell me it might be a toy. Small, metallic, looking more like a scale model than the real thing.

In that moment you don't care if it's a toy because it might be capable of killing you and that's the only thing your mental triage team will let through.

I clutched Keith harder and said, "Stop screaming." When that didn't work, I put my hand over his mouth and he stopped, eyes wide and white and terrified.

The young man who'd wanted to know about the Hays Code stood in my doorway over Josh's body, teeth seeming far too large in his mouth, gun seeming far too small in his hand. He kicked Josh's body, suddenly, for no reason, and Josh didn't move. Keith tried to get out of my grip, but I wouldn't let him and the intruder with the gun made a *tsk* sound.

"Oh, he's not dead. Where would the fun be in that? I just had to take him out first, since he's the big bad alpha." Another kick and Josh's body jolted. "Fucking alpha males, am I right? They're always such douche bags." The gun waved toward Keith, who shrank back. "I thought this was gonna be a lot harder, but so far three isn't harder than one. He would have been a challenge, but I knocked his ass out! Man, did you see that shit? I'm fucking unstoppable."

He bounced from foot to foot like an excited child waiting in line for Disneyland. An excited child with a gun.

"What do you want?" I demanded. I was afraid, but I was also enraged. This was my home. And that was my friend on the ground.

"What do I want?" All motion stopped. He stared straight at me, as if astonished by the question. "Shit, Cameron Rheingold. I'm the La Vista killer. What do you think I want?"

Keith tried to break away again, but another kick at Josh's stomach stopped him.

"Kind of a feisty little twink, aren't you? Sorry, we haven't been introduced. I've seen you, of course. And I know where you live." He smiled, that appalling parody of happiness stretching across his face. "I tracked Cam over there one night, and he did stay awhile.

Naughty." The gun motioned, indicating us. "Sit up. Slowly. Both of you. I want you sitting on opposite sides of the couch with your hands on your thighs so I can see them."

Keith started to struggle again, but the young man kicked Josh and used his gun to gesture to us. "If you want him to stay whole, you'll do what I say."

The words *La Vista killer* ricocheted through my brain, but I forced Keith's face to mine. His eyes were the only color left in the room. "We have to sit up now. Okay? I'm going to let go of you and we're going to sit up and everything's going to be fine, Keith, okay?"

Cary Grant would talk like the happy ending was right around the corner, even if you could see he didn't believe it. I didn't know if Keith could tell I was lying, but he nodded, and I let go of his mouth.

The gun wavered between us as we moved, and only when we were sitting perfectly still did the young man step all the way inside and shut the door. "That's good. Let's all stay calm and have a nice little talk." He nodded to Keith, as if they were at a bar. "I'm Joey."

Keith stared uncomprehendingly back at him.

"You know, you and I could have been friends. I get hooking up with the alpha male. I understand the attraction there." He glanced down at Josh's body, which still showed no signs of regaining consciousness. "I guess maybe he wasn't as tough as I thought, but I bet you don't feel the same." He laughed, a short, ugly sound. "Yeah. You like being his little bitch, right?"

"Go to hell," Keith said.

The smile froze. And the gun lowered until it was pointing at Josh's head. "Maybe I should shoot him right now, get him out of the picture. As long as he's still breathing, he might wake up and disrupt my fun."

"No—no, please don't."

"If you really loved him, you'd beg me to shoot him." Now the smile dropped. "If you really loved him, you'd give me anything to spare him what he has coming."

Keith shifted, maybe about to rise, but Joey squatted down to press the gun right against Josh's temple. "*Don't.*"

I sucked in a breath, trying to pull his attention away from Keith. "Why do you hate us?"

"Hate you? I don't hate you, Cameron Rheingold. You shouldn't take this personally. Think of me as . . . pest control, that's all. It's my job to get rid of you, like it was my job to get rid of them, and I'll do it." A flash of that smile again as he popped up from the floor. "I'm lucky enough to love my work."

"Pest control," I echoed.

"Here's the thing." He took up a more casual post, leaning against the wall like he had all the time in the world. And why wouldn't he? No one would come looking for me. Josh—and Keith by extension—wouldn't be missed until it was time for church in the morning.

Hours. All night. He could hold us all night, and as long as he had a gun on one of us, the others would do what he wanted. Until he decided he'd had enough and started shooting.

"It's like this. The way things used to be, everyone knew their place. Everyone stayed separate, and that was best. We're like different species, you know? We're not meant to mix. The gays, the lesbians, the mongrel in-betweeners. The fucking *gender benders*, whatever the hell they call themselves." He shook his head. "I'm just removing the outside influences, that's all. That 'drag king,' with her fucking attitude, like she was so much better than me. I showed her exactly where she was meant to be, didn't I? At my *feet*. And that fucking travesty, that she-male horror show. That can't be tolerated. You understand. There are lines that shouldn't be crossed, and they crossed them." Joey, gun loose in his hand now, started pacing, never turning away from us completely. "We fought for decades to get here, and suddenly all these fucking people come out of the woodwork, want to be included, want to take the rights that we bled for. You know what I'm talking about."

I could feel my chest getting tighter as he continued to talk. The worst of it was how rational he sounded, as if everything he was saying made perfect sense, when it didn't even make historical sense. Drag queens had beaten back police at Stonewall. Lesbians had nursed dying men in the early AIDS quarantine wards. And Joey, voice disturbingly sane, had erased everything that didn't fit into some lost ideal of gay male nirvana.

"Club Fred's should be a place for us, but every time I'm there I see too many freaks. Listen to me. This is important: *there are too many people.*"

Maybe he wanted to talk. Maybe I could start a conversation with him, convince him to let us go. I glanced at Keith, whose face was pale and expressionless, teeth digging into his lower lip. We had to get out of here. I had to come up with some kind of plan to get us out of here.

Joey cocked his head to the side, as if making a vital point. "They had to die. You understand."

My heart plummeted. *Be Cary Grant. Be unperturbed.* "You mean people like Honey Jansen."

The gun swung toward me. "I don't care what their names were," he said sharply. "But you don't get it. Of course you don't. I thought, maybe, you could be saved."

Such a small gun. I'd always imagined guns as imposing, heavy items in a room, as if the potential violence in even the smallest derringer would impact the space. But despite the fact that I felt certain this gun could kill me, it still looked bewilderingly tiny and inconsequential as Joey pushed away from the wall.

"But I've been watching you, Cameron Rheingold, and you corrupted them. It was bad enough when you sat there at the bar and *read a book.* Like you were above it all, like you were better than everyone else. But then you touched them, and I watched it, I watched the way you pulled them in, the way you tainted them with your stain."

My heart thudded distantly in my chest. "I don't know what you mean."

"*You.* You, Cameron." The gun slid to the side, settling in Keith's direction. Joey didn't look away from me. "You're the reason they have to die. They were perfectly normal until you, and now I can't be sure you won't spread your—" he hesitated "—your *poison* to them."

"Cam isn't poison!" Keith's voice was high and offended.

Joey advanced on Keith. "That's the problem. You don't see it. He has some pull over you, and now you can't see what's right in front of your face. We were made to fuck. We were made to defy the whole fucking world just to be together. And what does he do? He goes to a bar and *reads.*"

"You want to kill Cam because he likes to read? Jesus. You're sick."

He was fast. He was so fast. He swiped the side of Keith's face with the gun, and I wasn't even quick enough to think about lunging for him before he'd turned it on me. "*Get back*. I will shoot either or both of you and still have my fun with him unless you *fucking behave.*"

I should have tried something while he was distracted. But by the time I was thinking that, he was already backing away again. He kicked Josh in the gut, maybe to make sure he was still out, maybe because he wanted to.

Joey looked back at Keith, grinning, and kicked Josh again. "I can't wait to torture your boyfriend until he prays for death. I can't wait until he wakes up so I can kill you right in front of him."

Keith inhaled a sob, a thin trail of blood trickling down his face.

I never imagined that I would be a hero, but I'd never imagined having the opportunity. Now I was there, and the best I could do was hope that Josh would start moving. If Joey got distracted again, I would do something. Anything. Anything that wasn't sitting here waiting to die.

"You don't fucking understand, okay? This is my *job*. I was put here to fix what's wrong, to cleanse the community of the unclean." His movements were more jagged now. The gun hand cut through the air, no longer controlled. "Like that little prick, that boy, acting like I was a fucking leper just because I came on to him! Acting like I was some kind of monster, when he's the one who came with me, isn't he? He wanted it, he wanted it so fucking bad, and then, 'Oh no, no, I can't, I'm scared.'" Joey sneered. "I showed him what to be scared of, didn't I? I showed him what fear really was."

My vision, all dull grays and lackluster blacks, narrowed until all I could see was the gun. If I could get the gun away from him, we might have a chance. He was good at fighting, but there were two of us, and if he didn't have the gun we might be able to overpower him.

It was the only chance we had. I tensed my muscles, studied the angles, and got ready.

The next time he turned halfway I went for him, but he was fast, so fucking fast, and he had me on my back with his foot on my chest, pressing down so I could hardly breathe.

He didn't point the gun at me. He pointed it at Keith and looked right into my face.

"I only wanted you. You were the plan. I used to watch you sitting at the bar, so fucking smug, like you were above it, like you were better than everyone else there."

I gasped, struggling for breath, trying to wrench his leg away. "Let them go, then! They didn't do anything wrong, let them go. Please!"

"Oh, it's too late for that. I saw you. I saw you, when you thought no one was looking. You were there the whole time thinking you were better than us, and you're not, you're not better than me. And now you've gotten them killed, too." He leaned down harder, so hard I thought he'd break my ribs. "You're not better than me!"

The weight on my chest disappeared, and I didn't have time to be grateful before he was kicking me. Again, and again. "Why can't you be normal, like me, like they were before you?" I curled instinctively, trying to absorb the blows, when suddenly I heard a shout.

The gun fired. I ducked my head and covered it with my arms, but the gun fired again, and I couldn't lie there while some madman shot up my home. I raised up my head, and Keith— Oh god—

He was lying by the dining room table. No pool of blood, but it was such a small gun. I scrambled across the floor—

"Don't fucking move!"

I froze, fingers inches away from Keith's body. He was breathing—I could see his chest rising and falling—but he was very, very still.

"You fucking whore! You little twink bitch!" This time Joey wasn't kicking or hitting someone else; the gun waved precariously while his other hand, fisted, slammed into his own head. "Goddamn it, goddamn it, fuck! You don't understand!"

Keith had gone for him with a candlestick, which now lay just beyond his body. The seconds it had taken him to grab a weapon were probably why he hadn't managed much more than seriously pissing Joey off, but something had shifted; Joey's energy, which had been solely externally focused before, was now wildly unbalanced.

"I'm making things better, damn you! I'm fixing it! *I am a proud gay man and I'm sick of seeing the fucking freaks everywhere like they're normal!*" He was shaking, and the barrel of the gun had me transfixed. He'd shot twice. Did a gun that small have six bullets, or was I making that up from too many TV shows? Could I get him to shoot more if I jumped at him? Probably, since he was so unstable, but I couldn't guarantee he wouldn't hit Josh or Keith.

I really wanted to touch Keith, who was so close. Was he unconscious? I couldn't rule out that he might have been shot, but his breathing was even and rhythmic and fast.

He was awake. And lying there.

If this were a movie, what would happen next? One of us would be the distraction while the other would attack. *What would Cary do?* I tried to breathe slowly and brace myself, waiting for an opening.

Joey's rambling was getting more intense, with interjections of *fuck* and *unnatural* at varying intervals. He was a monster with a plan, with a code, with a goal in mind.

"I watched you." The gun swung down toward my eyes. "I watched and watched and I could have taken you that night you walked to your car late from their apartment. I could have taken you on one of those nights you left the theater last. I watched, and I watched, but then I saw you with them, saw that you corrupted them, that they were fine, they were normal, until you." His hold on the gun was unstable and his legs were shaking. "They were normal, until you screwed everything up! If it wasn't for you, they could live, but now look at them! You did this!"

"I'm sorry," I whispered, trying to concentrate on the shades of silver and gray and black in the gun. "I'm so sorry."

"Sorry? You're an abomination! Why did you have to be so fucking smug? Why does everyone think they're better than me?" The gun hand came up to rub at the side of his head. "Ow. I can't believe that little bitch attacked me. Like fucking Togg. You have no idea how hard I had to work him, how many weeks I spent, flattering him, making him think I was in awe of him, that fucking piece of shit. And he still almost got away. I made him pay, after I shattered his legs, but that fucking bastard hurt me. I couldn't go to the hospital, I had to hide from my parents—he could have gotten me caught!"

He looked so genuinely annoyed by this inconvenience, as if he expected me to sympathize.

"But you—you—what the fuck is *wrong* with you? You just sit there, *reading*, like you don't need anything, like you're so fucking evolved the rest of us are fucking ants in comparison." Joey stepped closer and stuck the gun right in my face. "Do I look like an ant to you now, motherfucker?"

I didn't hesitate. I grabbed the gun and twisted. I wasn't strong enough to break his grip, but I got him off-balance and lunged. The gun clattered across the floor, but Joey grinned, like he didn't have a care in the world.

We grappled, but I was never one for physical fights. Pain registered somewhere in the back of my mind, impact, a gasping sense of knowing I would lose, that Joey would win and I would die.

And judging by that toothy, feral smile, he knew it too. He quickly got the upper hand, pinning me to the ground. "You're not so good now, you—"

The candlestick took him hard on the temple and his neck snapped to the side. He roared and tried to go for Keith, but Keith was way too far gone to care. He swung again, cracking Joey hard enough to at least temporarily stun him, and when he fell over I jumped on top of him, trying to keep his arms and legs contained.

Keith kept hitting him, as if in a trance, bringing the candlestick down again and again until Joey was no longer moving.

His blood was bright, inescapably red, and my brain snapped to attention. "Keith, call 911." When he didn't move, I spoke louder. "*Keith*. Call 911 and get the gun. Right now."

He blinked at me for a long moment, but at least he dropped the candlestick.

"The gun," I said again, lowering my voice. "And your phone. Call 911. But hide the gun somewhere first in case he gets away."

Keith, eleven years younger than me and way more entrenched in the world of cell phones, managed to do both at once, holding his phone to his ear with one shaking hand as he deposited the gun in my freezer.

"We need help." His voice shook. "Help. Please. Oh my god, *Josh*."

I tried not to relax. It could be a trick, though some part of my brain registered that Joey had taken an awful lot of blows to the head. "Keith, c'mere. Put it on speaker." I wanted to reach out to him, but I didn't dare let go of Joey.

Keith started to cry in a quiet, frightening way. He put his phone on speaker and placed it on the floor. Then he went to Josh, huddling protectively over him.

"Sir?" the operator said. "Sir, are you still there?"

I cleared my throat. "My name is Cameron Rheingold. We're calling from 22405 Mooney, the apartment upstairs from the gift shop, next to the Rhein Theater."

"I have units on their way to you now, sir. Is anyone hurt?"

It seemed like such a stupid question suddenly. I laughed. "Yes. Everyone's hurt. Everyone here is hurt. I think we caught the La Vista killer."

"Sir? The what?"

"The man who's been hunting and killing queer people in La Vista. I'm sitting on him. I don't think he's dead, though." I should stop talking. I knew I should stop talking.

"Help is on the way, sir," the woman's smooth, controlled voice said. Nothing even betrayed that she was interested in what I was saying. She probably heard crazy people rambling all day long.

"That's good. We definitely need help."

Keith's small, muffled sobs almost broke me. I wanted to go to him, comfort him, but I was afraid if I moved at all Joey would spring up and we'd have to live the whole thing over again. We were trapped inside a spell, holding us in our places, each where we should be: Keith holding Josh, keeping him together with his bare hands, and me holding Joey, who I thought with every second might kill me.

Response time, Ed later told me, was twelve minutes. By the time the police and paramedics arrived, I was shaking with the effort of holding Joey down, Joey was found to be unconscious, Keith was in shock, and Josh was just beginning to wake up.

CHAPTER 21

They went to the hospital. Keith went with Josh (though he needed to be checked out, too), and once I'd explained to the police what happened, an officer went with Joey.

"But you won't—you won't let him get away, will you?" I asked, and even to my ears I sounded hysterical.

The female officer, with an air of always being The One Who Comforts Traumatized People, sat beside on my sofa. "We won't let him get away. We have a lot of work to do before we can charge him with all the rest of those crimes, Mr. Rheingold, but I'm looking right at the evidence we need to charge him for what happened here tonight. Will you go over it with me one more time?"

It wasn't one more time. I told her the story, and then they had me go down to the hospital to get checked out, where I told a nurse, and then some kind of counselor. My phone didn't work inside, so I couldn't tell where Keith and Josh were or how they were doing. Were they repeating themselves like I was? Was Josh okay?

I sat alone on a collapsible bed in a curtained-off section of the ER, waiting to be seen. When a nurse came to get my vitals, she said I was shaking, but I didn't feel anything at all. I told her that her scrubs were gray, but she didn't get the joke and I had to pretend I could see color so they wouldn't think I had a head injury.

I asked about Josh, but no one told me anything. Confidentiality. I hoped they at least let Keith stay with him.

Hours passed. Time dripped, drizzled, dropped here and there; sometimes an entire minute would pass without me looking at my phone. Sometimes I looked a hundred times and the digital readout seemed to have frozen. I forced myself to listen to all the sounds around me to prove that other things were happening in the world, that time had not stood still, because printers were printing and phones were ringing and carts were being wheeled down hallways, and curtains were being brushed aside on their metal rails somewhere nearby.

Eventually they told me I was all right, that I needed rest, and did I have somewhere safe to go?

I went to the theater. There were still people in my house—police? crime scene?—but I didn't go upstairs. I let myself into the lobby and grabbed a few of the army surplus blankets we kept in our little modified emergency supplies cupboard (just in case, Dad always said, though I doubted this was what he had in mind). I curled up under the desk in the ticket booth, and drifted in and out of consciousness for a couple of hours.

Whether you could call that state "sleep" was debatable. I didn't wake up so much as my brain and my body made a mutual pact to stop pretending. I was chilled. I felt heavy and achy, like I'd been in a fight.

I'd been in a fight.

I checked my phone, desperately scrambling to see if Keith had texted, only to discover it had died at some point in the night.

The charger was upstairs. Were the police still here? I didn't know. I didn't want to know. The theater was still locked up tight, so it wasn't nine yet. If I got out now, no one would know I'd slept there.

I folded the blankets, put them away, and slipped out while the alarm system beeped its warning at me. Except I had nowhere to go. Two cruisers were still parked on the street outside, so I walked the opposite direction. When I came to the Volvo, I got in.

Most of that morning was a blur when I tried to remember it later. I went to a discount store and picked up a black coat with a soft lining. It wasn't high quality and looked more like something Merin would wear than myself, but I didn't care. It was warm, and I needed something I could pull around me. I needed something that could hug me back.

I also got a charger for my phone. I ripped it open in the attached coffee shop and plugged it into the first outlet I could find.

Three text messages.

Keith: *Phones don't work in the hospital and my battery's dying. You okay?*

Ed: *I just heard what happened. I'm coming over.*

Ed: *Where are you? I'm at your apartment. Please call me, Cam. I'm sure you're at the hospital or something, but I'm worried.*

I knew I should call Ed. But I wanted to talk to Keith. I wanted to hear his voice. I wanted to hear his voice tell me that Josh was okay. When I dialed their phones, they went straight to voice mail.

As I was sitting there contemplating the wrongness of being out of touch in a hospital, when it seemed like circumstances might dictate people wanting to remain in touch, my phone rang. A local number, but not one I knew.

The police. Asking me to come down to give a statement. Did I need a ride? I assured them I did not need a ride. And yes, I'd come down. I had nothing better to do. I told them to give me an hour, and bought a cup of coffee, which burned in my stomach while I cradled my phone and prayed for it to ring.

Detective Green showed me into a conference room and gestured me into a chair with threadbare pink upholstery that might have been red, in some distant past. He took the chair on the short side of the table so that we were sharing a corner.

He was probably in his midforties, Filipino, and a pair of reading glasses was hooked on the collar of his shirt. He looked exhausted, though I figured I probably looked worse.

"Mr. Rheingold, we spoke once over the phone. Do you remember?"

"You called me about the boy. Steven Costello." He'd been nice on the phone. Direct, but not unkind. I glanced around the room, wondering if this was where they put you when you were a witness, or if it was where they put you when you weren't but they wanted you to think you were.

"You were photographed with him. Do you want to see the pictures?"

"No. I remember. Ed was a nuisance with his phone, but I guess if it helped the case at all, I'm glad he took all those pictures."

Green nodded. "Tell me about last night."

I went over it again. This time I was more collected, and I mentioned that I thought I'd seen Joey before, but I didn't immediately connect his appearance.

"So you knew him."

"No. He'd asked me about a movie I'd shown. Kind of... lingered, past when everyone else left."

"Did he make you uncomfortable?"

"No. Well, maybe. I was happy when he left, but I—I don't always know how to talk to people, or how to kind of—" I shook my head. "I didn't know how to get rid of him. A few friends showed up, and he kind of took off on his own. But last night I didn't immediately realize it was the same person."

Green raised his eyebrows. "What made you think it was?"

"I'm not sure. I guess he talked a lot about watching me. And then I was trying to sleep and I kept replaying things, even when I tried not to, I kept seeing it all over again, his face, this horrible smile, the gun—"

"It's okay," Green said. "Take a few breaths."

"Sorry. I'm sorry. I know it's over, I know it wasn't even that big a deal. But I haven't talked to Keith, and I don't know how Josh is, and I really—I really just want everything to be normal again." I focused on the worn upholstery, willing it to stay pink. "I'm sorry."

"I understand. Tell me a little bit about your relationship with Keith and Josh. Were they the friends who interrupted you when you talked to Joseph Rodriguez the first time?"

Joseph Rodriguez. He had a name. A full name. "Joey" could be anyone; Joseph Rodriguez was somebody's son.

"No," I said faintly. "No, that was— Actually, that was Ed and Alisha. Ed Masiello, who's the one who took all the pictures."

Green blinked at me for a long moment. "Ed Masiello also knows Rodriguez?"

"No, no. No, he didn't—" I paused, remembering the bags of food, the smell of turkey, Alisha's voice. Ed, frowning, staring out the front windows of the theater. "Wait. He thought Joey looked familiar, but he couldn't remember from where. Oh god. This means you have to talk to Ed again."

Green wrote something down. Probably *Call Ed Masiello.* "We have to investigate all leads, Cameron. Do you mind if I call you Cameron?"

"I just want to get this over with. I don't care what you call me."

"Let's keep going, then. Tell me about your friends, Keith and Josh."

My throat closed up for a second, then released. "What do you want to know?"

"What's the nature of your relationship with them?"

I wanted to lie. I wanted so badly to lie I could taste the words on my tongue. How could he know anything about our relationship? We'd barely gotten home before everything had happened. The most incriminating things in my apartment were two seasons of *Project Runway* and a computer with a few films I'd illegally downloaded to make sure I wanted to lease them to show at the Rhein. And they probably would have searched. Any secrets I had personally, they likely already knew. This was about Josh and Keith, damn it, and they didn't have to know everything.

Except when they asked Josh, when they asked Keith, both of them would tell the truth.

"Cameron?"

"I'm sorry. Yesterday I thought I understood what I was doing, what my place was, and today . . . everything's changed. Josh and Keith are friends of mine. Close friends."

"Meaning there is a sexual relationship between you?" He said it like he'd expected it.

"Yes. Yes, there is."

"And last night, was that why they were in your apartment? To continue your relationship?"

"Last night they were in my apartment because they're my friends, and it was the last night of the film festival, and we were celebrating. I have no idea what would have happened if Joey hadn't barged in, hit Josh."

"And you say that you didn't invite him in?"

"Invite him—no. I'd been trying to get rid of him. He had more questions, about *Notorious*, but his questions felt off."

"Off how?"

"Off like your question was off when you asked if my relationship with Josh and Keith is sexual," I said. "Off the way a question's off when someone already knows the answer. Did you talk to them? Are they okay? Can you—can you at least tell me if they're all right? Please, Detective." I bit down hard on my lip.

Green sat back and put down his pen. He cracked his knuckles, which looked bruised. I wondered if he'd been in a fight recently, or if he was a boxer of some kind. He wasn't tall, but he was the kind of skinny that sometimes meant strength you couldn't see.

"I spoke with them at the hospital. No permanent damage. But I need you to keep answering my questions, Cameron."

I wished I hadn't granted him permission to use my name. It turned out it did matter, after all. "Thank you."

"I'm not judging anyone here. If you invited him up, it's still not right what he did to you, or to them. But I need to know."

"I didn't. I don't know him. I don't invite strangers into my home. I own the Rhein, Detective Green. I've spent some portion of every single day of my life in the theater, around people. When I go home I want peace, not chaos. I want familiarity, not—not strangers." I didn't want to cry, so I closed my eyes. "I tried to get rid of Joey politely, but he wouldn't leave. Josh came down to open the door for me because I'd given him my keys."

"He doesn't have a key of his own?"

"To my apartment? No. No, why would he?"

"I'm trying to understand the nature of your relationship. Are you dating them, Cameron? Is it just sex, some kind of friends with benefits thing? Is it an experiment?"

"I don't know what it is. But I—" I rubbed tears out of my eyes. "I care about them a lot. I don't have a word for what I am to them, I only know that it's good, whatever it is. And we don't need a word to know that."

"What happened after Josh opened the door?"

I'd been over this so many times I was numb to it, like I was reciting the plot of a movie. "I was relieved, because it meant Joey would leave me alone. I didn't know his name then. So we went up the stairs, I went first, then Josh, and he—Joey—must have blocked the door or something, and we went inside—"

"You went inside first?"

"I went inside and Keith—" I didn't want to remember this part. It was the best moment of the night. "Keith kissed me," I murmured. "He kissed me. We moved to the sofa. And Josh laughed. And they said—I don't know—they were playing with each other, and Josh started to say something and that's when Joey hit him. He fell to the ground, right in the middle of his sentence."

Green pushed a box of tissues across the table.

I took one, trying to get my breathing under control before I had to keep going. "I'm sorry. I know we're all—we all lived, so it's okay, but it was so scary, it was just so scary, and I thought we were going to die and it was my fault—"

"Cameron, why would it be your fault?" He leaned over the corner of the table. "If you didn't invite him in, why would it be your fault?"

"Because he said it was. Because he said if it wasn't for me, he wouldn't have hurt them. He—he wanted to kill me, not them. They were— They just happened to be there. Because of me."

This time it was harder. I attempted to maintain some sense of dignity while blowing my nose and damming up a seemingly never-ending supply of tears, but it still took a few minutes before I could pull myself together.

"I'm sorry," I said again. "The things he said were horrible."

"Tell me more about what he said."

I repeated everything I could think of, and probably said the same things over and over. Green wanted to know which of the victims Joey had spoken about specifically (he never said they were *Joey's* victims, just "the victims"). I told him Joey had seemed fixated on Anderson Philpott, and resented him for fighting back.

We talked about Joey, and his madness, for what felt like an hour. Then, as if in the same flow, Green said, "How do Keith and Josh get along?"

"Really well. Better than most people."

"Do they ever have problems?"

"What kind of problems?"

He waved his pen. (When did he start writing things down again? I hadn't noticed.) "Normal problems. They've been together . . . I think three or four years, they said. Surely they have problems. Or maybe they keep their problems private."

"No. I mean, I don't think they're putting up a front, if that's what you're saying."

"I'm saying all couples have problems, Cameron. How do Josh and Keith handle disagreements?"

"What does this have to do with anything?"

He shrugged. "Maybe it doesn't. But somehow Joseph Rodriguez got into your apartment. You and Josh Walker have both stated that the inner door was still open because you had just walked in, but that the outer door should have been locked. If you didn't invite Rodriguez in, maybe Josh did. Maybe it was a surprise for Keith." His eyebrows went up a little. "Does inviting someone new in sound like the kind of surprise Keith would like, Cameron?"

I could sense the trap, but I couldn't feel its edges, didn't know what would spring it. I fell back on the truth, because it was simplest, and because it was what they'd want. Even though I hated to share anything of them with the detective (or anyone else).

"Josh would never surprise Keith by inviting a stranger in. Never."

"They invited you."

"We were friends first. And I was friends with *both* of them. You don't understand how this works." I bit my lip. I couldn't explain this to him, to anyone. I couldn't find the words to explain how important trust was, how sometimes it was almost tangible in the room, like a ribbon that connected the two of them, with a thin, silken line stretching from them to me.

Green leaned back in his chair. "Hey, I may be old, but I get that you kids live a wilder life than I did at your age."

"*No*. That's not what this is. Listen, everything about this—about having a person with them—everything is about trust. The three of us talked about stuff endlessly, because we had to all be on the same page. You can't—you can't do this stuff without that."

"What stuff, Cameron?"

I shook my head. "Nothing is more important than the two of them. Whatever we do, it begins and ends with them. And Josh wouldn't have invited anyone in without talking about it with Keith.

Not ever. I swear to you, whatever you think, that would have never happened."

"Okay. All right. I hear that. You said that Rodriguez took out Josh first, with one hit?"

Damn it, this again. I'd already tried as hard as I could to remember anything—a sound, a weapon that wasn't the gun—but I couldn't. "I don't know how he did it. No gunshot, we would have heard that. I don't remember anything except Josh falling to the floor. He was talking and then he was on the floor. I thought— For a second I thought he was dead and I couldn't do anything, I couldn't move."

"And Rodriguez said something about Josh?"

"He said he'd taken out the alpha. The alpha male." I was chilled remembering his words, his self-congratulatory tone.

"Was Josh the alpha male?"

"I don't even know what that means, Detective. Do you?"

"Oh, I think I get it a little. Big, swaggering guy, a little bit arrogant, always in control. Does that sound like Josh?"

"Josh lives for two things," I said, because I couldn't say *Yes, he swaggers, and yes, he can be arrogant, and yes, he's always in control.* "He lives for Keith and he lives for QYP. That's it. He's not a bully."

"Does he have a temper?"

"A temper? No, if one of them has a temper—" I stopped myself.

"So Keith has a temper."

"Most people do." I gritted my teeth, feeling that every one of my reactions betrayed them.

"What does Josh do when Keith gets pissed off?"

Ties him up, blindfolds him, and makes him feel until it's the only thing he can think about.

"He takes care of him. Same as you do for anyone you love, I assume."

"I'm just trying to get to the bottom of all this."

"I've already told you everything," I said, somewhat desperately.

"Not everything, I don't think." Green held up a hand. "I have a suspect who claims that he was invited upstairs for a sex party and then the three of you attacked him. He managed to get Josh down, in self-defense, because he thought Josh was going to kill him. He said he knows for a fact that Josh hits Keith, and he said he didn't know how you'd gotten tangled up in all that, but he wanted to help."

I started to open my mouth, but he shook his head.

"When he was examined at the hospital, Keith showed signs of physical abuse, which he explained as consensual acts between himself, his boyfriend, and you. When I ask you, you don't mention anything like that. I need to know what really happened, Cameron. Stop hiding things from me and this will be over a lot faster. I have to arrest Josh if I determine he's assaulted his partner. I don't have a choice. Keith doesn't have a choice. You don't have a choice. Tell me the truth."

I rubbed at my face and forced myself to keep breathing, even though my chest felt tight and my throat hurt. "It's not abuse. They have . . . whips, paddles, things like that. It's the furthest thing from abuse that anything could possibly be. And Joey—" How long had he been watching us? How had he known? "I don't know how he figured that part out, but we didn't invite him anywhere, and he and I aren't friends. He was trying to kill me last night. He was trying to kill them because they got in his way."

"But why wouldn't he just wait until you were alone?"

"I have no idea. Except I think he thought he'd win. I think he thought it was . . . raising the stakes. Killing Philpott raised the stakes. Killing the three of us raised the stakes. But you have to understand, Keith is telling the truth. Please, you have to—you can't arrest Josh. Josh is— Josh only does what Keith asks him to do."

"Cameron, listen to me. I have a young man with obvious signs of physical abuse, and he's a member of a community that has typically smothered that kind of bad press. Don't tell me that's not true, either, because there are statistics and I have them. This young, arguably vulnerable man has an older, bigger, stronger boyfriend, who shows a pattern of inviting other men into their relationship."

"It's not *men*, it's just me—"

"Both of them said there was another man before you," he countered, voice hard.

"But they didn't— That didn't work out. It was one guy and he took off when they—"

Green waited.

"He didn't want what they want."

"Okay. Maybe they came on strong. Maybe it was too much for this other guy. Give me an example. Does Keith hit Josh with this—with whips and paddles and whatever, too?"

"No, that's not what they want."

"What about you?"

"What about me?"

"Do they hit you, Cameron? Is that what they like? Do they enjoy hitting other people?"

"*No*. It's not like that. We do what they want. What *Keith* wants. I mean, Josh likes it too, but Keith is the driving force."

"And the other man they approached didn't like that force."

"No. I guess not."

"But you do."

"I— Yes. I do. I want whatever Keith wants, for as long as he wants it. You don't understand how brave they are. You don't get what it takes to trust people the way they trust each other."

"Do they trust you?"

I closed my eyes, picturing them, trying to feel them as if they were beside me. "The marks on Keith's back were made by a tipped single-tail whip he got Josh for their anniversary, Detective. Did you see them?"

"I saw the pictures."

"Well, I saw it in person, and it was . . . an act of love, of devotion, of beauty."

"It looked like an act of brutality."

"It wasn't. Every time Josh stopped to soothe Keith, Keith's the one who asked for more. Over and over again."

"And you just stood there while all this was going on?"

I wanted to keep this part for myself. It might be the last memory I ever had of them and I wanted to keep it for myself, but I couldn't. Because it might help.

"Keith was in their doorway, holding on to the pull-up bar. Josh was behind him. And I was on my knees. In front of him. *Blowing him*, Detective, while Josh marked up his back. It wasn't brutality."

"They didn't tell me that part."

I knew my cheeks were burning. "Because they wouldn't have wanted to embarrass me, and this does. But I don't care. You can't arrest Josh. Josh is all Keith has, and Keith would never forgive himself." I dashed tears from my eyes again, hating this day, this conversation, and everything that had happened since I left the theater the night before. "And it would be my fault. Because Joey was after me."

"All right." Green put his pen down once more. "I think I have what I need. And they released your apartment."

"Thank you."

He stared at me for a long moment. "Sounds like the Rodriguez kid did a number on your head, Cameron. Don't believe everything gun-wielding nutjobs say when they're trying to kill you. None of this was your fault."

"So you believe me."

"By your own statement and everyone else's statements who I've talked to, you didn't do anything illegal. None of the rest of that stuff is my business."

"And Josh?" I asked warily. "Do you think he did anything illegal?"

"I have a few more people to talk to on that one. I'm gonna need an official statement from you, if you're willing." He waved a hand. "We can start with what happened last night. If I need more than that, I'll call you."

"An official statement."

"You can do it now, or we can make an appointment for tomorrow or the next day, but sooner is better."

The last thing I wanted was to draw this out longer than necessary. Or go home. I checked my phone. I'd already called someone in to take my shift; technically I had the rest of the day off. "Now is fine."

He nodded. "Can I get you a cup of bad coffee? Or a water?"

"Coffee, please."

Three hours later I walked out of La Vista PD into a too-bright, too-cold day. Somehow it wasn't midnight, though according to my body it should have been. My teeth were unbrushed, my stomach was sloshing with coffee, and every time I happened to touch my face I was reminded that it had been well over twenty-four hours since I'd last shaved.

I had absolutely nowhere else to go. I got in the Volvo and drove home.

CHAPTER 22

Nothing about my apartment felt right. I'd cleaned it top to bottom and erased all signs of the night before. I'd have to find a rug to cover the bloodstain on the floor, which I couldn't completely remove. At least it was finally dark by the time I was done.

I'd told Ed I didn't want company each time he asked. I was just closing my three remaining candlesticks in a drawer when my phone rang again. The annoyance hit before I looked at the screen, and then the relief.

"Keith?"

"Oh my god, it's so good to hear your voice. Oh my god, Cam, I can't believe—" His voice dissolved into tears and there was fumbling.

"Cam, you okay?"

Josh. I sank into the nearest chair and pressed my fingers to my eyes, trying not to cry. "I'm not the guy who was knocked out. Are you okay?"

"Fine. Concussion. I've taken a few hard hits, so I guess I pass out real easily now or something." Pause. "I don't know how he got the drop on me. I'm sorry. I should've heard him coming."

"Don't be ridiculous. He's been honing his killing-people skills. We didn't even know we should have been practicing our not-getting-killed skills."

"Yeah, well, I really wish I hadn't left you two alone for all that." His voice moved away from the phone. "Babe, you gotta calm down or they'll come in here and threaten you with a sedative again."

I smiled a little. "People are threatening Keith with sedatives?"

"They have good intentions. But Keith's been lecturing the nursing staff on exactly how healthy his emotional responses are, and how their attempts to muffle him are interfering with his healing. Or something. He's the reason we have temporary phone privileges right now."

Keith's voice in the background rose, and Josh laughed. I pulled my legs up as if I could curl around my heart, protect it from feeling.

"He also gave the police a pretty good lecture on risk-aware consensual kink, which you should have been here for."

For a moment I'd forgotten. "I told them— I probably said too much, but the conclusions they were drawing were so offensive—"

"Hey, we know. Keith almost blew a gasket when someone suggested he was a victim of domestic violence. No, babe, I don't think we really need to rehash—"

"Those fucking bastards!" Keith had clearly taken back the phone. "Plus, you don't get marks like this from any asshole with a whip! Josh is a fucking *expert*, damn it, how dare they— No, I don't need a sedative!"

"Keith," I said. "Keith, talk to me. Calm down and talk to me."

"Sorry. God, I'm so fucked up in the head right now. Cam, I can't stop thinking about it, it's in my head all the time."

"I know. Me too."

"How are you functional, like at all? If I didn't have Josh here basically holding me half the time and letting me freak out the other half, I wouldn't even be upright."

"I cleaned my apartment."

"Aw, you should have waited so we could help."

I wanted them. I wanted to be with them so much it was beginning to feel like a need. Oxygen. Or human contact. Something no one could live without for long. I curled in harder on myself and bit my lips to keep from begging.

"God, I'm so fucking desperate to get out of here, you have no idea. We're supposed to leave soon anyway. I think we could have left earlier, but they wanted to observe Josh a little bit longer." He paused while Josh spoke in the background. "Oh, you're right. Yeah, that was probably bullshit they made up while they tried to decide if I was a battered spouse. Damn it. Listen, why don't you come with us to Josh's folks' house? Have you eaten? His mom's probably going to make enough food to feed most of La Vista."

I needed them, but there was no possible way I could go to Josh's parents' house like this, shaking and afraid. I forced myself to say, "No, it's okay. I have food here."

"Well, yeah, but you could come anyway. The Walkers are great. They'll coddle us and stuff us and totally overreact to everything." He sounded like he was looking forward to it.

"No, it's okay." *Don't cry, don't cry.* If I cried, they would come for me no matter how much I protested, and while part of me ached for them, a far more rational part of me needed them to not see me like this, huddled on my sofa, trembling, all the lights on.

I looked like a madman.

"Josh says it's no big deal. We can pick you up on our way to his folks' place."

"I'll be fine here." The words choked me. My throat ached as I said them.

Sounds over the line. "Are you absolutely sure you don't want to come over, Cam?"

"Absolutely sure," I repeated. I shoved my fist in my mouth and bit down hard.

"The doctor's coming in, hopefully to set us free. Promise me you'll stay inside where you're safe tonight? I can't even deal with the thought of you getting hurt."

I was going to cry. I could feel it rising in me, about to boil over. I mustered one final moment of composure. "Sure. Take care."

"Love you, Cam. From Josh, too."

Click.

The exchange rate of grief was unpredictable and extreme. When Keith hung up the phone, his casual *Love you, Cam* still echoing in my ear, I felt as if my last lifeline to the world had been severed. I cried as I lurched up from the sofa. I cried as I turned out all the lights, then scared myself with thoughts of what might be lurking in the dark and turned them back on.

I wept into my knees in the corner of my shower with the water on as hot as I could stand. When I had to get out, because the water had run cold, I was absolutely convinced that if I left my bathroom, Joey Rodriguez would be standing there with his gun and that huge, terrifying grin on his face, waiting to kill me.

I'd forgotten my pajamas, which under normal circumstances meant that I'd be a little cold as I rooted around in my dresser. But tonight it was unbearable. I stood at the bathroom door for a long, long time, shivering in my towel, trying to convince myself to go out.

He couldn't be there. He was in jail. And even if he wasn't in jail, I was behind two locked doors. He couldn't get in. Except what if he had a key? Had I left my keys anywhere? Could he have copies? Maybe that's how he'd gotten in last night, maybe he had a copy of the door key—

Except I never left my keys anywhere. They were on my dresser until I put them in my pocket, and in my pocket until I put them on my dresser.

And he hadn't had a key.

And even if he had, the cops would have taken it as evidence, so that was that. He hadn't had a key, but if he had, it was locked up in the police station right now.

Joey Rodriguez was not in my house.

But it was so fucking hard to open the door. My hand went numb on the knob before I could convince myself to do it. If I'd had more towels, I would have made a nest in the bathtub, an idea that sounded far more reasonable than opening the bathroom door.

Finally, eventually, I realized that if he had gotten in my home, I would have been far easier to kill in the shower, totally unaware, than I would be out in the apartment, which had already proven to have weapons strewn about. The bathroom door wasn't locked. He could have just walked in.

Clearly he wasn't actually in my apartment. Even though it felt like he was.

What they never tell you about your instincts, about the powerful primitive part of your brain that tells you when to fight and when to run like hell, is that sometimes it fails you. Sometimes your entire body *knows* you're about to die, but you aren't.

I crouched on the floor of my bathroom and opened the door very, very slowly. The hallway was empty. I was glad I'd left all the lights on; I could see the kitchen and half of the living room, both of which were empty.

My heart felt like it was drumming right out of my chest. I eased out into the hall and listened closely. Nothing. No sounds in my apartment.

I checked every closet, every cabinet, behind every curtain. I looked under my bed. Then I did another round, in case someone was there and had somehow eluded me the first time. My phone had died again. I plugged it in, but left it powered down. I doubted I'd need my alarm to wake up before eight.

Locking the bedroom door and hiding under my covers didn't make me feel safe. I fell asleep at one point and woke up, sweating, from a nightmare in which Joey kicked Josh's body again and again and I couldn't move to save him. Keith wasn't there. It was just me, and Joey, and Josh's body taking blows.

I ran to the bathroom and dry heaved into the toilet, but then I had to go through the entire apartment again to prove that no one was there. And even though it was stupid, ugly-stupid, unforgivably ludicrous, I grabbed one of Mom's candlesticks and brought it into the bedroom with me, behind the door I closed and locked and pushed a chair against.

I was grateful when the sun finally came up.

CHAPTER 23

Ed was waiting for me outside the theater in the morning.

I eyed him as I unlocked the front doors. "Shouldn't you be at work?"

"My excuse is interviewing the victim of a violent crime, if anyone asks." He hugged me tightly. "Are you okay? What the hell am I saying, of course you're not."

"I'm fine, Ed, really." I felt better with my keys in hand, deactivating the alarm, unlocking the booth, booting up the computers. "Josh and Keith took real hits. I'm fine."

"Yeah, I'm on my way to the center after this."

I stopped everything. "QYP is open? They're *working* today? They got out of the hospital like twelve hours ago!"

Ed rolled his eyes. "You can talk."

"I didn't have a concussion!"

"Cam, come on. You should be recovering or something."

"I am recovering. My job's not actually that strenuous."

"Detective Green said you were a little roughed up, too."

That had been one of the worst parts of the statement. Removing my shirt, letting them take pictures of the couple of bruises I'd gotten from the fight. Impossible to ignore them when they were right there on my skin.

"What else did he say?"

Ed shot me a baffled look. "Off the record, Joey Rodriguez is fucking nuts. On the record, they're investigating a suspect who may have a connection to a string of local beatings. Not murders, *beatings*."

He followed me as I turned everything on, got coffee brewing, unlocked the doors for the early staff. When I returned to the booth,

Ed took his usual seat and I took mine. The routine was supposed to be making me feel safe and secure, but in truth I felt a bit nauseous instead.

Ed cleared his throat. "You not talking is beginning to weird me out."

"I don't know what to say."

"You could tell me what happened, if you want. If it would help."

"Don't you mean you're dying to know?" His wince told me both that I'd hurt him, and that I was right.

"I really want it to be him. I want this to be over. Alisha keeps telling me that if I let things take over my life like this, it won't matter when they end because there will always be something else, but I want to prove her wrong."

I thought that sounded pretty accurate, but I didn't say anything.

He shook his head slightly. "I'd met him before. Joey Rodriguez. That's why he looked familiar the night we saw him leaving here. It's probably why he left so fast. I work with his dad at the paper."

"Really?" What a strange, small world.

"Yeah, uh, he was kind of my mentor. Or maybe he still is, though after this— I don't know if you ever get over finding out your kid's a murderer. Especially if you've been reporting on his murders for like ten months. And the kid, Joey, was friends with Philpott, or at least they knew each other."

I shuddered. "He had no friends. I don't think he even had the capacity for friends."

"So you think it's him, Cam? No doubt?"

"He told us he was fixing the community. He was weeding out everyone who didn't belong."

"Huh." Ed nodded. "The drag king, the trans woman. Stephanie Hawkins was bisexual, that might have pissed him off. Felipe Farraway was flamboyant, I guess. But what about you and Steven Costello?"

"I read books and think I'm better than everyone else," I said. "I'm not sure about Steven Costello, except that he was scared, which Joey found offensive. Joey seemed to have a very narrow, limited idea of what being a gay man looked like. 'A proud gay man,' he said."

He looked a little green. "You're kidding."

"No. He was culling the herd. He was a . . . separatist, I guess. A gay male separatist. And everyone who didn't fit in with his idea of what was 'natural' needed to be destroyed."

"That's creepy as hell. You know, the only time I ever spoke to him, he said something weird, about simplicity. About how he was old-fashioned, that all he wanted was a beer and a hot guy."

My chest tightened and I forced myself to breathe. "Apparently my failure to want either of those things offended him. I'm not sure why he went after Philpott except that by then it was about something else, almost like he got hooked on it. Instead of needing more drugs for the high, he needed a harder target."

"Cam—I am *so* sorry this happened. Like, I can't even imagine how scary it must have been."

Still is. How scary it still is.

"I'm fine, and Keith and Josh are fine, and for a while there I thought none of us were going to survive, so it's good. It's all good." I couldn't pull off the phrase, but Ed let it slide.

"I think we're going to postpone our trip. So you know, you should come over Saturday. Have dinner with us."

"Why?"

"Cam. Saturday is Christmas Eve."

"Oh." Christmas Eve. Right, of course, right where it always was. And Christmas the following day. The full picture came into focus. "What? No, you and Alisha are going out of town for the holiday. You told me that."

"We were going to, but we don't *have* to. We could go just as easily some other weekend."

"Absolutely not, Ed. I'll be fine. I'm already fine. There's no reason to delay your trip and I flat-out refuse to come over, so if you do, you'll have wasted it."

"Cam—"

"I'm fine. We're showing *It's a Wonderful Life* like we do every year, and I'll eat snack foods, and make myself sick. It's a good tradition, and I'm not interrupting it so you can feel better about me being alone."

He sat back in the chair. "Alisha said that's what you'd say. More or less."

"Well, it's true. I'm fine."

"Come on, Cam. You can't be 'fine' like nothing happened."

"Maybe I'm lucky that way. Now go back to work. If you get fired over this, I'll be irritated."

"Yeah, okay. But first I have to fix something, so hold still."

I held still, and when he started unbuttoning my waistcoat I went even more still. My heart began to race and I could feel heat under my skin, as if Ed's proximity burned. I stared at the blue wall behind him and held the shade in my mind so it couldn't slip away.

"Your buttons are skewed and it's been bugging me the whole time. There. Better."

He backed off. Which meant I could breathe.

"Fine, I'll go. But I don't believe you're fine, so you better return my texts when I check in or I'm coming back here."

"I will."

We hugged. He was the wrong person to hug; doing it only made me feel a little less stable, a little more distant.

"Take care of yourself, Cameron."

"Of course I will," I lied.

Ed went away and I went, blessedly, to work.

I wanted so desperately to find an excuse to go down to the drop-in center on Monday that I forced myself not to. Nothing I wanted this much could be healthy, and I couldn't escape the notion that I was bad for them, that I'd called this down on them. Keith and I exchanged a flurry of text messages late in the day, and I hoped they might decide to visit me unannounced, which would save me the agony of deciding, until I realized that they were returning to Mr. and Mrs. Walker's for at least another night.

I felt gutted. The ritual of checking the house for intruders took longer. I kept thinking I'd missed something, or heard something, and I'd have to start over. It was better, I told myself. Better that they stay away from me, and I them. Better that they not see me this way: skittish, jumping at car doors slammed too hard, or shouts on the street. I drifted in and out of sleep, nightmares, sometimes realizing that the sound of the candlestick hitting flesh was really a bass line in a car driving down Mooney, sometimes jolting out of bed before I knew I was awake.

The next morning it was harder to fake "okay," but Ed didn't stop by, so there were fewer people who needed to believe it. On the whole, I decided I was fine. I was managing.

I'd dodged a phone call from Hugh Reynolds, but in the afternoon he called again and left a brief message: "Unless you want me to drive to the theater and stand there until you talk to me, call me back."

He was a therapist, and probably a good one, but his habit of being both nosy and overbearing was a lot older than his license. After my first boyfriend broke up with me, Hugh had come out to the theater one night, bought a ticket to whatever we were showing, then sat in the booth with me through the whole thing. We hadn't talked. He just sat there, beside me, watching the movie on the monitor. At the end he'd given me an awkward hug and said good-bye.

I called, resigned, and suffered through a volley of questions I recognized as testing my psychological well-being. I answered them honestly, but in as few words as possible. Yes, I had experienced nightmares. Yes, I'd had a few flashbacks. No, I wasn't thinking of harming myself or anyone else. Yes, my body was healing just fine, practically healed.

"How are your friends? They're the ones I met, aren't they? The paper named them, but I couldn't recall."

"They're the ones you met. Josh had a concussion, and Keith had a cut on his face, but they're fine."

Hugh exhaled on the line. "PTSD is a real thing, and the right therapist can talk you through it."

"I know it's a real thing, but I'm sure I don't need therapy, Hugh. It was all over so fast." I wanted this to be true, I willed it to be true, even though every time I was in my apartment it felt like it was happening again, endlessly repeating.

"I think you're in denial. Do you feel vulnerable all the time? Like the world is a thousand times more dangerous than it was before?"

"It— Yes. It feels that way. I know it isn't."

"In a sense, it is. Or rather, before you didn't know how dangerous it really was, and now you do." He paused. "Cameron, I know how you're feeling. Please contact me if you need anything. Day or night.

My phone is always on and I'm telling you, I've been there. You have to find a way to feel safe again."

"I'm fine," I murmured.

"You *will be* fine. But right now I'd be very surprised if you were anything even remotely resembling 'fine.'"

"I'll live, then. I need to go back to work."

"Liar."

I smiled. "Thank you for calling."

"It's so easy to feel alone, Cameron, for men like you and me. You aren't alone. Don't isolate yourself reflexively; it makes it so much harder to ask for help when you need it."

"Bye, Hugh."

"Good-bye."

I'd meant to go down to QYP that day, but I was too exhausted after the call with Hugh, so instead I sat in the theater and watched whatever we were showing (one of the big movies of two summers before). It seemed like a good idea until I realized that once people started filling in the rest of the seats, I was too paralyzed to move and too unsettled to enjoy the movie. He could be any of those people, any of those silhouettes. Joey Rodriguez could, even now, be sitting in my theater, laughing at the funny parts, gasping at the scary parts.

How many times had I sold him a ticket and missed the hungry way his eyes took me in? How many times had he sat here in the dark, thinking about how he wanted to hurt me?

I waited until every single human being had left the theater. Then I walked out as quickly as I could and went to my apartment, where I spent another near-sleepless night jumping at random noises and shadows and dreams.

Keith: *You okay?*

Keith: *I think you aren't okay.*

Keith: *You keep saying you'll come down to see us, but it's Thursday and you haven't.*

Keith: *Cam? You there?*

Cameron: *I'm here. I'm okay.*

Cameron: *Just keep getting overwhelmed.*
Cameron: *But I'm fine.*
Keith: *When are you working today?*
Cameron: *Closing.*
Keith: *Okay, we'll come over.*
Cameron: *You don't have to do that, I'm okay.*
Keith: *We miss you.*
Keith: *Don't you miss us?*
Keith: *Cam?*
Keith: *Cam, where'd you go?*
Keith: *<3 <3 <3*
Keith: *Cam?*

Ed and Alisha had stopped by to bring me dinner before they took off on their holiday weekend. I'd gotten a few phone calls from people—Zane, Jaq, Obie—checking in, which was nice, I guess, though every time someone checked in made it harder to forget all of it had happened.

I shouldn't have ignored Keith's texts. But seeing them made me want to cry, and I couldn't cry in the ticket booth. I left my phone in my pocket on vibrate. Then I turned it to silent so I would stop thinking about Keith, and Josh, and how I'd keep it together if they visited.

The nine o'clock movie was just letting out when they slipped inside. I was aware of them, but pretended not to be, helping concessions close, telling a few people what movies we'd be showing next week. When I allowed myself to notice them, from across the room, they were standing under the *White Christmas* poster, as if they'd planned it, as if they were highlighting how much I'd lost. Christmas was a time for grief, and it looked like this year would be no exception.

I walked over, taking steady breaths, trying to keep my face calm when I wanted to throw myself at them.

"You *are not* okay," Keith whispered harshly. "Oh my god, Cam."

"Hey." Josh put an arm around him, but kept looking at me.

"I'm almost done if you want to stay for a few minutes." I couldn't meet their eyes.

"Yeah," Josh said.

"Okay."

A few of my staff waved hello to them when they went to sit on the sofas while we closed. I couldn't bring myself to give them keys this time. What if he was upstairs right now? He wasn't, he wasn't, I knew he wasn't, he was in jail (a fact I'd confirmed with Detective Green every day since Sunday), so he couldn't be upstairs, *but what if he was?*

It was exactly like I'd pictured it the first time: the camera rolled backward as we walked toward it, me, then Keith, then Josh, up the narrow staircase, me unlocking the door (testing it to make sure it was still locked first), holding it open for them.

I bit down hard on my tongue as I shut it quickly and locked it, not breathing until the dead bolt slammed home.

"Oh my god, why didn't you come see us?" Keith hugged me fiercely. "Every day you say you will and then you don't."

"I'm sorry."

"Don't be sorry." He tugged me to the sofa. "Shit, it's hard being here, Cam. Are you going out of your mind?"

"I cleaned. A lot. Cleaning helped." That wasn't a lie. It had helped—a little. A very little.

Josh sat on my other side. "Do you guys want to talk about it? It might be cathartic or something."

"No," I said, as Keith was saying, "Maybe someday."

"Yeah, all right." Josh's hand reached out to rub my back, and now I was biting so hard—on my tongue, my cheek, whatever I could get between my teeth—that I tasted blood. "Cam, you're all kinds of tense."

"I'm okay." I twisted away from him, afraid that if he kept doing that I'd dive into his arms and fall apart. I had to stay calm so they wouldn't know. I needed them not to know how scared I was all the time. I needed to not be more of a problem for them than I had been already.

"Cam," Josh said. "What's up?"

"Nothing. Do you guys want anything to drink? Or no, I don't—I don't really have much."

Keith shifted, pulling his legs up so he could face me. "We don't want anything. I mean, except for you to look at us and stuff."

"We finally gained release from the convalescent care of Dr. and Mr. Walker, so we're heading home. Why don't you come with us?"

Home. Their apartment, which I'd so vividly pictured when I was in the police station giving my statement. The apartment I'd unwittingly led Joey to. I shook my head.

"I'm so tired. I just—I need to get some sleep. That's all."

"Are you sleeping okay?" Keith asked after a few seconds, in which I thought both of them were trying not to argue with me. "I wake up a lot. I really—you know—I really freak out a lot in general right now."

"It's not freaking out." Josh reached across me for Keith's hand. "The doctor said it would take a while before you were on an even keel again."

"Yeah, I know. But in my head, it definitely *feels* like freaking out. They gave me some pills that are supposed to help with sleeping. Do you want a few, Cam?"

"No, thank you." Because what if I was so deeply asleep I didn't hear him moving in the apartment? He could kill me in my sleep. No. He wouldn't be in the apartment. He was in jail. He was still in jail. I had the sudden urge to call the police department and ask someone to confirm.

"Cam," Josh said. "Come home with us."

"I can't." I wanted to. I'd been waiting all week for them to go home so I could retreat to the security of their apartment, the perfect comfort of their voices, their bodies. But now that it was real, I just wanted them to go, so they'd be safe, so they'd be out of the line of fire. Having them in my apartment felt like tempting the fates to try again.

He reached out with his other hand, and I knew he was about to take mine like he'd taken Keith's, but I couldn't let him. I scrambled up, breaking through their arms, heart pounding. Had I heard something in the bedroom? No. No, I hadn't, I couldn't have. No one was here but us.

"You guys should go," I said, with all the firmness I could muster. "I've been going to bed early, so . . ." There. That sounded reasonable.

Now leave before he comes out here. No, he was in jail. Jail. Jail, damn it. He wasn't in the bedroom. He wasn't lying in wait.

He wasn't going to kill me the second the door shut behind them, but on the off chance he was, I wanted them safely on the other side.

"This doesn't feel right," Keith murmured. He stood. "You're jumpy. Why are you jumpy?"

"I'm just tired."

"Because I'm jumpy, and I know why, but you're acting like nothing even happened."

"I'm trying not to think about it too much. And I'm tired. You know." *Please leave before I disgrace myself. Please leave before he hurts you again.*

Josh stood as well, and they moved toward the front door. It took all my strength and resolve not to cry. This was what I wanted, what I needed: them outside and safe. It was my only goal. I couldn't go with them. I was the one who put them in danger.

"Love you." Keith kissed me. "And I'm not fooled, like even a little. I know you're all fucked up. When you want to talk about it, I'm here."

"Thanks."

Josh took my face in his hands and said nothing at all. He kissed me, and I couldn't look into his beautiful eyes, eyes that had reminded me of the kinds of things in my life that had never let me down, never wavered.

I locked the door behind them and utterly lost control, muffling myself in my arms until I was sure they were gone. I took another one of my habitual showers, and when the water went cold, I let it. I couldn't feel. I didn't care. Only when I was stiff and shaking did I get out, wrapping myself in a towel. I didn't hesitate. This time I opened the bathroom door and said, "Kill me if you want to. Go ahead."

No one was there.

I fell, still wet, into bed.

Three hours later I woke up, panicked, from a dream in which Josh had been awake, and both he and Keith had been on their knees, begging for their lives. I didn't understand how I could move around but I wasn't trying to help them—until I realized I was the one they were begging. I was the one trying to kill them.

I got dressed, went downstairs, took a stack of emergency blankets out of the cabinet, and went to sleep in the booth.

CHAPTER 24

K eith texted me all day on Friday. I could tell he was trying to make sure I was okay, so I kept responding, even though every text I sent felt more dishonest. I wasn't okay. It wasn't okay to jump whenever someone wanted to buy tickets. It wasn't okay to dry heave in the bathroom because a car backfired outside and for a second I thought Joey was shooting.

I didn't have to google *PTSD* to be pretty sure that's what was happening, but knowing it didn't help.

Of course they invited me over. And of course I said no. I went to the grocery store, which was too bright, too loud, with far too many colors, and bought enough almond milk and bread and peanut butter to last me for days. I didn't have to leave the apartment Saturday unless I wanted to. Or Sunday. We'd show *It's a Wonderful Life* at two and *White Christmas* at six. When it was over, we'd close for the night. But the weekend staff—who'd volunteered to work Christmas Eve and Christmas, same as they did every year—could handle it without me. We had a few gallons of eggnog and dozens of cookies to give out to the people who made our holiday showings a family tradition.

My parents had loved it. All my Christmas memories were in the theater. I'd neglected to decorate this year, but someone had managed it: the ticket booth was bedecked with shiny green garlands, and concessions had had a holiday makeover as well, with little holly berries and menorahs and a symbol I didn't recognize but figured by process of elimination probably related to Kwanzaa.

The theater, like a living organism, had a life of its own, a role to play in the lives of people, in the town itself. I, Cameron, despite owning the Rhein, was largely redundant.

I told Keith good night early so he'd think I was going to bed, then ate a peanut butter and jelly sandwich sitting at my bedroom window, waiting to see the staff go home. When everyone was gone, I ventured downstairs. The ticket booth was an uncomfortable place to sleep, but at least when I woke up with a stiff neck and an aching back, I knew I'd actually slept.

Saturday. The first Saturday after the Cary Grant Film Festival ended. Christmas Eve.

Hiding in the apartment was a stupid idea. I was growing slowly to hate the apartment, where I never felt safe anymore. I was growing to hate myself.

I dressed in a good suit, put on a mistletoe pin someone had given me as a joke, and made myself a fixture in the lobby. I lingered, hoping to see them walk in. Keith liked Jimmy Stewart; I maintained a fantasy that they closed the drop-in center and came to the theater for *It's a Wonderful Life* long after the movie started playing. I drank way too much coffee. I couldn't find a place where I felt comfortable sitting for longer than five minutes. The ticket booth was off-limits because my staff was using it, concessions was running fine without me cluttering it up, and the back office was so stuffed with boxes and other "storage" items that I couldn't even get the door all the way open.

I should clean it. Maybe use it as an office again. Or, my mind continued ruthlessly, I could move in there, put up a camp bed and a hot plate. Since it seemed more and more clear that my apartment was about to become a glorified closet and pantry.

In the end, the old projector booth was the best place to hide. It was no good as a permanent living arrangement (the floor sloped, and my parents had been relatively certain that the ceiling was full of asbestos), but I could hide there for a little while.

I fell asleep. Not too long. I fell asleep sitting in my dad's old chair, drooling on my suit.

When I was somewhat awake and presentable, I went down into the lobby, but by then *White Christmas* was clearing out. Eight thirty. I sent Iliana home early and started helping close. I could have sent all of them home and done the rest of the tasks, which would have at the very least killed some time, but I thought they might find it odd. The weekend staff were old-timers, and I didn't like them to wonder if I was all right, so I put up a significantly better front than I'd been able to for Keith and Josh.

It worked, too. I even fooled myself for a little while. I was on my knees, spraying down the display case, when a perfectly normal thing happened. Someone came up beside me to ask a question. An entirely mundane event: "Do you need anything, Cameron?"

The sudden, unexpected proximity of another human being so startled me—terrified me—that I yelped and fell backward, the spray bottle shooting out of my hands while I scrambled away in a clumsy crab crawl.

Toni, who certainly hadn't meant to scare me, took a step back. "Sorry. Floors are done. Anything else?" Her eyes took in my sprawl, but she didn't mention it.

I knew it would make the rounds of the weekend staff, but hoped it wouldn't penetrate all the way to the relatively newer (more in awe of me) weekday staff.

"No. Thank you." I got up and brushed myself off, heart pounding, aware that now the red *Sandwiches and Snacks* sign was a dirty gray. My skin was tingling and saliva flooded my mouth. "No," I said again, and bolted for the bathroom.

Since I hadn't eaten, there wasn't much in the way of stomach contents, just bile and acid. When the wave passed, I dried my eyes as well as I could (I hadn't cried again, but being sick brought on its own kind of tears), and made my way back out.

They made a good show of not having been talking about me, but of course they had been. I pretended not to notice the extra attention of their looks. Ten minutes later everyone was gone and I was standing outside my securely locked theater, wondering if I should give up and go back inside.

My apartment. My parents had helped me paint it. The window in the bedroom still had a roller mark from where Mom had slipped while doing the wall. There was a scuff on the hardwood in front of the fridge where Dad and I had come down too hard when sliding the fridge into place and gouged the floor. Suddenly I was bitterly angry that the safest place in my world was now the most frightening.

I had to take it back. I unlocked the outer door (and shut it firmly behind me). I walked up the stairs. I unlocked the inner door. I locked it behind me. I stood there in my living room, damn it, full of my things, my gorgeous red velvet sofa, my deep-indigo curtains—

And started hyperventilating almost immediately. I'd stood here. He'd come in through the door, at first standing in the shadows, then emerging, right there. He'd had a gun, and I'd seen it so close I could still picture it, I could still remember how it smelled when it fired. Even better than the sound, I remembered the slightly acrid smell, the way my taste buds wanted to recoil from it.

I held him down right there, *right there*, near the dining table, behind the sofa. I could almost still see us. I could almost still see Keith with Josh's head in his lap. I could still hear him crying.

Something moved. No.

Yes.

Something moved in the corner of my eye and I spun around, but nothing was there, of course nothing was there, but something had moved, hadn't I seen something move?

I slid to the ground and pulled my knees to my chest, too afraid to go anywhere else.

I couldn't do this. I couldn't do this right now. I couldn't stay here, hiding in a corner of my own apartment.

Back to the theater, then. The booth. I knew I should eat. I hadn't eaten. I could make a sandwich. Or I could drive somewhere. What was open Christmas Eve? Not much. I could drive around. I could drive out to the pier and stand there and think about Josh, and Keith, and how we'd walked there once, weeks ago. It would be cold and dark and I wouldn't be distracted by the lack of color in the world.

Or.

I could go to them.

My chest began to loosen up at the thought. I could go to them. I knew they were not overly religious about the holidays (I'd asked Josh), so it wouldn't be like I was intruding on traditions.

Maybe it would be.

It was a bad idea. It was a bad idea, the worst, far worse than going down to the drop-in center in broad daylight, a plan I'd made and scrapped so frequently in the last week that all the arguments played out in my head without meaning.

I should go. I can act normal for an hour, then they won't worry.

I can't go. I'll lose it if I even see them. I'll lose it if they hug me. If they even come near me.

I have to go. I have to show that everything's fine.

I can't go. Everything isn't fine, and the minute they see me, they'll know.

I was ruining my suit, sitting on the ground, crying on it, puking while wearing it. Sweating the ugly sweat of fear and despair. I shoved my fist in my mouth to keep from screaming—for a second I didn't think I'd be able to stop myself—and once I'd bitten down, I couldn't help biting down harder.

I needed it all to stop. Biting helped, but I couldn't chew on my hand all night.

This was bad. But I needed to see them, and if I couldn't hold it together, I'd have to hope they would be too kind to kick me out. It was barely 10 p.m. and I couldn't stand the idea of an entire night, an entire twelve hours, with nothing in the middle of it except nightmares.

I'd take them their *Project Runway* DVDs. I could return them, and they'd have me in, and maybe I could find a way of asking if I could stay the night on their sofa. I knew I'd actually sleep if I wasn't in the apartment, and while I could stay in the booth again, it was cold, and loud, and I was afraid to stand up or move around, because I didn't want anyone to see me and call the police. I couldn't crouch on the floor of the booth for twelve hours, anyway.

It would be fine. Once they were asleep I could have my little fit, quietly, and they wouldn't have to know. I just needed to keep it together until then.

But a blanket, and a sofa, and a place where there were other people nearby, where there had never been a man with a gun. Where every sound didn't remind me of him, where I didn't see things out of the corners of my eyes.

I had a plan. I dusted myself off and splashed water on my face (in the kitchen, because I couldn't afford to be stuck in the bathroom right now). I put the DVDs in a cloth grocery bag. I had my keys. I put on my overcoat.

My eyes teared up as I went down the stairs because I so clearly remembered the first time I'd let them in, the first time they'd come over, when we'd lit candles in my mother's candlesticks. They'd fit perfectly into my space, not disrupting it at all. I'd seen it as great tidings that I had friends who so eased into my life that I couldn't remember the line, before which they had been strangers and after which they were friends.

It all seemed innocent and lost now. I started the Volvo with shaking hands and waited until the heater was blasting hot air to pull away from the curb.

They weren't there.

I slid in the door when someone else went in. I was grateful for the suit, and the coat, and my general appearance as "unthreatening middle-class white male," and I wondered, if I'd been Josh, if I would have received the same smile, the same "Oh, of course, go right ahead." I went right ahead, to their door, where I knocked again in case they hadn't heard the buzzer.

I didn't text. I leaned, then I sat, and I considered texting or calling, but no, the moment I did that I was committed.

They weren't home, which might be a sign that this was a very bad idea. It was almost certainly a sign. QYP had been closed for over an hour. There was no reason for them to be gone right now. So. This was a sign.

But still, I waited. I had nothing else to do. Nowhere else to go. I waited until eleven. Then I waited until it was nearly midnight.

They were at Josh's parents', of course. They were probably spending the night. Mr. and Mrs. Walker (or was it Dr. and Mr. Walker?) were the type of people who really *did* Christmas. Maybe they had some grand breakfast planned, all hands on deck, everyone with a job to do, gathering at the same moment to share in a feast at a big table, with more food than the four of them could eat. No, wait, hadn't they said there was more family than that? Josh probably had cousins and aunts and uncles, all of them gathering at this table, taking part in the holidays, in tradition, in ritual.

In family.

I rubbed my eyes again and finally forced myself to stand. I couldn't sleep in the hallway leaning against their door. It was pathetic, and eventually someone would call the police. I'd find myself in the conference room again, trying to explain myself. Trying to tell the story in a way that didn't make me seem desperate and crazy, though it was coming up on an hour and a half of sitting there, so "desperate and crazy" was, at this point, the baseline of my behavior.

I'd managed to create a bubble of heat with my body hunched over my knees. It popped the second I stood up, and I was shivering as I walked two flights of stairs to the ground floor. Slowly. I shuddered when the first blast of wind hit me. This was it. I looked both ways down the street, but no, they weren't just now approaching.

They weren't coming home.

I could text, but at this point I needed to forget I'd ever been here if I wanted to maintain any shred of dignity still remaining. I braced myself and made slow tracks down the sidewalk. Parking was about the same as always in downtown La Vista; I was a block and a half away, but grateful to not be on some side street up a hill.

I could sleep in the Volvo. The Volvo was safe. But no, too cold. And while in the ticket booth I was a little cold and a little worried someone might see me if I moved around too much, I still had access to a bathroom, to running water. In my car I wouldn't have any of that, and I was pretty sure I'd end up in the conference room at the police station if I was busted on Christmas, asleep in my car.

The keys were warm in my hand for half a block. Then they were cold, so cold, like they sucked in the chill wind and transmitted it through my fingers. I'd be numb by the time I finally got to where I'd parked. Numb, and trying to unlock the car, though at least the heater still worked—

"*Cameron!*"

My heart stopped, stuttered, restarted.

"*Cam! Wait up!*"

No. I was dreaming. I was imagining this. I would turn around and they wouldn't be there. They couldn't be there. It was too ridiculous, the timing too convenient. (Though it would have been a hell of a lot more convenient if they'd showed up when I was still marginally warm.)

No.

Except.

"Cam! Cam, wait up!"

I waited. I held my breath. I turned around.

They were jogging. Not just walking briskly—actually jogging toward me. But it was them. No amount of blinking made them dissolve.

"Oh my god, what're you doing?" Keith slammed into me and held me up all at once. "I thought you were going to keep walking!"

"I thought you were a dream."

"What? No way. We are so not a dream. We're for real, look." He kissed me, to prove his realness.

I leaned my head into his neck and started crying.

"Damn it," I heard Josh say. "I knew it. I knew I should have made him come home with us. *Damn it.*"

"Well, he's here now." Keith rubbed my back. "Come on, Cam. Come upstairs. It's okay, you can keep crying, but let's get you a little bit warmer."

I didn't want to look at them, and I resented the lights of the building, the stairs, the hallway I'd recently left.

I fell to my knees the second we were inside and said, "Please don't make me go back there tonight. Please. I can't." Then I was sobbing too hard to speak, and Keith was hugging me and Josh's hand was in my hair and absolutely nothing else had any meaning in the world but the two of them holding me in place, making me real.

CHAPTER 25

W hen I could breathe again, Keith pulled me up and pushed me onto the sofa, then climbed on top to sit in my lap, straddling me, eyes all over my body like he was searching for everything I hid.

"What is *wrong* with you? Why didn't you call me?"

"Keith, let Cam have a minute before he tells us what's up." Josh turned away, muttering, "I fucking *knew* it."

He came back with steaming mugs of almond milk hot cocoa. Keith shifted to the side so he was sitting more stably, but his legs were still over mine, almost as if he expected me to run away.

"We were at Josh's mom and dad's house for Christmas Eve dinner," Keith said. "That way we get out of Christmas Day."

"Though we usually end up over there later anyway, but we aren't obligated to be there for the gifts in the morning."

"Yeah." Keith nudged me. "If we'd known you were here, we could have come and gotten you. When's the last time you ate?"

The idea of facing people made me want to dive into my cocoa.

"Or we could have left earlier," Josh added. "Cam. Talk to us."

It should have been easy, the relief of confession, a pouring out of sins and secrets until I felt cleansed in their wake, a catharsis of words and shared burdens.

It was nothing like that. I didn't want to tell them too much. I thought I could simply apologize and that would be enough. But everything I said seemed only to be the tip of something else, and finally I was forced to explain all of it, what I'd said to the detective, how I'd revealed more than I wanted to reveal, how scared I was for them, how sorry I was that I'd gotten them caught up in it, how much I'd missed them, longed for them. After a silence that should have marked the end of my confession, I told them more. About hiding in the bathroom that first night, knowing that if I left it, Joey would be there and he'd kill me. About how my house felt haunted by him, that every sound was him coming for me, every shadow was him lying in wait.

It was difficult. I'd always imagined that once you started talking the words would just flow, a broken dam letting all the water through, but perhaps my dam was too thick, too wide. I merely sprang leaks, here and there, and through each crack I had to force the words until the pressure was finally off.

I told them about the nightmare where they were begging me for their lives, and Josh wrapped his arms around me so I could cry into his shoulder.

"But we were here the whole time," Keith said softly, sounding sad and grieved.

Josh's hand smoothed up and down my back. "Cam's not used to thinking like that, babe. But it's okay. We'll teach him."

I shook my head. "You can't. It's—it's dangerous. You should stay away from me. I brought back your *Project Runway* DVDs, and you—you shouldn't—you can never go back to my apartment, because I don't want him to kill you too—" I knew these were the kinds of things I shouldn't say out loud, but in the moment I couldn't stop myself. I was far more concerned for their safety than I was for my sanity.

"Cameron." Josh kissed my forehead, my cheeks. "He's gone. He's locked up. Listen to me." He kissed my lips. "He's not coming back. He killed six people."

I wanted to believe him, but I could hear the doubt in my voice. And the fear. "What if they can't prove that, though?"

"They'll prove it. They'll hold him for what he did to us, and they'll make their case for what he did to everyone else." He kissed me again. "I knew I should have pushed it when you said you didn't want to come with us. Damn it. Every instinct in my body was telling me to push it, but I didn't want to like—you know. I didn't want to *force* you, even though I knew you needed me to. Goddamn it."

"Every instinct in my body was telling me that Joey was in the bedroom and I had to get you out of there so he couldn't hurt you."

"Aw, Cam—" He kissed my forehead again and held me to him.

"But—" Keith's voice came from the darkness on the other side of my eyelids. "If you thought he was there, then what'd you think he was going to do to you once we left?" He paused. "Oh my *god*. You fucking *idiot*! I'm going to kill you myself, you jerk, how could you think that way?"

Then Keith was pressed up against my back, and I thought I'd emptied all my secrets out, that I was free of them, that sharing them would magically make everything all right.

Except it wasn't quite all of them. Not yet.

"I needed you to be safe. I needed to protect you. Because all of it was my fault. And because—because I love you, both of you, even if—if for you it's something else, that's what it is for me, so I knew I had to keep you safe. I'm sorry. I'm so sorry."

"You"—Keith thumped a fist down on my back—"are"—*thump*—"so"—*thump*—"irritating. Nothing was your fault. Are you talking about all that crap he said when he was telling us how he'd kill us? Because seriously, Cam, your bullshit detectors need realignment if you really took all that as truth."

Josh's hands framed my face, but I refused to look at him. "We love you too, Cam."

"As I've, like, actually *said*," Keith mumbled.

I shook my head. "It's not the same. And it shouldn't be. You have each other. But I— For me it's different. It's something else. And I—I keep thinking that I'd do anything to keep you safe, even if it means— even if I can't—"

"You won't come over, and you won't let us stay with you." Josh kissed me lightly. "Because Joey might be lying in wait, about to kill you. Oh man, Cam, you had a shitty week."

"Can we get back to this thing where you think we don't love you? Because fuck you, we can love whoever we want."

"I think we should demonstrate." Another kiss. "But Keith's right. Did you think we thought of you like a teammate, that we're fond of you but ultimately you're interchangeable? Because you aren't."

I didn't say anything.

"All right. We are addressing this and everything else in the bedroom."

"I shouldn't stay—"

"Oh, yeah. You're staying. Don't bother trying to get out of it, because after all this I think I've decided to trust my instincts more when it comes to you, and my instincts say you need this, Cameron. Don't you?"

"What?"

He tilted my head so I couldn't avoid his eyes. "You know what."

"Help," I whispered. "Please help."

"We have you. We won't let anyone hurt you. Unless you want them to. Come on."

They took me into their bedroom and only turned on Keith's glittering fairy lights. More than enough light to see both of them. More than enough light for them to see me.

Keith's fingers began at the buttons of my waistcoat while Josh hung up my coat, my jacket. Josh took it off my shoulders, and Keith went to work on my shirt.

They'd seen me before, but this time I felt so much more exposed, standing there, bare from the waist up. Keith went to his knees and I shuffled away, uncertain.

"Get your ass back here." He smiled, eyes twinkling. "Come on, handsome. Let me at you."

"I told them you had a temper. I didn't mean to. They said Josh had a temper like he might—"

"Oh, I know what they said. And if you were talking to the same guy I was talking to, news that I have a temper would not have been a shock to him."

"You should have heard Keith going off. I thought for a minute *he* was going to be the one arrested for assault."

Keith stood, taking my hands, tugging me toward the bed. "I do have a temper. It's okay. They found— I don't know, Josh, did we decide for sure if that other detective was kinky?"

"Do you think she was a detective? She was definitely kinky. She closed the curtain and looked at Keith's back and when they came back out she looked at me like she wanted to say 'Good job.'"

"But what she actually said was, 'Green, you've clearly never whipped anyone. No way someone pulls a job like this off angry.' So he apologized for the personal nature the investigation had taken and wrapped it up."

"When was that?"

"Sunday. Afternoon? No, later. We'd eaten dinner."

"Yeah, right before they let us leave. She didn't look thrilled to be there, either," Josh added.

"I wonder if you get that all the time if you're into BDSM and you're a cop. Like being a doctor: 'Hey, take a look at this guy's back and tell me if it's the good hurt or the bad hurt.'" Keith pushed me gently backward. "The good hurt, always the good hurt. You want to feel it, Cam? You curious?" He climbed over me, holding me down.

I was scared all of a sudden. It was too much like grappling with Joey, like the moment I'd known I was losing control, that he'd get away and—

"Whoa, it's okay." Keith shifted, rolling me to the side, pressing himself against my back. "Hey, it's okay, Cam. You're okay."

"No, you're not." Josh had undressed, completely, and knelt beside the bed, all long muscles and smooth skin. "You are not okay. It only happened a week ago. You aren't okay yet. Cameron." His thumb peeled down my lower lip, and it was strange that something so unrevealing could make me feel splayed open, as if the inside of my lip, my gums, were somehow a window into my everything.

Josh's thumb rubbed back and forth, holding me open. "I want to take everything away from you right now. I want you naked on your knees with your hands behind your back. I want to bind your thighs so you can't get up."

I trembled, but he held fast.

"I don't want to blindfold you or gag you or take away your hearing, Cam. But if we don't make you hold still, I get this feeling like you'll never let us show you how we feel because you're always running away from it. Let us show you."

Keith kissed the back of my neck. "Let us in. And then believe us."

"But we don't have to do any of that." Pressure, keeping me open, not letting me speak. "We can hold you here between us without any other reason than we like having you here. And you don't get to tell us we don't, Cam. You understand me?"

I nodded, his thumb still holding my lip.

"So what do you want?"

He took his hand away, and I immediately missed the awkward sensation of restraint. "I want to stop being afraid all the time. Can you give me that?"

"We can damn sure try. What about the rest of it?"

I searched Josh's eyes. He'd meant every word. "I don't think I'm as brave as Keith is."

"If you mean you can't take the shit he takes, join the club. I'd be weeping like a little baby if he ever doled out to me what I dole out to him. But that's not what we're talking about, Cam, and I think by now you get that."

Keith's breath warmed my neck. "It isn't the same for everyone, you know."

I did. They'd shown me that. And all the spaces in between.

"I might lose it if you—if you put my hands behind my back. If you make it so I can't move. Not that— I mean, he only had me down for a second, and I know worse things are happening every minute to people all over the world, I shouldn't even be complaining—"

Keith's hand stole over my mouth. "Shh. Listen to me. It's not about how bad it was on some objective scale where you only get to complain if someone tore your fingernails out and killed your cat in front of you and busted your kneecaps and kicked you in the balls. A totally normal-looking guy followed us into your apartment, knocked out Josh because he figured you and I didn't pose much of a threat, terrorized us with a gun, and talked a whole bunch of shit. And it took us two tries to bring him down, Cam, okay?" I could feel how fast he was breathing. "It took two tries and the entire time it was happening I just wanted someone to save us. I wanted Josh to wake up, or the police to come, or fucking Superman, I didn't care. I wanted someone to save us from dying, because I knew, I *knew*, he was going to kill us."

"Me too," I whispered.

"But no one did. It was you, and me, and we saved ourselves."

"He hurt you."

"Yeah, he did. And he hurt Josh. And he killed Philpott and all those other people. And he hurt you too, Cameron. He hurt you too."

"I didn't even—I didn't even get a cut. I barely got a bruise. I was fine."

Josh's jaw tightened. "I got a really bad headache, but on the whole, that's probably better than having a head full of memories. I wish I could have saved you both. I know that's bullshit, but it's true. I'm so pissed at myself for passing out when you needed me."

"You didn't have a choice," I said.

"Right back at you."

"But now you do." Keith tipped me so I was on my back, but this time he didn't climb over me. "Now you have the choice. You can let him win, you can let all the shit he said to us rule you, or you can choose to do something else."

"I can't sleep. I've been sleeping in the ticket booth because when I'm in the apartment I can't stop thinking he's going to kill me."

"Jesus! Why didn't you *call me*?"

Josh touched Keith's arm, but looked straight at me. "Because he was trying to protect you, and he thought he had to keep you away in order to do that. Cam, that whole thing is over now. You get that next time you call us when you can't sleep, and you come over here, and you do not go down and sleep in the theater. Right?"

I closed my eyes. "I could say that I'll do that, but in the middle of the night, when I know I'm making it up—I won't disturb you. I know I won't."

Josh growled. "You really seriously make me want to hurt Keith."

"Ha!" Keith laughed and tugged him in for a kiss over my body. "Any time, slugger. And it's fine. We'll just make Cam stay here until he can commit. Or maybe we spend some time over there. I really don't know how you've been in your apartment alone, Cam. If I even think about it, I start to wig."

"I have an idea for that," Josh said. "Are you up for rearranging? I think if we can change the feel of it, maybe it won't be so triggering."

"I'll try anything. I hate being scared all the time."

"We'll work on that tomorrow. Tonight, we're busy." Josh lifted one of my hands above my head and held it there. "I won't tie you. I'll let you stay loose, but I'm gonna hold you just like this."

Keith drew my other arm up, and Josh pinned it.

I made myself take slower breaths. I wasn't panicking this time—at least, not yet—and I was grateful for my trousers. They didn't hide much, but they certainly hid more than nudity would have.

"Angel," Josh said.

"What do you want me to do? Or not do?"

"I want you to do the things you haven't done before. I think we held back because we didn't want to scare Cam away, and he took it as we didn't have strong feelings for him. So we gotta show him now."

"Yeah, good." Keith leaned in to my neck and inhaled. "You always smell so good to me. Even when you're, uh, a little ripe, FYI—"

I tried to get my hands back, but Josh held tight.

"Oh, hey—" Keith's fingers stroked my throat. "Shh. I was joking. I mean, not that you aren't ripe, but it doesn't bother me."

"It bothers *me*," I said. "I don't like that you're seeing me this way. I don't let people see me this way."

"Well, that just makes me feel way more special now." He sniffed again. "Cam, you're amazing. That first night, you dropping your index cards and saying you had trouble with your teleprompter? Oh my god. So hot."

"It's true. Keith wanted to jump you right then."

"And then you were so sweet. You're always so sweet, but like you don't even know it, like it's something you just are, without trying."

His fingers seemed to be dragging along my skin, waking up my nerve endings. He kept talking, but I couldn't track all of it because I was busy watching the way he touched me, Keith's fingers an extension of his voice, both casual and also deliberate, always so far from accidental. He touched my nipples, grazing over them, and I jolted.

Josh moved so he could pin my wrists with one hand and put the other on my stomach. His hands didn't move, a perfect firm counterpoint to Keith, who never stopped moving.

Or talking.

"It's so weird, being watched, being seen. Like, until I met Josh I don't know if anyone ever saw me, I didn't get that there was someone to see. I thought, you know, I thought that this kind of overachieving, privileged, just-like-everyone-else boy was all I could ever be, that anything else, any other part of me that didn't fit into that, was false." He brushed his cheek over my sternum. "Then I thought he was the only one who could see deeper than that, you know? But he wasn't. Him seeing me allowed me to see myself differently—better, or maybe not better, just more accurately. And other people, too. Like I shed my skin, snake-style, and the person underneath was suddenly visible to everyone else."

I breathed into the weight of Josh's hands and let myself fly a little with the sensations of Keith's, now lightly scraping over my clavicle, now drifting up my arms where they were above my head.

"And it's cool that other people, you know, maybe they don't write me off as much anymore. But you see something else again. The thing I thought only Josh could see, and only with my clothes off. You see everything I always thought made me weak, but to you it makes me brave. Which I don't understand at all, but I like it. I want it to be true."

"It is," I told him, arching between the fixed points of Josh's hands. "It is. I see you, Keith."

"Yeah." He kissed me, hard. "Well guess what, Cam? I see you, too. I see how much you want this, how hard you tried to cover it up. I saw how scared you were in the beginning that you'd do something wrong—"

Josh squeezed my wrists just slightly. "Or say something wrong, or have the wrong look on your face—"

"—and how you focused everything on me to try to keep from feeling anything yourself. Cam, you didn't have to. We didn't mean for you to do that."

I looked away. "It was the right thing to do. Prioritizing you—your relationship—was the right thing to do."

Keith squared himself up to my face, so close I was caught by how blue his eyes were, how I could sense their blue even in low light. "What our relationship wants is you. Oh my god, Cam, I fell for you, like, before we ever introduced ourselves. Josh fell for you when you got Merin's pronouns right."

"And then, with the candlesticks." Josh's hand stroked the skin of my abdomen. "I was so nervous that night that we were going to make everything into this deep, heavy thing, but you lit candles. That made it perfect." He kissed my cheek without letting up on my wrists. "We aren't asking you to feel everything right now—"

"Speak for yourself. I'm *totally* asking him to do that. No, I'm *demanding* it."

Josh ignored the interruption. "Just maybe stop trying so hard to protect yourself, protect us. Let it be whatever it is for a little while."

"I told Detective Green we didn't need words to know it was good," I said.

"Exactly. We don't." He kissed my cheek again. "But let's do naked time now, okay? Keith's really got a lot of things he wants to do, and, since it's Christmas, this seems like a good time for him to do them."

"Oh hell yes. Merry Christmas, let me rim you."

I squirmed and both of them laughed. "You *are not* rimming me until I've showered."

"I'm down for showering, too. We should shower together."

I appealed to Josh, whose grin held absolutely no promise of mercy. I tried anyway. "Your shower isn't big enough for two people."

"Oh my god, of course it is! You just gotta be friendly about it."

"Keith . . ."

Josh released me. "I think Keith's idea is good. You guys shower. I'll wait here and think really hard."

"You'll wait here and not touch yourself until we get back, mister."

I rubbed at my wrists, which weren't actually in any form of discomfort, and tried to think through the haze of arousal to come up with some reason why I needed to shower alone. "Keith, come on, I—I have to wash— I should be alone for that—"

He coaxed me up with kisses, holding my head to his and backing away until he was at the wall. I stood close enough to press him harder against it, though I didn't.

"I'll close my eyes if you're shy. But when you're alone your mind goes bad places, so I'm not leaving you alone. It's not up for discussion."

"And leave the door open," Josh added. "So there's no barrier, no moment when you have to choose to make yourself vulnerable."

"Yeah, good call. C'mon, Cam."

I went, with one last backward glance at Josh, who sat on their bed, naked and hard, smiling at us.

Keith washed me, except for the more private locations (which I washed while he turned his back). I expected everything to get very intense, and sexual, and serious, after we returned to the bedroom, but it didn't.

They kissed each other, they kissed me, sometimes all three of us were connected, sometimes it was only two, while the third watched, touching himself, enjoying the sight. Most of the time, that night, it was me they touched; I was the one never on the outside, never looking in. I knew they were doing it that way on purpose, though they didn't have to. I hadn't minded being on the outside.

But this time they seemed to want me on the inside, and it was a separate pleasure, sweet and precious and unforeseen.

CHAPTER 26

W e spent Christmas at my apartment, moving furniture, which is how everyone always imagines a kinky threesome: lots of grunting and groaning and the occasional cry of pain (or triumph; my sofa was heavier than it looked).

I would have quit halfway through, because it wasn't working. The living room area wanted to be where it was, in front of the door. The dining room area wanted to be where it was, next to the kitchen. And moving the bookcases seemed like madness to me. Taking all the books out, unscrewing the cases, moving them, finding studs so we (Josh) could screw them back in. Then, of course, putting all the books back in.

Except a strange thing happened once we'd shifted the bookshelves. The front part of the apartment, which now had a table and chairs, was starting to look like a dining room. A real dining room. Not just an "area closest to the kitchen, so might as well put the table there" dining room.

"This is cool." Keith flopped into one of the chairs. "This is totally gonna work."

"Now we just gotta fix the rest." Josh circled my furniture—sofa, two armchairs, coffee table—and walked the perimeter of the space. "It's longer and more narrow than how you had it arranged over there. How do we do this configuration for a long and narrow living room?"

It took at least another hour, but the simplest idea ended up being the only one that worked. We kept trying to run the sofa longways. Then Keith, finally, in desperation, turned it shortways, so the longest part of the sofa was along the shortest part of the space, and for some reason, everything felt bigger.

"Oh hell yeah. We got this now!" Josh, doing some kind of interior decorating victory dance, vaulted over a chair. "Hell, Cam, you got room for more furniture if we do it like this. You could have stools up at the peninsula!"

"Okay, cowboy, you can slow right down." Keith, far more methodical than Josh or I, went back to the dining room and adjusted the position of the table, turning it slightly at an angle, which seemed like it should have been wrong, but wasn't. "The thing that's making the space feel small is all the lines. Rectangular table, all these squared off edges to the dining room chairs, the kitchen's all clean lines without curves. Stools would actually help. But let's do this for right now."

Josh and I moved everything into minutely different configurations while Keith watched, made comments, walked around, entered the room from the front door, then the hallway, seeing it from all angles.

Finally, after what felt like a thousand very slightly different attempts, Keith told us we were done.

"Good. Because we haven't eaten and I'm starving." Josh strolled into my kitchen and started opening cabinets.

"I don't have much," I said apologetically.

"Peanut butter and jelly sounds good to me. Keith?"

"Are there bananas?"

"Peanut butter and banana for Keith."

After lunch they inspected my bathroom and made me put out the "company" towels, which I argued were only for special occasions.

"You are a special occasion," Keith said.

"Just change it up for now," Josh added. "What about sheets?"

"You two are not—"

They changed my sheets. I shrank a little, unsettled and emotional, worried that none of it would help. I'd managed not to think about it too much, but now I was, and the world was getting smaller, beginning to crowd out all the good moments.

When they were done, Josh pulled on my hands and brought me back to what was now the living room.

"We're going to do something else before we leave, and then you're coming home with us."

I didn't fight with him. I wanted to go with them. Back to their apartment. This had been good, and I thought it would help, maybe, but tonight I wanted to know I was okay.

When he reached for my clothes, I balked.

"We're in my living room."

"And I admire whoever designed those high windows, because it means we don't even have to worry about people watching us from the street." He did twin *come back here* gestures with his hands. "Cameron."

"What—what are we doing?"

"We're reclaiming your space. This is where he made you sit, isn't it?" He stepped forward. "I'm sorry I wasn't with you."

"He kicked you. When you were . . . lying there. It happens in every single nightmare, him kicking you while you just lie there."

"Mine too." Keith took my hand and laid his head on my shoulder so both of us were looking at Josh. "In some ways it was scarier than the gun, though I guess the gun was kind of the point. He held a gun on us and we couldn't protect you, we couldn't fight him. He made us *watch* while he hurt you, and you couldn't defend yourself."

"Classic bully. Never starts a fight unless he has all the advantages. Babe, c'mere."

Keith stepped forward, allowing Josh to undress him and fold his clothes with care on the coffee table. Then they switched, and their mutual reverence still made me wonder if I should even be present while they did things like this, while they stared at one another as if no one else mattered.

Until both of them, naked and aroused, turned to me. As if I was the only one who mattered.

"I think I saw a spare blanket." Keith kissed my cheek before he walked away.

"What—what are we doing?"

"Being in love with each other in your living room, Cam. Come here now. Let us show you."

They were so gentle, so soft, so sweet. Taking off my clothes, revealing me as if it were the first time, as if I was a gift to them from each other. Keith spread out the comforter that had graced my parents' bed for most of my childhood, and it should have felt wrong, but it didn't. It felt like the most safe thing in the world, lying back, letting them touch and kiss and lick and rub against me, no one on top, no one on the bottom, no one in charge.

It didn't escape me that we were exactly where I'd held Joey down until the police arrived. That Keith had placed us here on purpose. That you couldn't be any more deliberate about reclaiming space than having sex on the spot where you once imagined dying.

It might have felt like a cheap bandage over a gushing wound. It didn't.

CHAPTER 27

I spent the better part of my days at QYP for the next couple of weeks. Anytime I wasn't specifically needed for a shift at the theater, I was at the center. At first I felt ridiculous, and juvenile, as if I needed a babysitter. But sometime in that first week I realized I could be helpful. Keith was brilliant with numbers and spreadsheets, and Josh was brilliant at telling the stories of QYP in such a way that people wanted to help out, but I'd been running a business by myself for eight years, and I'd been an apprentice to it all my life. I reorganized their files to make tax season less gruesome and went over their insurance, which didn't cover them in the ways they should be covered.

I knew I'd finally been accepted as part of the family when Merin came over to the kitchen while I was making sandwiches.

"Hey," he said. "You raid my wardrobe or something?"

Merin had never initiated a conversation with me. I had been, until that moment, somewhat convinced he disliked me.

The jacket I'd bought myself still felt like safety and comfort, so I tugged it in tighter. "I think it suits me."

"Yeah, something about you just screams 'thug.'" He paused before vaguely gesturing to where Josh, Keith, and Zane were sitting in the little conversation nook. "I can't stand that lady."

"Zane? Why?"

"She is *relentlessly happy*. It bugs me. Like, can't she keep it to herself? Why's she gotta shove it in my face all the time, that she's happy and well-adjusted? It's insulting."

I studied Zane from across the room. She'd stopped by to show Josh and Keith houses she was scouting for them. Apparently Josh's parents wanted to give them twenty-five thousand dollars toward a down payment on a house (or maybe they wanted to take a loan out on their behalf for twenty-five thousand dollars, I was unclear on the details). They would have preferred to put the money into QYP, but the Walkers had been firm. And it was smart, too, forcing them to think of something outside the drop-in center.

"You think she's relentlessly happy?" I asked. "I don't know."

"Nah. I don't really think that. It's more like she's all up in my face about how happy she is because really she's fucked up in the head."

"And being fucked up in the head somehow annoys you? What, you don't like the competition?" I held his gaze through the flash of anger, thinking about how remote he felt most of the time, and how much he liked it when Josh challenged him.

"You're hilarious. Speaking of fucked in the head, what's your deal?"

"Guy tried to kill me. And Keith and Josh." I shrugged like it was nothing. "Apparently I'm allowed to be a little fucked in the head for a while. What's your deal?"

"My dad wants to beat me into the girl-shaped kid I never was and my mom wishes she'd had that abortion she always wanted."

"That must be disheartening."

He barked a laugh, cut off almost immediately. "Yeah. It's fucking *disheartening.*"

I wasn't sure if I should say it, but after a second I did. "I call you 'him' when I talk to them. Do you want me to do something different? Keith said maybe you didn't like those pronouns. Or that you didn't use them."

He looked away. "I don't want to make a big thing about it. They want me to live with them. But I'm not a kid, you know?"

"On the other hand, they probably can't afford to pay you enough for you to afford your own place. It's in their best interests to ensure you can continue working at QYP, don't you think?"

"You think like Keith thinks. I mean, he wouldn't say that, but I know he's got a plan. He's always got something brewing in his fool brain."

"Do you graduate this year?"

"Yeah."

Would a kid like Merin celebrate graduation? Kids like Merin were the ones who worked the hardest just to survive high school, but I bet he didn't have plans to honor his efforts. "Are you and Keith going to have a joint graduation party?"

He rolled his eyes, then sighted across the room again. "Very fucking funny. By the way, you hurt them and I swear to God, I'll fucking kill you."

"Someone already tried. Shouldn't you be telling me to stay away? I'm the reason they got hurt before."

"No, stupid. Crazy's the reason they got hurt before. You start taking responsibility for crazy and you'll be pretty fuckin' busy. At least that's what Josh is always telling me. Anyway, I gotta go. See ya, Cam."

"See ya." The colloquialism felt round and lightweight on my tongue, as if it made me a more casual person even to speak it.

He left the kitchen and saluted. Keith waved, Josh returned the salute, and Zane called, "Don't think I don't know how much you secretly like me, Merin!" I was decently certain he muttered "Jesus fuck" on his way out the door.

Keith gestured me over, so I stacked some sandwiches on a plate and brought them to the table, where Zane was in the middle of what seemed to be a monologue.

"This wedding is killing me, boys. If you two ever get married, leave me out of it. To be honest, I had no idea they were asking me to plan the thing. When Jaq did a wedding, she just had to show up early to help set the thing up, not spend every waking hour of her life— Oh, food. Thanks, Cameron."

"You're welcome."

"So." She looked at all three of us. "You caught the killer."

"We didn't catch him as much as we got caught by him." Keith peeled open a peanut butter and jelly, but I grabbed his hand and put it on the sandwich I'd made for him (even though putting banana in a sandwich felt wrong). "Aw, you are totally the best, Cam."

I kept my eyes on my tuna and certainly didn't preen.

Josh tousled Keith's hair. "I had nothing to do with catching the killer, but these two are heroes."

"Any word on what's gonna happen now?"

"I don't think they've officially charged him with the murders yet," I said. "At least, I think Ed would have mentioned it."

"How about Ed? The *Times-Record* website has never been this up-to-date."

I nodded. "They're making him assistant online editor."

"That's great. The kid deserves it."

We all agreed.

"I wish Philpott was around to see it go down, though," Josh said. "He was always annoyed that the *Times-Record* didn't do enough with its site, and he's part of the reason they are now. Because Togg's not around to pick up the slack."

"I still can't believe that half the time. Philpott was Togg. Togg was Philpott." Zane wrapped half her sandwich in a cloth she pulled out of her bag. "I'm off to do something with floral arrangements. Listen, you three take care of yourselves, got it?"

"We will," Keith said. "Thanks for showing us those places, Zane, though we still have kind of a lot of thinking to do about it."

"It's my job, kiddo. And anyway, keep dropping me ideas, and I'll keep my eyes open." She stood. "Hey, do me a favor and go to Club Fred's at some point this week. Tom wants to shake your hands, and Fredi will probably comp your drinks. And business has been a little slow for the holidays, she said, so hopefully all this will—you know. Get things back to normal."

Josh nodded. "Hopefully. Let me walk you out, Zane."

Josh went with Zane. Keith turned and propped his legs on mine.

"I'm excited about tonight." He held up a finger. "And *don't* tell me we don't have to do it. We want to. End of story."

"Merin said I could use 'he' and 'him.'"

"Oh, way to change the subject, Cam. So smooth."

"Also, are you two thinking about adopting him?"

"We think about a lot of things. But yeah, just to give him something stable, though now that he's eighteen he probably wouldn't agree. It wouldn't work now because we only have a one-bedroom. But if we had a house, maybe. And a locking closet or wardrobe or something in our bedroom. Wink, wink."

"Did you just . . . verbally emoticon at me?"

He grinned. "Anyway, tonight's going to be amazing. Mostly because you're going to let your guard down and beg us to defile you."

"*Keith.*"

"Hmm? Did you say something?"

I blushed, even though no one else had heard him. "We have no idea if this will work."

"Listen up, handsome: we are spending the night at your apartment. If the nightmares get worse, for either of us, then at least we'll be there for each other. Right?"

"Yes, but we really don't—"

"Oh my *god*, stop talking." He leaned forward and put his hand against my chest.

The door opened. I jumped, but it was only Josh coming back inside.

Keith did not move his hand. "I know the scariest thing is that it might not work and you can't make the apartment okay again. I know that, Cam. But it hasn't been long enough for us to know if that's true, so tonight we're trying this."

Josh slid in on my other side. I anticipated, and felt, his hand on my back. "He's trying to get out of it again?"

"Yeah. Make him stop."

"Only one way to do that. Let's close early and go now."

"You can't close early!" I said. "You have two hours left!"

"It's a Saturday night. I don't think we've ever, in the history of QYP, had anyone come in on a Saturday this late. Plus, we have to adjust our hours. We've been talking about it for weeks. This schedule's not sustainable."

"Truth." Keith yawned.

"But—but your signs—"

"We'll reprint the signs." Josh's hand moved up to my neck. "Cameron. Time to go home."

I shivered, maybe because of his hand, maybe because of the words. "Okay."

"This feels like cutting school," Keith said, suddenly awake enough to spring out of his seat. "Let's go, come on, we're wasting time!"

And just like that, we wrapped the rest of the sandwiches, put them in the fridge, and trooped out to the cars. Keith rode with me, and when I accused him of monitoring my movements to make sure I actually drove to the theater, he didn't deny it.

The new arrangement of furniture helped. The apartment no longer felt like the same space where all of it had happened. But it smelled the same, and at night, going to the bathroom, I still became unreasonably frightened.

I left lights on now. I'd already told them, but I worried that it would still seem wrong, or weird. I worried that my eccentricities, now amped up by trauma, would be too much to take in real-time.

"How did Cary Grant pick his name?" Keith asked, brushing his teeth after dinner.

They had never stayed overnight at my apartment before. I'd bought toothbrushes and a comb I'd seen Keith use at their place, and presented all of it bashfully, worried they'd think I was taking this single night too seriously. But of course Keith immediately called "the red one" and tore into the toothbrushes, while Josh asked where I'd found the comb, because apparently it was a point of contention how specialized that particular model was.

I'd gone to three stores looking for it. I didn't mention that part. At least—I didn't mention it right away. I mentioned it later, when Keith tried to claim it was a normal comb and that it could be found everywhere. It really couldn't.

"Archie Leach was an okay name for vaudeville, but once he got serious about performing in motion pictures, the studio suggested he change it. So he took the name 'Cary' from a character he'd played, and 'Grant' from a list of potential surnames supplied to him by the studio."

"It'd be weird to go by a different name all the time, I think." Keith surrendered the sink to Josh. "Like, I don't know, to choose your name as an adult? That's such a trip to me."

"I think it's kind of cool," Josh said.

"Yeah? What name would you choose?"

He thought about it, spat, rinsed his mouth. "Joshua Benjamin Walker. I think. Off the top of my head."

Keith swatted him with a hand towel. "What about you, Cam? Would you change your name if you could?"

I thought about the theater's marquee, and the ways my name had been woven all through people's memories. "I used to want to change Cameron to Charles, when I was a kid. I thought Charlie was a way better nickname than Cam."

"Seriously? I love Cam. Ha, see what I did there?"

Josh sighed heavily. "Have to be blind not to—"

"Hey! I'm pretty sure that was ableist, Josh."

"I take back my ableist language." He tugged Keith in by the towel he was still holding. "What about you, babe?"

"Not really. I don't mind my name. But if I had to—like if we couldn't be successful at the center unless I changed it—I would."

"Cary Grant took it really seriously." I led the way to the bedroom with more confidence than I felt. Even at their apartment I hated this moment, this commitment to sleep that so frequently led to waking up in a cold sweat with my heart pounding.

"You mean like playing Cary Grant was his most important role?"

"I think it kind of was, in a way. I'm not sure he did it dishonestly, or anything. But it meant something to him that he'd crafted this image, and that he lived and died by it. He ended his career without really telling anyone because the roles kept coming, but he felt he was too old to play the leading man pursuing the young ingénue. So he just . . . stopped."

"He dropped the mic," Josh said, pulling back the covers on my bed. "Damn. That's actually really cool. There are some actors now who I kind of wish would do that, you know?"

"It might have been easier for him because 'Cary Grant' was such a deliberate construction that he could make business decisions that were based around what was good for 'Cary Grant' the brand, more than the person."

"Like you make decisions for the Rhein that are different than the ones you'd make for yourself." Keith slid into the sheets and patted the bed. In the middle.

"Kind of. Though I never actually think I'm the Rhein."

"But in a sense, you are. You're the living embodiment of everything the Rhein is, was, or ever will be. No pressure." He patted the bed more insistently.

I hesitated. "What if I can't do this?"

Josh's arms came around me. He held me close, a move he'd only been doing in the last few days. A move I used to long for when he did it with Keith. "Can't spend the night here? Or can't be the Rhein?"

I didn't know how to explain that, in a way, they felt like the same thing. Insurmountable goals. "The Rhein's not in that much danger. But five years from now? Ten years from now? I don't know."

"All you can do is adapt. You'll adapt your business. You'll adapt your lifestyle. It might be harder to do the things you used to do, so you'll do different things."

"Like us," Keith added. "You'll do us. A lot. Over and over."

But that was the worst, most terrifying of my fears. "And what if I can't?"

Josh kissed my neck. "You already are."

"It takes a while to stop worrying about it all the time." Keith, apparently sick of waiting for us, got back out of bed so he could kiss me. "At least, for me, I thought it was all going to disappear for a long time, that I'd wake up and Josh would be a stranger. But it's never happened yet, and eventually you just kind of . . . get used to it. Get used to the idea that maybe you get to have this thing that is good, that makes you feel good."

Josh's hands caressed my stomach, my sides. When he spoke, his voice was lower. "Get used to the idea it won't be stolen from you in a night."

"Every time I let myself hope for a second, I think about it," I admitted.

"Come to bed." Keith tugged and I followed, and Josh followed, and then we were lying there: Josh on his back, me on my back, Keith on his side facing us.

"Do any Cary Grant movies end in bed?" Josh asked.

I ran through movie endings. "I guess *That Touch of Mink* sort of does. It ends—sorry, spoilers—with him in a hotel room having an allergic reaction to love."

"Is that as . . . dumb as it seems like it is?"

"Yeah. Pretty much. I kind of don't like that role they kept casting him in where he's the shallow playboy redeemed by the love of a good woman."

"But—" Keith laid his hand on my chest. "Isn't that sort of what *An Affair to Remember* is?"

"No. No, the transformation in that, for both of them, is that love's not enough to make everything work out. You have to change, and change is hard, and there are no guarantees. I mean, that's what makes it so good, so believable. Because we want to believe that change is possible, and that hard work pays off."

He kissed my cheek and snuggled closer. I put my arm around him, feeling impossibly intimate, nestled on both sides by men for whom I cared deeply.

Josh turned, propping himself on one arm. "I believe all that. I believe we transform ourselves, and that no matter how hard it is, it pays off in the end."

"Me too," Keith said.

I wanted to say, *I do too* and let it rest, but I couldn't lie to them. Or to myself. "I'd like to believe that. I'm trying to believe that. I don't think I do, yet."

Josh slid his hand over Keith's until I could feel both of them. "I admire that about you. It's easier to work at it every day when you're convinced it will all be good in the end. But you work at it every day on the strength of your hope, Cam. And that's pretty damn amazing." He kissed me.

Keith kissed me.

"Thank you for coming over tonight," I whispered, when really I meant, *Thank you for materializing in my life and making everything before you seem like monochrome.*

"Anytime," Keith said. "Literally. I love your stove. I'd kill for a gas range. Can we have a gas range in our house you're gonna buy us, Josh?"

"*We're* buying it, and hell yeah. And maybe one of those barbecues that's hooked up to the propane line so we don't have to keep exchanging tanks."

"Ohhh, and can we have heated floors in the master bath? I've always wanted heated floors!"

"Yeah, as long as we find a contractor who accepts payment in tuna sandwiches."

The three of us settled in, still talking about their dream house (three bedrooms, two and a half baths, small fenced yard if possible, downtown would be ideal, but they'd probably have to look in the suburbs). We planned what we'd do the next day after Josh came home from church, and I almost asked if I could go with him, but the idea of staying in bed with Keith was a little too hard to pass up. We talked for what felt like hours, until my eyes were closed and it was increasingly hard to make the words assemble in my brain and force them out my mouth.

The last thing I heard was Josh saying, "I think he's asleep."

Fingers brushed my hair. "Yeah. Sweet Cam."

I let myself go, drifting, my breaths mingling with theirs like currents in deep water, flowing together, flowing apart, all eventually joining to move in the same direction, as inevitable as the tides.

Explore more of the *Queers of La Vista* series:
riptidepublishing.com/titles/universe/queers-la-vista

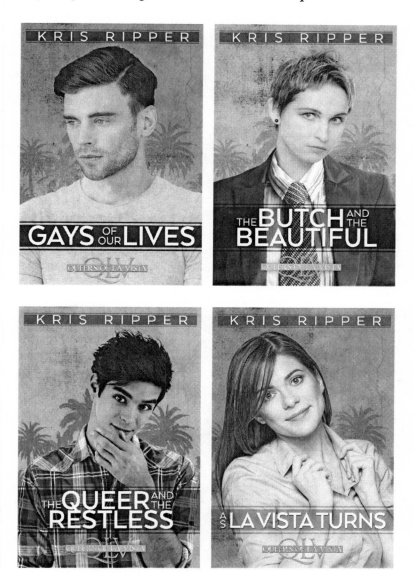

Dear Reader,

Thank you for reading Kris Ripper's *One Life to Lose*!

We know your time is precious and you have many, many entertainment options, so it means a lot that you've chosen to spend your time reading. We really hope you enjoyed it.

We'd be honored if you'd consider posting a review—good or bad—on sites like **Amazon, Barnes & Noble, Kobo, Goodreads, Twitter, Facebook, Tumblr,** and your blog or website. We'd also be honored if you told your friends and family about this book. Word of mouth is a book's lifeblood!

For more information on upcoming releases, author interviews, blog tours, contests, giveaways, and more, please sign up for our weekly, spam-free newsletter and visit us around the web:

Newsletter: tinyurl.com/RiptideSignup
Twitter: twitter.com/RiptideBooks
Facebook: facebook.com/RiptidePublishing
Goodreads: tinyurl.com/RiptideOnGoodreads
Tumblr: riptidepublishing.tumblr.com

Thank you so much for Reading the Rainbow!

RiptidePublishing.com

ACKNOWLEDGMENTS

Oh, the toil of the writer, the endless research, the agonizing fact-checking...

Full disclosure: my research for this book was watching many hours of Cary Grant movies. Other things as well, but that's the only part I remember now.

Cam gets a little emotional telling the story of the key in *Notorious*, stolen from the set by Cary Grant, passed on to Ingrid Bergman, and eventually to Alfred Hitchcock. I challenge you to watch the clip on YouTube and not get emotional yourself: youtu.be/74Mzt-DTHsk

Whether or not there's really an "original" ending to *Suspicion* is up for some debate. Was it written, but not shot? Was it shot, but not edited? Was it edited and complete, but rejected for the softer, less disturbing ending? We only know that the film differs from the book; who made those decisions, and whether they were challenged, is lost to time.

For a little more about the great American juggler Bobby May, check out his page at the Juggling Hall of Fame: www.juggling.org/fame/may

Sometimes inspiration arises in strange places. I learned about the existence of the tuna strainer from the marvelous Liz and Tracey Jacobs. TUNA STRAINER. You don't know it's necessary until you use it. Then you realize you can never live without it.

For my fellow *Goonies* fans, there does (or at least did) exist a discontinued *Goonies* oven mitt on Ebay. I did not make that up. And now I kind of want to write a scene where Cam, Keith, and Josh watch the movie.

Eagle-eyed readers may recognize the, ah, "murders at a fashion show" book. But I'm certainly not giving it away.

And finally, a little bit about community.

I've always been an uneasy player in queer spaces. Some of it is gender, some of it is my decided lack of allegiance to the rigid roles of "gay" and "lesbian" and "bisexual" as those terms were defined when I was coming up, and some of it is merely that I am uneasy, and awkward, in general.

Queer folks have a lot of shifting loyalties. Our place in the world is constantly changing, and the lines between us seem to be perpetually erased and redrawn, factions aligning and realigning, sometimes in deep disagreement, sometimes in tenuous accord.

And sometimes, of course, we align as a family in which water is much thicker than blood, conflicts and all.

Joey Rodriguez isn't modeled on any one person; he's a composite of a lot of different people I've known, and a lot of different people I've encountered through their written words. He's not a random murderous gay, and he's not really a madman, though that word is applied to him. He's a guy who feels that part of his birthright—a certain role he was meant to play, a way he was meant to be seen by others—has been stolen from him by a rapidly changing world.

People feel that way in all countries, in all walks of life. There is nothing very special about Joey, except that he takes matters into his own hands and tries to force the world to conform to the way he wishes it was. In his mind, he's a damn hero.

The most compelling villains are always the ones whose perspective you can kind of see, if you tilt your head to the side and squint. Or, as Hitchcock says, "[Audiences] want an ordinary human being with failings." Joey's a decent kid from a good family; he could be the boy next door, or the guy you went to school with. He could be pretty much anyone, and he's probably not as much of a stranger as you wish he was.

But the moral of this story isn't *Be afraid. Be very afraid.* Cam's story is all about what we do when fear finds us where we live and we can't shake it off.

Be brave. Be very brave. And let the people you love return the favor.

ALSO BY

KRIS RIPPER

Queers of La Vista
Gays of Our Lives
The Butch and the Beautiful
The Queer and the Restless
As La Vista Turns

Scientific Method Universe
Catalysts
Unexpected Gifts
Take Three Breaths
Breaking Down
Roller Coasters
The Boyfriends Tie the Knot
The Honeymoon
Extremes
The New Born Year
Threshold of the Year
Surrender the Past
The Library, Volume 1

New Halliday
Fairy Tales
The Spinner, the Shepherd, and
the Leading Man
The Real Life Build
Take the Leap

The Home Series
Going Home
Home Free
Close to Home
Home for the Holidays

Little Red and the Big Bad
Serial One
Serial Two

The Erotic Gym:
Training Mac
The Ghost in the Penthouse

For a complete book list, visit: krisripper.com

ABOUT THE
AUTHOR

Kris Ripper lives in the great state of California and hails from the San Francisco Bay Area. Kris shares a converted garage with a toddler, can do two pull-ups in a row, and can write backwards. (No, really.) Kris is genderqueer and prefers the z-based pronouns because they're freaking sweet. Ze has been writing fiction since ze learned how to write, and boring zir stuffed animals with stories long before that.

Website: krisripper.com
Newsletter: krisripper.com/about/subscribe-what
Facebook: facebook.com/kris.ripper
Twitter: twitter.com/SmutTasticKris
YouTube: youtube.com/user/KrisRipper

Enjoy more stories like
One Life to Lose
at RiptidePublishing.com!

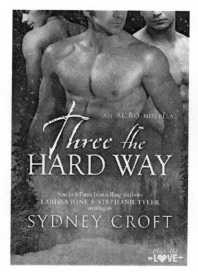

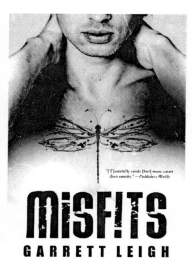

Three the Hard Way
ISBN: 978-1-62649-234-9

Misfits
ISBN: 978-1-62649-247-9

Earn Bonus Bucks!

Earn 1 Bonus Buck for each dollar you spend. Find out how at RiptidePublishing.com/news/bonus-bucks.

Win Free Ebooks for a Year!

Pre-order coming soon titles directly through our site and you'll receive one entry into a drawing for a chance to win free books for a year! Get the details at RiptidePublishing.com/contests.

CPSIA information can be obtained
at www.ICGtesting.com
Printed in the USA
LVOW11s1547211216
518286LV00004B/710/P